NHL1 EIP

We hope you enjoy this book. Please return or
renew it by the due date.

You can renew it at www.norfolk.gov.uk/libraries or
by using our free library app.

Otherwise you can phone 0344 800 8020 -
please have your library card and PIN ready.

You can sign up for email reminders too.

Also by Domenica de Rosa

The Italian Quarter
The Secret of Villa Serena
One Summer in Tuscany

As Elly Griffiths

THE DR RUTH GALLOWAY MYSTERIES

The Crossing Places   *The Woman in Blue*
The Janus Stone   *The Chalk Pit*
The House at Sea's End   *The Dark Angel*
A Room Full of Bones   *The Stone Circle*
Dying Fall   *The Lantern Men*
The Outcast Dead   *The Night Hawks*
The Ghost Fields   *The Locked Room*
              The Last Remains

THE BRIGHTON MYSTERIES

The Zig Zag Girl
Smoke and Mirrors
The Blood Card
The Vanishing Box
Now You See Them
The Midnight Hour
The Great Deceiver

OTHER WORKS

The Stranger Diaries
The Postscript Murders
Bleeding Heart Yard

FOR CHILDREN

A Girl Called Justice
A Girl Called Justice: The Smugglers' Secret
A Girl Called Justice: The Ghost in the Garden
A Girl Called Justice: The Spy at the Window

Elly Griffiths writing as

Domenica de Rosa

The Eternal City

QUERCUS

First published in Great Britain in 2005 by Headline Review
This paperback edition published in Great Britain in 2023 by

QUERCUS

Quercus Editions Ltd
Carmelite House
50 Victoria Embankment
London EC4Y 0DZ

An Hachette UK company

A CIP catalogue record for this book is available
from the British Library

PB ISBN 978 1 52943 435 4
EB ISBN 978 1 78087 953 6

10 9 8 7 6 5 4 3 2 1

Typeset by CC Book Production
Printed and bound in Great Britain by Clays Ltd, Elcograf S.p.A

Papers used by Quercus are from well-managed forests and other responsible sources.

For Andrew

Then out spake brave Horatius
The Captain of the Gate:
'To every man upon this earth
Death cometh soon or late.
And how can a man die better
Than facing fearful odds,
For the ashes of his fathers,
And the temples of his Gods.'

Thomas Babington, Lord Macaulay,
Lays of Ancient Rome: Horatius

'O Rome! my country! city of the soul!'

George Gordon, Lord Byron,
Childe Harold's Pilgrimage

FOREWORD TO THE ETERNAL CITY

I wrote *The Eternal City* in 2005. It was my second published book, following *The Italian Quarter* in 2004. *The Italian Quarter* was a fictionalised version of my father's life, following his parents' migration from Italy to England and his internment as an 'enemy alien' during the Second World War. *The Eternal City* starts with the death of a beloved Italian father. My dad died in 2002. He didn't live to see me become a published author, unless you count a little book about Shakespeare and Food, which I don't.

I wanted to be a writer for as long as I can remember. Even before I started school, Dad used to make me tiny books which I'd fill with pictures. An early attempt was called 'The Ship of Mystery'. I'm pretty sure I spelt it wrong but not a bad title for a six-year-old. Later on, I would draw book covers in my notebook, often deploying my favourite Shakespeare quotations. 'The Prince of Darkness is a Gentleman' by Domenica de Rosa. I always hoped that my beautiful and memorable name would be an asset when it came to getting published. It wasn't at first. I had many rejections before *The Italian Quarter* was accepted by Headline Review. Three other books followed, all about Italy, families and identity. They were: *The Eternal City*, *Villa Serena* and *Summer School*. The last two were retitled as *The Secret of Villa Serena* and *One Summer in Tuscany* when my current publisher, Quercus, reissued them.

It was while I was writing *Summer School* that I had the idea for a book about a forensic archaeologist called Dr Ruth Galloway. My agent suggested that I come up with a 'crime name'. Her thinking was that Domenica de Rosa sounded too romantic, also possibly made up. Maybe she just wanted to give me a fresh start after the somewhat disappointing sales of the first four books. Without thinking too much about it, I opted for Elly Griffiths. My maternal grandmother was called Ellen Griffiths. She died when I was five, but I'd always been told that she loved reading. I thought she would have liked to see her name on a book. My first crime novel, *The Crossing Places*, was published by Quercus in 2009. Since then there have been twenty-eight Elly Griffiths books and I have become much better known by that name. Hence the rather disconcerting line on the cover of this book, 'Elly Griffiths writing as Domenica de Rosa'.

The Eternal City follows the story of Gabriella de Angelis and her two older sisters as they travel to Rome to scatter their father's ashes. All have different ideas about his final resting place, and all have different relationships with the dead Enzo. It transpires, over a tearful and boozy lunch near the Spanish Steps, that they all thought they were his favourite. Gaby thinks about this later: '"I have three daughters", Dad used to say, "and I love each one better than the other." I used to hope that it was a cumulative thing . . . Now I see that this might not have been what he meant, that it was something altogether more profound. That he loved Anna, Maria and me in a kind of circle: the more he loved one of us, the more he loved the other two. That his love was everlasting.'

The book is certainly a love letter to my father, Felice, but it's not autobiographical in other ways. Like Gabriella, I'm the youngest of three sisters but Anna and Maria in the book are not like my older sisters, Giulia and Sheila, apart from seeming impossibly glamorous when I was growing up. Gaby's mother is certainly not my warm and wonderful mother, also called Sheila, although she too was an English woman married to a charismatic Italian. It's funny, as my first books were written under my own name and often in the first person, people assume that they are based on my real life. In fact, there is probably more of me in the Ruth books.

Rereading *The Eternal City*, I was struck by how many themes recur in the Ruth series: history, family, myth, religion and motherhood. There are Roman remains here, haunted churches and complicated family dynamics. Jonathan is the first in a line of tormented priests; Bob one of many witty red-heads. I hadn't long become a mother myself when I wrote this book and there are heartfelt feelings that I revisited when Ruth has her baby, Kate (very similar in name to Kitty). Of course, I had twins, which surpasses either of them, but my wonderful offspring, Alex and Juliet, are far too amazing to be believable in print.

In some ways, this is a book of its time. Some of the characters have mobile phones but, extraordinary to us now, they mostly use them to phone people. A text is unusual enough to become a plot point. However, I do hope that some of the themes, like Enzo's love and the title itself, are eternal.

Domenica de Rosa

2023

PROLOGUE

She knew, of course, that if you spoke with the communion wafer in your mouth, you would die. Maria had told her. 'If you touch it with your teeth, you die. If you think a wicked thought with it in your mouth, you die. If you speak before you swallow it, you die.'

'What if the church is on fire and I have to call for help?'

'It's better to die in the fire than commit a mortal sin.'

Now, sitting on her mother's bed, having her hair brushed (it had to be smooth so the wreath would sit on top), she thought about the myriad dangers in front of her. What if she chewed it by mistake? What was the difference between chewing and swallowing anyway? What if the wafer got stuck to the roof of her mouth? She had swallowed it once before, during practice; she remembered the dry, papery taste.

But that wasn't a consecrated Host, just a piece of bread. Was there a difference anyhow? What if God knew her secret thoughts about Sister Immaculata and wishing Anna lived somewhere else and struck her dead all the same? Would you go straight to heaven if you died with a communion wafer in your mouth?

Her mother lifted the wreath of white silk flowers and placed it carefully on her head. One of the wire stems stuck into her. 'Ow,' she said, but quietly.

'Keep still,' said her mother indistinctly, her mouth full of hairpins.

She kept still, smoothing out the skirt of her first-communion dress with careful fingers. It was beautiful, she thought. You couldn't tell that it had been Anna's and Maria's before her. Briefly, she wondered what it was like to be Anna, to have things when they were new, before anyone else had worn them. Mummy said things were more special if someone else had worn them first, like an heirloom, she said. 'Heirloom,' she said to herself. It was like a word from a fairy tale.

Her father appeared in the doorway. 'I'm sorry, Your Highness,' he said politely. 'I was looking for Gabriella de Angelis. I didn't know this was a princess's boudoir.'

'Oh, Daddy.' A giggle seemed called for, so she giggled.

Daddy sat beside her. The bed dipped right down and Mummy tutted through her pins. He put his arm round her, crushing the puffed sleeve of the dress. 'You look beautiful, *bambina*.'

'Mind the dress, Daddy.'

'I've got a present for you, *bella*,' He put something into her hand. It made a sort of clinky slither and she hoped it was a necklace.

'It's my mother's rosary. Made of ivory. Apparently it was blessed by the Holy Father himself.' He gave the funny little nod that he always did when he mentioned the Pope. The Pope lived a long way away in a town called Rome, where Daddy was born.

'Thank you, Daddy.'

It was lovely, even if it wasn't a necklace. A plain gold cross, satisfyingly heavy, hung at the end of the ivory beads. It crossed her mind to wonder why Anna or Maria hadn't been given the rosary first, like the dress or her school jumper or the bicycle that was too small for her now. Maybe there had been three rosaries from Nonna, one for each of them.

Her mother had finished at last and, with a little push, set her on her feet. She gazed at her reflection in Mummy and Daddy's long mirror. It was odd: having seen first Anna and then Maria in this dress, she had thought she would look more like them. But she looked like herself. Anna's hair had been longer and her fringe gave her a severe crusader's look, despite the wreath of flowers. Maria's hair was lovely and curly but the dress had been slightly too short for her and you could see her school shoes underneath. Gaby, with her dark, wavy hair and round cheeks, looked like a doll. On her, the dress came right down to the floor, like one of those dolls that hid the loo roll. She smiled.

Outside, Daddy took pictures of her on her own by the bird-table and one of her standing between her sisters. Anna and Maria were in ordinary clothes, of course, but as it was such a special day they wore their best outfits. Anna was in a long gypsy skirt and a white blouse, Maria wore a black dress with lots of buttons. Daddy hadn't wanted her to wear black but Maria had said it was either that or her jeans so he gave in.

'Smile, girls! It's not a funeral, you know.'

At the church, the first-communion children stood, as Sister Immaculata had told them, in alphabetical order. Gaby was behind Michelle Daly and in front of Michael Edwards. Sister Immaculata had also given them little pointers to look for in the church so that they knew if they were standing in the right place. Gaby's was the picture of Salome holding St John the Baptist's severed head on a plate. She looked round and shuffled forward half an inch so that she was in line with Salome's foot in its jewelled sandal.

'Gabriella de Angelis.'

She stepped forward. Father O'Hagan seemed twice as tall as normal. She knew one of the altar-boys standing beside him. He fancied Maria and passed her notes on the bus.

'Body of Christ.'

'Amen.'

The dry disc on her tongue. She closed her mouth and swallowed as hard as possible. It stuck in her throat, just beyond her larynx. She gulped frantically as she paced slowly back to her place. ('Walk reverently,' Sister Immaculata had said. 'Don't stroll or skip. Walk as if you are holding some-thing very precious in your hands.') She reached her pew, still gulping. What if it never went down?

'Sweet sacrament divine,' sang the choir. 'Dear home of every heart.'

Oh, God, prayed Gaby, please let me swallow it. 'Pray silently,' Sister Immaculata had said. Well, she was praying now, all right, harder than she ever had before in her life. Suddenly her mouth filled with saliva and she swallowed. The wafer went down. Gaby lowered her head in relief. 'Gabriella de Angelis,' Sister Immaculata said the next day, 'was the only one of you who looked as if she was really praying.'

Later, when Daddy got the photos developed, there was Gaby by the bird-table, looking like the loo-roll lady, with Nonna's rosary in her hands. And there she was between her sisters, in her bright white dress, with Maria's fingers forming two little horns behind her head.

CHAPTER ONE

My father died on the day that my daughter was born. 'Well, we know whose place she's taken,' said my Aunt Ena, sitting knitting by my bed like one of those women at the foot of the guillotine. I thought at the time that this was unfair, as if Kitty had deliberately pushed in front of her grandfather in some cosmic dinner queue. Poor little thing, she didn't even know her grandfather. And now she never will.

At first, nobody told me that Dad had died. During the boring, agonising hours of labour (funny how pain can be extremely boring) my husband Bob was called away for a telephone call. He came back looking rather pale and shocked. 'Where the hell have you been?' I shouted unattractively.

'Nowhere.' He squeezed my hand.

'And don't bloody squeeze my hand.'

Even after the pure hatred of Bob, men and life in general had been replaced by the dreamlike euphoria of the birth, he still didn't tell me. It was the next day, when I sat up in bed looking at Kitty's little round face and wondering if she was going to have my nose, that Bob said, 'Gaby, I'm so sorry. Enzo's dead.'

At first I didn't understand what he was saying. Bob hardly ever called my dad by his name. It was always 'your father' or, when he was pretending to be a Cockney, 'your old man'.

'Who?'

'Enzo. Your dad. He had a heart attack two days ago. I'm sorry.'

I stared at him stupidly. 'Two days ago. He died two days ago?'

'The day Kitty was born. I'm sorry.'

I looked down at Kitty, at her wrinkled forehead and furiously shut eyes. When I first saw her olive skin and sparse black hair, I said to Bob, 'She looks just like my dad!' I remembered now that he didn't answer. 'Why didn't you tell me before?' I whispered.

'I didn't want to upset you. Just after the birth and all

that. The nurses said to wait until you were breastfeeding properly.'

I cringed. Another thing to add to the long list of Things I Wish I Had Known Before I Gave Birth was how incredibly *difficult* breastfeeding is. It may seem amazing but even the death of a father fades into the background compared to the monstrous, stomach-clenching tension of trying to get a newborn baby to suck. Before I had Kitty, I used to think of breastfeeding as lovely and natural. A bit embarrassing on the bus or at a dinner party, maybe, but essentially an easy, casual thing. My sister Maria breastfed her two youngest children until they were practically able to go to the pub for themselves. At the time, I thought this was typical Maria – hippieish, smug exhibitionism. Now I saw it as an amazing feat, comparable to building the Great Wall of China.

I peeled back the honeycombed hospital blanket and looked at Kitty's little clenched hands. Tears stung behind my eyes. 'I didn't say goodbye. Bob, I never said goodbye to him.'

Bob sat awkwardly on the edge of the bed and put his arms round me. 'I know,' he stroked my hair, 'but it was quick. That was a good thing. Your mother went out into the garden and there he was. Lying in his rosebushes.'

'He loved those roses.'

'There you are, you see. It was a good way to go.'

Kitty woke up and started crying.

I had to stay in hospital for five days because Kitty had a spot at the base of her spine and nobody knew what it was. It was a strange, dislocated time. I watched mothers come and go with their new babies, feeling like the Ancient Mariner, the woman in the corner who never got to leave the hospital. Some of the mothers, on their third or fourth baby, were so casual and blasé about it all. They hardly bothered to unpack their cases and were off as soon as the baby had been washed, weighed and nappied. They breezed out, hobbling slightly, holding their older children by the hand, the fathers following behind, carrying the latest baby as if it were a piece of luggage. I watched them with shocked fascination and envy. Would I ever be so casual with Kitty that I could give her to someone else to hold *without even looking round at her*? It seemed as remote as being able to pee without crying.

On the second day, my mother came to see me. I had already had a visit from Bob's parents, as well as Aunt Ena, nervously offering congratulations and condolences and telling me that Kitty looked just like Bob ('Only prettier,' his dad added kindly). But the space left by my parents seemed vast, unfathomable. My least favourite midwife, the one who looked like a vole, with watery eyes and a twitching nose, kept asking me if I'd seen 'Mum' yet. I noticed that even women with no discernible husband or partner had their mothers in close attendance. They were so involved, holding the babies, advising on feeding, dispensing chocolate and copies of *Hello!* from giant handbags. I longed for one to come up to me, take Kitty from me and tell me to have a good long sleep. But they ignored me, invisible in my corner.

But eventually my mum did come, very smart in a blue blazer and white trousers. I could sense the other women marking her down for lack of mumsy cardigans and light reading matter. She was carrying a small bunch of flowers and looked very tired. I stared at her. It was incredible, impossible, that Dad was not downstairs, parking the car ('Only an Italian can park in a space this small') or following her, hanging back with the embarrassed smile he reserved for exclusively female occasions. If I didn't say his name, perhaps it wasn't true.

'Oh, Gaby.' She smelled just the same. It couldn't be true.

'Here's Kitty.' I put the baby into her arms. Kitty's hands were opening and shutting like sea creatures. Mum hadn't mentioned Dad.

'Oh, Gaby,' Mum looked at me, her eyes swimming with tears, 'she's just like him.'

'It's not true, is it?' I whispered.

In answer, Mum put Kitty back into my arms. 'She's a beautiful baby. Your dad would have been so happy. He loved babies.'

And that past tense confirmed everything.

For five days, doctors were wheeled in to examine the spot at the base of Kitty's spine. They pulled her and prodded her and twisted her but said nothing. Nightmare scenarios chased each other round in my mind. Kitty suffering from some mystery disease, fading away before she had even left hospital. One night, I walked up and down the hospital corridor for hours, holding Kitty against my shoulder, convinced that if I just kept walking she would survive. Fire extinguisher, trolley, broken drinks machine, watercolours of the Lake District: Windermere, Ullswater, Ravenglass, Coniston. Up and down, all night.

Husbands were allowed in only for a few hours in the

morning. They brought flowers and younger children and an almost palpable sense of the world outside. Bob was always the first to arrive: I would see his red head through the frosted glass of the ward door and, for a moment, everything was all right again. He held me and comforted me and told me that Kitty would be fine. 'Look how beautiful she is. Just like me.' Once he told me a feeble joke and I laughed for hours, until I cried uncontrollably and the vole-faced midwife came over to complain about the noise. Bob even tried to help with the breastfeeding, propping Kitty on cushions to try to get the exact, scientific angle so that she could perform the miracle of 'latching on'; he fed me spoonfuls of disgusting hospital food to keep my strength up, carefully not suggesting that I call it a day and offering to run down to the shops for a vat of formula milk.

Finally, a new consultant in a smart pin-striped suit arrived to tell me that Kitty had a condition known as 'Mongolian blue spot'. 'It's quite harmless. Nobody knows what causes it. Tradition has it that it only occurs in people directly descended from Genghis Khan.' He smiled nervously.

'Genghis Khan?'

'Yes. Mongolian hordes and all that.'

I looked down at Kitty. I wished he hadn't said 'Mongolian'. Bob put a hand on my shoulder. 'Genghis Khan?' he said mildly. 'Are you sure you don't mean Imran?' Bob loves cricket.

But the consultant was already backing out of the room. His work here was done.

In the afternoon, Bob brought the brand-new car seat to the hospital. I dressed Kitty in the yellow cardigan and hat that my mum had knitted for her. Although she was a good-sized baby, she looked swamped in her 'going outside' clothes. The hat obscured most of her face and her arms flailed uselessly inside the cardigan sleeves. Her head, with its jaunty bobble, reached only half-way up the car seat. I remember thinking how tiny it was when we bought it. Now it looked massive: the baby equivalent of the *Mastermind* chair. 'Name: Kitty Duncan. Occupation: Full-time baby.'

Then we said thank you to the nurses (including Vole Woman), picked up the baby seat and left the hospital. It felt like the most terrifying moment of our lives.

Back at our flat we placed the car seat carefully in the middle of the sitting room, which was full of flowers. I sat on the sofa. My stitches were burning and I felt terribly tired and terribly hungry. All week I had been longing for home, with the feverish intensity of a hostage. If only I could be at home, I kept thinking, I'd be able to feed Kitty easily. I imagined myself with my feet on our Mexican oak coffee table, drinking cold white wine like someone in a colour supplement. But sitting in my very own sitting room, with all our books and posters around me and the heavy scent of the flowers in the air, I felt worse than ever. It was a beautiful April day and the window was open, bringing sounds of reggae music and laughter from the street outside. The cherry tree in our neighbour's garden was covered with shocking-pink blossom. A long way away, I could hear a police car wailing. London in springtime. It is just that I didn't fit into the scene. I was a leaking, overweight woman with a baby in my arms. I belonged to a different house, one with stair gates and baby alarms and plastic toys in the hall.

Kitty started to cry. Bob picked her up. 'Do you want to try feeding her?' he said doubtfully.

I tilted Kitty's head towards my nipple and tried not to wince as she took it into her mouth. That's the other thing they don't tell you: it hurts like buggery.

Bob brought me a cup of tea, but I was too scared to drink it in case I spilt some on Kitty's head. My mouth felt like paper, beyond thirst, as if it had never been wet in my life. Kitty sucked and sucked, but I was sure she was getting nothing. Tears rolled down my cheeks.

The doorbell rang, making us both jump. Bob went to answer it. I was frantically drying my eyes on a cushion when he came back into the room with my sister Anna.

She was dressed all in black. Even in my bemused, tearful, strung-out state I wondered where on earth she could have bought black *earrings*. Long jangly jet ones, like those worn by Victorian widows. She wore a black lace blouse, long black skirt, black tights and black high-heeled shoes. I was sure that if she could have found a lace mantilla, she would have been wearing one.

'That baby's not latched on,' said Anna. She has always been good at saying the right thing.

I started to cry again. Kitty let go of my nipple and joined in, little newborn wails that nevertheless expanded to fill the room. Anna took her from me with a practised-mother swoop. Pressed against her large black-lace bosom, Kitty abruptly stopped crying.

'How are you finding the breastfeeding?' Anna asked.

'A bit . . . you know . . . uncomfortable.'

'Keep at it,' she told me sternly. 'Breast is best.' I could feel her putting it in capitals. The Breast. It seemed to loom over my life like one of those alien life-forms in science-fiction films. *Invasion of the Breast*.

Anna sat down next to me. Kitty slept traitorously in her arms.

'I'll make a cup of tea,' said Bob. Anna makes him nervous.

Anna looked at me with a kind of sorrowful intensity that I always find unnerving. 'It's about the funeral,' she said.

Dad's funeral was the next day. In one part of my mind I knew this; in another it seemed immeasurably far away. Dad was dead and his funeral was tomorrow, but, compared to this room and Kitty and the stupefying panic of motherhood, it felt unreal, as if it were happening to someone else's family.

'Are you bringing Kitty?' asked Anna.

'Yes,' I said defiantly. As I was her only source of food at present, where I went Kitty went. And I wanted to be there. Or, rather, there was nothing in the world I wanted to do less, but I had to be there.

17

Amazingly, Anna approved. 'I'm sure it's what Dad would have wanted,' she said kindly. 'He loved babies.'

I wanted to say many things. I wanted to say, 'How come everyone knows what Dad would have wanted?' I wanted to say, 'Please stop telling me how much Dad loved babies when he is never going to see mine.' I wanted to say, 'It doesn't matter what Dad would have wanted because he isn't going to be there. He is dead.' But I said nothing.

'I'm doing a reading,' Anna continued. 'St Paul, of course.' She said it as if he were a personal friend. 'Do you want to do one?'

'No, thanks.'

'Maria's doing a bidding prayer. She's writing it herself.' Briefly, she raised her eyes heavenwards. We both knew that the prayer would contain numerous references to Brother Sun, Sister Moon and the circle of life. 'Marco and Sergio have written a song.' They are Anna's sons, usually to be found plugged into iPhones. It would be amazing to see them without wires attached. 'What do you want to do?' prompted Anna.

'Do?' I echoed stupidly.

'At the funeral.'

'Nothing.' The dreary tears started again.

'You must do something. Why don't you write a little poem about Daddy?'

'For Christ's sake, I'm not one of your fourth-formers.' Anna is, of course, a teacher.

I had made a big mistake. I had mentioned the C-word. I had called on another of Anna's closest friends. Anna looked as if she were going to reply, perhaps to remind me that it was for Christ's sake, after all, but mercifully she said nothing. Instead, she patted me, rather clumsily, on the shoulder. 'Don't cry, Gaby. I understand. It's your hormones.'

I cried even harder, wanting to say, 'It's not my hormones, it's because my father's dead.' Why did everyone blame my hormones for everything? 'We've just had another weepy day,' the nurses at the hospital would say comfortably to Bob. 'It's nothing to worry about, just hormones.' And if I did have these things racing around inside me, making me cry all the time, wasn't that something to worry about? My father was dead, I couldn't feed my baby, my sister kept droning on about funerals – wasn't that something to cry about?

Anna kept patting my shoulder with firm downward movements, as if she were making bread. 'Don't cry,' she said. 'It'll curdle your milk.' And then I howled in earnest and Kitty joined in. Bob came in to find the room full of screaming women. To his credit, he didn't turn tail and run. Instead, he took Kitty out of Anna's arms. She stopped crying immediately. 'Gaby's tired,' he said. 'Perhaps you'd better discuss this another time.'

Anna is five years older than me. Now it seems like nothing (except when I see her dance), but when we were younger it was a huge gap. By the time I arrived in secondary school, Anna was in the fifth year, wearing make-up and talking about 'global capitalism'. Maria is two years younger than Anna and three years older than me. She is in the middle, but when we were children she was always closer to Anna. They shared a bedroom while I had the tiny boxroom to myself. They used to read *Smash Hits* and go to discos when I was still keen on being a Brownie. By the time I got to the Sacred Heart comprehensive, I was already known as 'Anna de Angelis's sister'.

Not that this was such a bad thing. Anna was a big star at school. Clever, sporty, great at taking on those thankless jobs like 'pupil representative' and 'chair of the debating society'. She was always organising things: petitions against abortion, collections for starving children in Africa, sponsored walks in aid of CAFOD. The teachers, particularly the nuns, adored her.

I was a disappointment – I grasped that immediately. Oh, I was clever enough, though mostly in subjects like maths and science, which were subtly considered (by my parents, at least) to be inferior to English and history. It was just that I lacked Anna's sense of showmanship. I was slow to put up my hand in class or in assembly. I never volunteered to do the reading at mass. I hated debating and hid at the back of the chorus in school plays.

Anna never had any such qualms. She was the star of the debating society, a mesmerising Olivia in *Twelfth Night*, a rather disturbing Titania in *A Midsummer Night's Dream*. No feast day was complete without the sound of her clear, calm voice reading the bidding prayers. I will always remember once, after I had stumbled through an obligatory reading at assembly, one of the nuns saying, 'Sure and He broke the mould after He made Anna.' At the time I dismissed it as one of those gnomic nuns' remarks that mean nothing. It was only afterwards that I thought about it and understood that they meant Anna was the original and best; Maria and I were only inferior versions of her. The standard in our family was going down: from Anna down to Maria and hitting rock bottom with me.

Anna was always sure to go to university and do great things in the world. 'I can see her as the first Catholic prime minister,' said Sister Anthony mistily, as Anna gave the vote of thanks at her leavers' dinner. There was no doubt that she would go far.

And, at first, she did. Anna got straight As at A level and went to Cambridge to read English. All was going according to plan: she bulldozed her way on to a variety of committees and it seemed it was only a matter of time before she would appear on *Question Time*, arguing passionately against the morning-after pill. But then she fell in love.

She announced it with typical Anna confidence. 'I've met the man I'm going to marry,' she told us, when she arrived home for the first long summer vacation. In fact, she announced it in the car on the way home from the station. I was only along for the ride (I was in my loafing-around stage: too young to go into town on my own, old enough to be bored by everything else) so I said nothing. Married, I was thinking. Leaving home, going to university, getting married. Isn't something missing here? Like the brilliant career?

'That's lovely, darling,' said my mother, after a pause. 'What's his name?'

'David,' said Anna. 'David Blackstock. I met him at the Catholic Society.'

I don't know why, but this information depressed us. Dad, trying hard, asked, 'What is he reading?'

'Philosophy,' said Anna unanswerably. 'After university, he wants to do VSO and teach in Africa.'

We all murmured appreciatively. Dad misjudged the turning into our drive and knocked off the Lancia's wing mirror.

When we finally met David, they were already secretly engaged, Anna wearing the ring on a chain round her neck, next to her crucifix. David was nice: we all liked him. He was a dark, intense-looking Catholic boy from Manchester. He wore John Lennon glasses and thought that Jesus was the first socialist. He impressed me by being knowledgeable about current music (Anna considered the Gregorian chant dangerously modern) and excitingly reckless on the Palace Pier dodgems. My parents liked him too. He talked to my dad about philosophy and economics and to my mum about feminist historians. He even helped push Dad's car when it refused to start in the morning (although he fell over and broke his glasses in the process). Why, then, did it seem such a bombshell when Anna announced their engagement. Coming down late one night to get a glass of water, I overheard my parents saying things like 'Let's be sensible, it may not last,' and 'I never thought we'd have this problem with Anna, the other two maybe' (thanks a bunch, Mum). Why was it such a disaster that Anna was marrying a good Catholic boy with whom she was manifestly in love?

I think it was just that they'd had such high hopes for her. She was marrying a nice boy and would no doubt start a nice Catholic family. It was unlikely that she would become prime minister. Anna married David straight after graduation, wearing the biggest, whitest dress seen in Lewes since the visit of Elizabeth I, some four hundred years earlier. There was no more talk of VSO or Africa. David and Anna settled in London, and Anna did a PGCE and got a job teaching English at the local comprehensive. She liked her work and was good at it, becoming head of department in three years. At about the same time, she had her first child, Marco. My parents were happy: they were proud of her, they liked David, they adored their first male grandchild, but there was still a lingering sense that it wasn't what they had expected for Anna, 'the clever one'.

Anna didn't seem unhappy, though. She achieved at motherhood in the same way that she had achieved at everything else in her life. Marco was the brightest, most stimulated baby in existence. When I went to visit Anna in her new house in Forest Hill (magnetic letters on the fridge, climbing frame in the back garden) she drove me mad by continually stopping what she was saying to me to answer one of Marco's countless questions. 'Yes, Marco, Auntie Gaby's my little sister. How can she be my little sister when she's all grown-up? Well, to me she'll always be my little sister. Just like Sergio will always be your little brother.'

Yes, Sergio followed Marco after two years. The perfect Catholic gap. Close enough that they might not be using contraception, but not so close that David looked like a sex maniac. Anna took the boys to church on Sunday, one child holding her hand sweetly, the other burbling in a pushchair. They were the ideal family.

Which would have been fine: the children *were* sweet,

Anna *was* a good mother, she and David *did* have a strong marriage. If only she could have been content with that. But, no, it was not enough that she and David were walking in the light of the Lord: we all had to join her in the heavenly spotlight. My dad was urged to renew his baptismal vows. My mother, who is not a Catholic, faced an almost daily onslaught of pamphlets and newsletters inviting her to 'Come and See. Join in the Catholic Journey of Faith.' 'Will Grandma go to heaven even if she's not a Catholic?' asked Marco, aged five.

'Only if she's very good,' said Anna darkly.

But it was Maria and I who suffered most. Since she had got pregnant at nineteen and divorced at twenty-one, Maria was already well on the way to fallen-womanhood. In fact, I suggested she changed her name to Maria Magdalene and had done with it. Funnily enough, though, it was when Maria remarried and happily started a new family that Anna really got on her case. Maria's second marriage, to Ray, involved a brief visit to the register office followed by a picnic on the South Downs where Maria, in an embroidered gypsy dress, talked about pantheism and stone-age fertility rites. Anna, rigid in a blue suit, sat on a hillock with an untouched mug of champagne beside her. I knew from her set, stony face that she was inwardly reciting the rosary. Could this really be counted as a marriage? Later, when Maria had Mosaic and Kyle, she did not have them baptised but invited us to their Native American naming ceremony. Anna refused to come, adding threateningly that she would pray for them. You could tell that, in Anna's mind, an education at various Montessori and Steiner schools would never make up for not chanting the Our Father and taking part in May processions.

With me, Anna's Christian zeal took the form of worrying about my morals. I had scarcely been at university a week when I received a letter from her. 'Dear Gaby,' it began, 'I hope you are enjoying university and that you are not too tired after freshers' week!!' The exclamation marks were meant to show that she knew what it was like: she had been to university and she understood the temptation of spotty youths studying environmental science. She was human but she knew her duty, which was to warn me. The letter went on: 'I know some of your friends will be sleeping with their boyfriends but I do urge you not to do the same. Save yourself for your husband.' I remember throwing the letter into the bin, then taking it out and tearing it into very small pieces. Saving myself for my husband indeed! If her behaviour with Stuart Wilkins was anything to go by, I was pretty sure *she* hadn't. How dared she lecture me?

Whenever I had a new boyfriend, Anna would sigh deeply and say she hoped 'this one is going to last'. But it was when I fell in love and got married that Anna's disapproval reached new heights. Bob and I even got married in a Catholic church but, for Anna, the Church's blessing could hardly have been more painful if it had been a black mass. Not only was Bob not a Catholic, he was also, according to Anna, 'a man without a spiritual connection.' Bob had scandalised her by saying cheerfully that he had been raised as an Anglican but he 'didn't mind' if the wedding was in a Catholic church because 'They're all the same, really, aren't they?' Anna was horrified. She would have preferred a Muslim or a Jew or even a downright atheist (lots of scope for conversion), anyone rather than this smiling heathen who just 'didn't mind'. He hadn't even got the necessary conviction to be anti-Catholic. He simply didn't care very much either way.

To be fair to Bob, there was no way, in Anna's eyes, that

he could ever live up to my previous boyfriend, Jonathan. He had been intelligent, good-looking, spiritual and committed. He was Anna's ideal man.

He is a priest.

CHAPTER TWO

The next day I thought of my wedding again, when I walked into the church for my father's funeral. The last time I walked up this aisle I was dressed in white (not such a fantastic affair as Anna's dress but still a bit of a meringue, all the same) and holding Dad's arm. I remember waiting at home with him for the car to arrive: he was pacing the room nervously, and I helped him retie his cravat (funnily enough, I wasn't nervous at all). When we got to the church, Maria's daughter Tara was waiting to meet us. She was nine and very serious about her duties as our bridesmaid. She came eagerly down the steps to take my train. As we began our slow walk up the aisle, she tripped and, with the terrible sound of tearing silk, my train came away in her hands. I will never forget Tara's yelp of dismay or Dad's shocked expression. Tara didn't know whether to laugh or cry, but suddenly Dad and I were shaking with laughter. In the front row, Bob turned round, grinning. Dad and I went back to help Tara and we walked back up the aisle in a threesome, all three of us crying with laughter.

Only Anna was disapproving. She said that, for her, it had ruined the moment. But by then I didn't care. I had married Bob.

But now, as Bob and I walked into the church, we were following Dad's coffin. He was dead and I would never hear him laugh again. Bob held my arm tightly as I clutched Kitty to my chest. Mum walked in front, with Anna and David at either side of her, as if she were under arrest. Behind us walked Anna's sons, Marco and Sergio, awkward in unaccustomed suits. Maria, in a bright purple dress ('It's a colour of mourning,' she had told Anna defiantly), came next, a child on each side of her. Mosaic, aged six, looked bright-eyed with suppressed excitement, and Kyle, four, was humming softly to himself. 'The wheels on the bus go round and round. Round and round. Round and round.' Anna hissed at him to be quiet but I was glad when he took no notice. I felt that the wheels on the bus were an excellent antidote to that grim, silent walk. 'Round and round. Round and round. All day long.'

At the front of the church was Aunt Ena in a terrifying hat. Behind her, two of Dad's friends from the university were crying quietly. I started to shake. Bob looked at me anxiously.

It was better when we sat down. The choir began a hymn and I looked round the church. Behind us was Dad's brother, Bruno. He must have flown over from Rome that morning. Next to him was his son, Franco, who is my age, thirty-five. Franco smiled briefly and touched my shoulder. Uncle Bruno gestured admiringly towards Kitty. Even at a funeral, Italians are ready for a spot of baby worship.

The priest, Father Simon, was young and nervous. Dad used to tease him by asking complicated questions about celibacy and the mystical body. Even now, it seemed to me that Father Simon eyed the coffin warily as he spoke about Dad: 'A brilliant man, a highly respected academic, much-loved father and grandfather.'

Anna stood up. She stared sternly at us from the lectern. 'A reading from the letter of St Paul to the Romans.' I was now shaking so hard that Kitty's head was rocking to and fro on my chest. The whole thing – the church, the single bunch of lilies on the coffin, the sound of Uncle Bruno sobbing quietly behind me – seemed like one of those weird Oriental tortures designed to discover, scientifically, how much pain the human body can stand.

'"Having died to make us righteous",' said Anna, with awful solemnity, '"is it likely that he would now fail to save us from God's anger?"'

The church swooped and swayed around me. I could see every individual mote of dust in the air.

'" . . . now that we have been reconciled, surely we must count on being saved by the life of his Son?"'

I swayed forward and had to hold on to the pew in front to stop myself falling.

'Gaby?' said Bob. His voice seemed to come from very far away.

I got up and stumbled out of the pew, heading for a door on my right. Kitty, disturbed by this activity, started to cry. I fell through it into the vestry and sat down on a chair. I had never been in here before. Vestments hung from pegs on the wall, and a pile of old newsletters sat on a box marked 'recycling'. I couldn't take my eyes off a pair of bright yellow rubber gloves on the table. Whose were they? Did Father Simon put them on when he was doing the washing-up? Surely priests shouldn't worry about keeping their hands soft. From the other side of the door, I could hear guitars. Anna must have finished her reading and Marco and Sergio were starting their song: 'Oh, Nonno, you were the best. You loved Arsenal better than all the rest.'

Kitty was still crying. Without thinking about it, I undid my black blouse, popped open my maternity bra and put her to my breast. The midwives were always going on about getting the angle of the baby's head exactly right, so that they could latch on properly but, in my disorientated state, I just shoved my nipple into Kitty's mouth. Somehow, miraculously, she twisted her head and I felt a great pull, coming not from my breast but from far deeper in my body, almost as if there were a string tugging upwards from below my stomach. Despite everything, great waves of love and happiness washed over me. We were doing it right. Kitty and I had passed the test.

'Oh, Kitty,' I said, 'oh, my sweet girl.'

When I turned my head, I saw Bob standing in the doorway. He was smiling.

The rest of the funeral passed in a blur. Then we were

singing 'Thine Be the Glory' and the undertakers carried the coffin out of the church. I twisted round so that I could see it one last time. We got back into the cars for the drive to the crematorium. It was a bright spring day and the Sussex countryside was at its most beautiful. The ceremony was brief: a few prayers, a sprinkle of holy water, a burst of taped music and we were emerging into the sunlight.

Father Simon shook my hand. 'God bless you,' he murmured.

'Thank you, Father,' boomed Anna loudly, from behind me.

Afterwards, there was a curious feeling of relief. In the car, on the way back to Mum's house (no longer Mum and Dad's), we loosened ties, undid shirt buttons and eased feet out of shoes.

'That went very well,' said Anna.

Maria snorted. 'Yes, it was great, Anna. Quite a treat.'

My mother was gazing out of the window and appeared not to have heard them. 'How lovely the daffodils look,' she said vaguely.

Back at the house, there was quite a party. Maria's husband Ray, who is good at this sort of thing, kept filling everyone's glass. Mosaic and Kyle played in the garden with Mario and Sergio, who had changed out of their suits. I fed Kitty again, sitting on a bench in the garden. The sun was warm on my exposed breast. Bob sat beside me and fed me small bites of sandwich.

Franco came over with a glass of red wine, like someone at a wedding reception. 'Congratulations,' he said. 'What a beautiful baby.'

I was gratified. I felt that Franco's praise carried extra weight because he is a paediatrician.

Franco sighed heavily. 'What a sad day. Poor Uncle Enzo. It must have been a terrible shock for you.'

'Yes,' I said. Dad was seventy-three but he always seemed in such good health. His hair wasn't even grey and he could still beat Marco at tennis. But it was more than that. I'm the youngest: I wasn't ready to lose my father yet. I wanted him to be around for a lot longer, I wanted him to be a grandfather to my children. For a second, I felt so angry I couldn't speak.

'My father is devastated,' said Franco. 'They were very close.'

'At least they saw each other recently,' offered Bob, 'in Rome at Christmas.'

'Yes.' Franco sighed again. 'Uncle Enzo was saying he wanted to come back and live in Rome.'

'Was he?' I said in surprise. This was news to me.

'Yes. He was saying that a Roman never feels truly happy away from Rome. He said he wanted to end his days there. I thought at the time he must be feeling . . .'

'Sick?' I asked anxiously.

'No. Mortal,' said Franco sadly.

When all the friends, neighbours and people from the university had gone home, I sat with my mother, Anna and Maria in the conservatory. Marco and Sergio had taken the younger children to the park. Bob and Ray were clearing up. David was driving Bruno and Franco back to their hotel. Kitty was asleep.

Suddenly it seemed odd to be alone with my mother and sisters. I couldn't think of the last time that it was just the four of us. In my mind it was always Dad with me, and Mum with my sisters. 'The girls,' Mum used to call them, just as Marco and Sergio are now 'the boys.' Once I heard her refer to 'the girls and Gaby.' 'I'm a girl,' I had protested hotly.

'Oh, I know you are,' said my mother quickly, perhaps fearing damage to my childish self-image (she read books about that sort of thing). 'It was just a quick way of speaking.'

I don't know if Anna and Maria resented being rounded up together in that way but I know that I didn't mind. I had drawn first prize: I had Dad. My mum would be supervising my sisters' homework while I watched TV with Dad. Mum would take Anna and Maria to the ballet; Dad took me to buy used cars. It was obvious who the winner was.

Even as adults there had always been husbands, children, relations, friends. We had never really been alone. Recently even my pregnancy came between us like another person. Now the room felt charged, as if we were waiting for something. My mother was sitting on an uncomfortable wicker sofa. Anna was wedged next to her, watching her solicitously. Maria was on the matching armchair, her purple skirts spread round her. I was sitting opposite with Kitty next to me, sleeping in her car seat. Suddenly my mother got up (hoisting herself out of the sofa with difficulty) and walked out of the room. Anna, Maria and I watched her in silence. We just sat there, wordlessly, until she came back, carrying a photograph.

'What's that?' asked Anna, in her new 'Mum' voice, compassionate yet bright.

Mum held out the picture. It showed Dad in Rome at

Christmas. He was standing outside the Castel Sant' Angelo, arms spread wide as if to embrace its splendour and somehow take credit for it. She looked at us. 'He wanted to go back,' she said.

'Back where?' asked Maria stupidly.

'To Rome. He wanted his ashes taken to Rome. He told me.'

Anna smiled. 'That's a lovely idea. We can arrange a mass. Gaby, Jonathan's still in Rome, isn't he, at the English Church? Perhaps he could do a service at the little church where—'

'Actually,' Maria interrupted, 'he told me that he wanted a pagan service.'

Maria. The middle daughter. She is 'the pretty one'. For reference, Anna is 'the clever one' and I used to be 'the cute one' or 'the youngest one', although now I am probably 'the one who became an accountant', which isn't quite so catchy.

We are all all-right-looking. Anna is tall and statuesque. She used to have wonderful hair, long, black and shiny, like an unusually attractive witch's, but now she is going grey and, typically, refuses to do anything about it. She just pulls her hair back into a ponytail or bun with the grey streaks prominent. Maria says it's tragic.

Maria is the opposite. She has black hair too, wavier and wilder than Anna's, but Maria is Henna Woman. Her hair has changed colour so often that it's a wonder anyone remembers the original shade. Or, as Bob once remarked, 'Maria's lucky to have naturally purple hair.' Since Maria got into natural fabrics and the healing power of jewellery, her look is very hippie chic: lots of purple and black layers edged with gold, fringed jackets, patchwork coats, strings of beads, friendship bracelets, vegetarian shoes. Her hair, now a sort of orangy-yellow, is usually worn in a messy knot on top of her head. She is still beautiful, nothing can change that, but she does look as if you should cross her palm with silver. Luckily she's keen on silver.

At school, Maria was a star. Anna was the teachers' favourite and the girl most likely to be prime minister, but Maria was a star where it mattered: among the pupils. 'You're Maria de Angelis's sister?' people would say, in an awed whisper. When I arrived at secondary school, Maria was only in the third year but she had already been out with all the best-looking boys. She was the centre of a group of achingly cool girls who wore their uniforms with the sort of throwaway style I could never achieve: socks rolled down, tie pulled tight, shirts tied round the waist, boys' names written on their arms. I don't know how Maria got to be so cool. Our parents weren't cool – they both taught at the *university*, for heaven's sake. Anna wasn't cool: she was clever, which is different. I tried hard to be cool but I was too timid and too scared of getting into trouble. Maria had her navel pierced before I even got round to having my ears done. She had her own lighter at the age of thirteen; I still hadn't smoked a cigarette by the time I went to university.

When she was about sixteen, Maria's cool reached new heights. She started going out with Lee Higgins. It is hard for me to describe what that meant. Lee was beyond cool. He was the school version of Brad Pitt, Leonardo DiCaprio and Ewan McGregor, all rolled into one. Dirty blond hair, rangy body, the brightest, most dissipated blue eyes ever seen outside a movie screen. Just to see him in the corridor was enough to make girls faint for a week. A smile from Lee (teeth very white, the most heartbreaking small scar on his upper lip) could mean a whole afternoon in Sick Bay.

Lee was in Anna's year, not that she had much to do

with him. They lived in different worlds: Anna's sphere of Oxbridge debates hardly ever overlapped with Lee's skiving off to hang around the café milieu. Lee went out with the two prettiest girls in his year, broke their hearts and moved on to girls outside school, who drove cars, had jobs and, it was rumoured, 'did it.'

Lee left school at sixteen and got a job as a trainee manager in a frozen-food shop. The first time I was aware of anything between him and Maria was when she started taking her books to school in a carrier-bag from the frozen-food place. I remarked on the uncharacteristic naffness of this bag and she said casually, 'It's from Lee's work.' Her friends, Shelley and Becka, nudged her and giggled madly. I was transfixed. The fact that Lee worked there made the carrier the height of cool, the Prada clutch-bag of carriers. Surely Maria was not on plastic-bag terms with the great Lee Higgins?

But she was. The next thing we knew, Lee had given Maria a gold necklace costing a week's frozen-food wages. He met her after school, leaning casually against the wall, scattering his cigarette ash in bland disregard of the teachers' disapproval. Later, in a truly glorious moment for Maria, he came to meet her on a motorbike, holding a spare helmet. Maria hitched up her (already minuscule) skirt, put on the helmet and climbed on behind him, putting her arms round his waist in a wonderfully casual gesture of togetherness.

Our parents hated him. They considered themselves tolerant and left-wing, but this did not extend to their daughter going out with a boy who worked in the Ice Palace Frozen Food Emporium (For All Your Cash And Carry Needs). Lee, with his motorbike, cigarettes and dragon tattoo on his shoulder, was every parent's nightmare. They tried to be clever about it. They didn't forbid Maria to go out with him. They tried to be friendly, inviting him round for tea or Sunday lunch, but to no avail. 'No, thanks,' said Maria. 'Lee doesn't do families.'

This almost reduced my parents to tears. To them families were sacred. I think for my father it was a natural, almost unconscious thing. Your family came first. He didn't see the need for any relationships outside the family. I remember many rows about this, particularly with Maria. Maria would say that she wanted to see some friend on Sunday (the most sacrosanct family day of all) and Dad would say, 'But don't you want to be with your family?' and Maria would answer sulkily, 'No, I want to be with my friends.' Dad didn't understand that. Friends were fine in their place but *family* was special. I really think that, for him, his wife, daughters and brother in Italy were enough. He didn't need anyone else in his life. Oh, he had lots of friends, at university and elsewhere, but part of his charm was that he didn't need them. He was quite happy with his family. He was a contented man and, of course, people were attracted to that.

For my mother, it was a more abstract concept. She was an only child and I think she sometimes found the reality of family life rather trying but, in principle, she was all for it. I wonder if it was one reason why she married an Italian, whose family, though sacred, was a long way away.

And now Lee was making Maria question the holy principle of The Family. 'Oh, well,' said my father stoically, 'it won't last. I give it six months.' But after six months Lee and Maria were just getting into their stride. After a year, Lee had 'Maria' tattooed on his other shoulder. After two years, Maria was openly spending the night at Lee's bedsit. After three, she was pregnant.

Our parents were devastated. This didn't happen to people like them, people with degrees and large houses with double garages. There was Anna at Cambridge, me keeping my head down at school ('It's hard to believe she's Maria's sister') and now Maria, pregnant at nineteen, like someone from the council estate. I remember whispered late-night discussions ('She's throwing her life away', 'She'll never go to university now'). My parents endlessly discussed the options: adoption, marriage, life as a single parent (but never, not once, abortion) but it was all pointless. Maria had made up her mind. She loved Lee, Lee loved her. They were married at Brighton register office when Maria was six months pregnant.

At first it still seemed cool. Lee and Maria lived in a little flat in Kemp Town with red walls and crazy posters. Lee was now a manager at the Ice Palace and Maria worked part-time in a bookshop (to my parents' disgust, she had flatly refused to go to university). I would sometimes go to stay the night and it was wonderfully exciting and grown-up. Maria would cook pasta or chilli con carne and we would eat in front of the TV (something my parents considered almost as evil as drug abuse). Afterwards we would go for a drink in the pub on the corner. Lee would come over from the pool table, put his arm round Maria and pat her huge, taut stomach. 'That's my girl,' he would say. 'How's the baby? How's my boy? Still kicking? He's going to be a footballer, this one.'

Except it wasn't a boy. After a long, agonising labour during which she called repeatedly for Mum, Maria gave birth to a girl. Perhaps Lee felt left out. Certainly I remember him hovering on the edges of the tight, all-female group of Maria, our mother and the baby girl, Tara. Shortly afterwards, Maria moved back home. 'Just for a while,' said Dad, wearing his doting baby smile. 'Just while the *bambina* is little.' I grunted sceptically. The baby was sweet but her crying didn't help with my GCSE revision. Also, I had quite enjoyed having my parents all to myself, and now Maria was back, with her blankets, baby paraphernalia and talk of 'posseting', 'cradle cap' and 'projectile vomiting'. It wasn't a very congenial atmosphere for a tormented teenager.

I'll always remember the last time I saw Lee. It was late one Saturday night. I had just got back from going to the pictures with a boy and was trying to avoid my parents' questions ('Do we know his parents?' 'Is he doing his A levels?'). Maria was watching *Parkinson* on the TV. She was in her dressing-gown, her dark hair spread on her shoulders, serene and quite astoundingly beautiful. Baby Tara slept in a Moses basket at her feet. For the moment, Maria seemed to have no urge to go out in the evenings. Brighton, the Mecca of our teenage years, had lost its charm. She was happy to sit in front of the television drinking cocoa and wearing fluffy slippers.

I got myself some cocoa and sat down next to her. I remember that Parky was interviewing some American actress from *Dynasty* and had tied himself into a huge knot of obsequiousness. We sat there, in the cosy glow of the TV, not speaking but enjoying one of those rare moments when it doesn't seem too terrible to be with your family. Tara mumbled in her sleep, Mum brought in a plate of biscuits, Parky seemed to be trying to get his right foot round his left ear. Then we heard a shout from outside. 'Maria! Maria!' I looked at Maria, who continued to stare at the TV in a kind of trance. My mum went to the window. 'Maria,' she said, 'it's Lee.'

'Tell him I don't want to see him,' said Maria, not taking her eyes off the screen.

'He's on the garage roof,' said Mum.

I joined her at the window. Lee was indeed on our garage roof. He stood there in the rain, arms outstretched, shouting, 'Maria!' like something out of *West Side Story*. I stared at him, fascinated. Maria stared at the television.

48

Then Dad came into the room, the ever-present book under his arm. '*Mamma mia!* What's going on?'

Silently, Mum indicated the scene on the garage roof. 'Maria!' shouted Lee. 'You're my wife! Come back to me!'

'He's drunk,' said Mum.

Dad looked at Maria on the sofa, then back at Mum. He put down his book and went outside. We saw him go towards the garage and speak to Lee, one hand shielding his face from the rain. We couldn't hear what he was saying. They talked on and on, Lee kneeling on the asphalt roof, his blond hair plastered flat, thin shirt soaking, Dad talking up at him, hands moving all the while. During all this time, Maria's eyes did not once leave the television. I watched, fascinated. There was a desperate pathos in the scene, which I don't think I recognised then. Lee, so cool, so certain, driven to such a ridiculous display of devotion. My dad, who disliked and despised Lee, standing in the pouring rain, pleading with him. What was he saying? To forget Maria? To come into the sitting room and watch *Parkinson* with us? To be a member of our family? I didn't know, but I did know that I had never aroused one-tenth of the passion in anyone that Lee was showing now. When I had finished with my last boyfriend, he had shrugged and said, 'OK. See you around.' No one had ever stood on a garage roof for me and I didn't think they ever would.

Eventually we saw Lee lower himself from the roof. He stood there for a few seconds, swaying, and then collapsed, sobbing, into Dad's arms. Much later, Dad drove him home. I never saw him again.

Maria lived at home until Tara was three. By this time I had gone to university. In snippets I heard that Maria was moving out, going to university, joining a commune, getting back with Lee. Finally she did move out, to a one-bedroom flat in Brighton. Much to my parents' relief, she also enrolled at university, put Tara into a crèche and proceeded to get a good degree. Of course, she had an affair with her tutor, but even that had a happy ending, of sorts. He left his wife and married Maria. Ray and Maria now live in a huge house beside Brighton College, full of stained glass and bookcases. They have had two children, Mosaic and Kyle, and Maria has become a fully fledged New Age thinker. 'It's not so bad,' said my mother philosophically. 'Some of it is very pretty. And they do have lovely wind chimes.'

CHAPTER THREE

Now Maria rearranged her purple skirts and looked at Anna with the clear certainty that she was right. As Anna was equally sure that *she* was right, this promised to be a long discussion. I got up and went to the window. Dad's beloved roses were in full bloom outside and, once again, I had the strongest feeling that he was about to come round the corner, carrying his trowel and wearing his Arsenal hat.

Now Anna was asking Maria what she meant by a pagan ceremony and Maria was saying that when Dad was staying with her ('that time you were in hospital, Mum') they talked about where they wanted to be buried.

'Sounds fun,' I said.

Maria turned her headlamp eyes on me. 'Actually, it was

beautiful, Gaby. We had a really lovely, deep discussion. I said I wanted to be buried in an ecologically sound cardboard box in a sustainable forest. Ray wants to be buried at sea. And Dad said that he wanted his ashes scattered near Trajan's Column. You know, in Trajan's Forum. In Rome. And I said, "It's not a very Christian place," and he said he didn't want a Christian ceremony. "Sacrifice a few goats," he said.'

Sacrifice a few goats. I could just hear him saying that. Not that he had anything against goats – he was sentimental about all animals, especially donkeys. When Marco was born, he adopted a donkey in his name and called it Pinocchio. No, it's the tone I recognised. When faced with either Maria's highminded mysticism or Anna's relentless Catholicism, he would retreat into faintly waspish irony. 'Sacrifice a few goats,' I could hear him say, smiling into his wineglass. But Maria, of course, had taken the comments at face value.

Meanwhile Anna was swelling like a bullfrog. 'It may interest you to know, Maria,' she said, with dangerous quietness, 'that Daddy told *me* that he wanted his ashes scattered at the church of Maria Assumpta in Rome. Where he was baptised.'

'When did he tell you that?' asked Maria quickly.

'When he came to stay for Marco's confirmation.'

'There you are,' said Maria triumphantly. 'That was last spring. He told me about the Forum in September. He must have had second thoughts.'

Anna looked as if she were about to explode. I decided to fill the breach. 'Actually,' I said, 'he told me in February that he wanted his ashes scattered in the Tiber. You know, like the poem: "O Tiber! Father Tiber! / To whom the Romans pray".'

Dead silence greeted this announcement. Then Anna said contemptuously, 'Pure doggerel.' She loves to remind us that she has an English degree.

'Dad loved it,' I said. 'You remember how he used to quote, "How can a man die better than facing fearful odds"?'

Anna is silent because Dad indeed loved that poem, with all its Victorian posturing:

> O Tiber! Father Tiber!
> To whom the Romans pray,
> A Roman's life, a Roman's arms,
> Take thou in charge this day!

I realised that I wanted desperately to put his ashes into the Tiber. Forums and churches are such dead places. Water is alive. If we put his ashes into the river, it would carry them to the sea. He would be part of something that was moving, changing, living. Isn't that why people used to worship the river gods?

'We have to have a religious ceremony,' said Anna stubbornly, at last.

'I don't see that at all,' said Maria, 'given that he expressed a wish to go back to a more ancient form of worship.'

'More ancient form!' scoffed Anna. 'Typical wrong-headed hippie thinking.'

At this promising moment, the conversation was broken up by the return of Marco and Sergio with Mosaic and Kyle. Mosaic was complaining that Marco didn't carry her on his shoulders like he did Kyle. Maria took Kyle on her lap; he is obviously her favourite.

'What are you talking about?' asked Marco curiously, sitting on the arm of Anna's sofa.

'We're talking about Nonno's ashes,' said Anna repressively. 'About where we'll scatter them. Which church.'

'Or other sacred place,' said Maria stubbornly.

Marco looked from one to the other as if he were watching a tennis match. I stood by the window, wondering if I was going to intervene again and whether anyone would listen to me. I had heard this debate so many times before: Anna on the side of the angels; Maria on the darker, more glamorous team. Where did I stand? Unlike Anna and Maria, I was not certain of my ground.

But I did have Kitty, who saved me by waking up and crying.

'Feed her here,' said Anna imperiously, as I got up to leave the room.

'Breastfeeding is natural,' chimed in Maria. 'You shouldn't have to hide.'

'Perhaps Gaby wants some peace and quiet,' suggested my mother mildly. It seemed the first thing she had said for hours. I nodded gratefully and left the room, Kitty clamped, wailing, to my chest.

In my parents' room, all was order and stillness. I was so desperate to feed Kitty, to check that the miracle of breastfeeding still worked, that at first I hardly noticed my surroundings. Then, as I lay back on the pillows, Kitty sucking happily, her toes wiggling with delight, I felt a chill of horror. I was lying on my parents' gravestone-smooth counterpane *on Dad's side*.

So many times, as a child, I had crashed in here after a bad dream, to find Dad rising up from this side of the bed: 'What is it, *bella*?' Always Dad, never Mum, who would just say calmly, 'Go back to bed, Gaby,' then turn over and fall asleep. But Dad would get up, tuck me into bed and sing me an Italian song about a cricket and a grasshopper getting married. With mounting panic, I looked round the room: at the louvred wardrobe that contained his shabby lecturer's clothes, his slick Italian suits for special occasions, his Arsenal shirt, the Hawaiian shirt that Bob and I bought him, which Mum hated. I could almost feel them behind the doors, like the Tell-Tale Heart, struggling to get out. On the chest of drawers was the box that Maria made at school in woodwork. I knew exactly what was inside: his cufflinks, his Italy tiepin and a broken earring of Mum's that he was always promising to mend. Next to it was the tiny ebony Madonna that his mother gave him. Someone (my mother?) had put a vase of roses on his bedside table; the petals were already dropping.

Kitty had fallen asleep so I got up and went to the window.

Outside, Sergio and Mosaic were playing football in the garden. They seemed to belong to a different world. A clock, kept ten minutes fast by Dad, ticked loudly. How could it still be ticking when he was dead? Wasn't the symbolism wrong here?

The worst thing about someone dying is also the most obvious: *the person is not there*. It's as simple as that. The horror of this sunny room was that Dad's clothes and cufflinks and Italy tiepin were here, but he wasn't. If that horrible space on his side of the bed could just be filled with his body, his corporeal presence, then everything would be all right again. Yes, we believe (don't we?) that his spirit lives on, but at that moment that seemed a poor exchange for my dad with his Arsenal shirt, his trilby hat and wonderful crinkly smile. I felt I would give anything, *anything*, for the scent of the lemon aftershave he always wore. Dad's dressing-gown hung on the back of the door. Desperately, I pressed my face into it. His smell was still there, embedded in the worn brown towelling, and I wanted to stay there, with my head buried in its comforting darkness, for ever.

On his bedside table, under the roses, was a picture of Anna, Maria and me. We were standing on a beach, possibly in Ostia. Anna was about ten, holding a beach ball rather aggressively, as if she were about to throw it at the camera. Maria was next to her: her hair was in long plaits – she would suck the ends and Dad used to say that he knew a girl in Italy who had died from doing that ('Her stomach became one big ball of hair'). I was standing slightly apart from my sisters and looked as if I had just sneezed. My hair was standing up in wild curls and I was wearing a horrible bobbly swimming costume. I must have been five, I suppose. 'I have three daughters,' my dad used to say, 'and I love each one more than the other.' As a child this drove me mad. What did it *mean*? Why couldn't he just say he loved me best?

On my mother's bedside table was my parents' wedding photograph. I picked it up. They looked so young. She was only twenty-five, he thirty. Mum had long straight hair and was wearing a blue coat and skirt. Dad was sporting a smart suit, obviously Italian, and a rose in his buttonhole. My mother's corsage was clearly upside-down. They looked casual, comradely, radiantly happy.

They met at the LSE in the late fifties. Dad was there as a PhD student, having taken his first degree at Rome University. My mother was studying history. They met on a protest march. As a child, I loved to hear about this: my parents as student activists, all long hair, sit-ins and drugs, bravely campaigning for a better world. The truth was that they were very mild rebels and couldn't even remember what they had been marching about. 'Rates,' my mother would say vaguely. 'Lower rates or something.'

'Equal rights for all,' my father would say, magnificently comprehensive.

Anyway, whatever the cause, the significance of the occasion was that Jane Shawcross, a pretty Birmingham girl with long hair and a placard, met Enzo de Angelis, a dashing Italian with a leather jacket and a good line in patter. He offered to carry the placard for her, but after a while they got tired of it and left it propped by the side of the road while they went for coffee. Coffee bars being another exciting new thing in fifties London.

'Did you fall in love at first sight?' I used to ask Mum.

'Yes, I suppose so,' she would say dreamily. 'He was very good-looking, you see. He had broad shoulders and a tiny waist. English boys didn't really have waists.'

My father was more forthcoming. My mother was the most beautiful woman in the world, he said. She had wonderful hair, so long she could sit on it. As children we found this fascinating, even slightly indecent. 'You used to sit on it?' we would say. 'You used to *sit* on your hair?'

'Of course not,' my mother would say. 'It was long, but not that long.'

'What happened when you went to the loo?' Maria would ask, and we would all collapse into giggles. Then my mother would sigh, perhaps wishing that we had inherited her seriousness along with her hair.

They got married and moved to Brighton, where Dad had a job at the new Sussex University. My mother gave up her London teaching job to go with him. Women did that in 1961. They lived in Brighton in a top-floor flat with a tiny roof garden. My mother told me that they used to sit up there every morning, drinking coffee and feeding the seagulls with toast crumbs. They were very happy. Then Anna was born and they moved to Lewes.

My mother hated Lewes. She hated the dinky little streets full of bookshops with quirky names like the Bag O' Nails. She pined for Brighton, with its seedy hotels and windswept seafront. She told me that she used to stand by the road sign that said it was seven miles to Brighton, with Anna in her pushchair, and cry and cry. She felt that she was missing out on the sixties. She was the only mother at her mother-and-toddler group to wear a Mary Quant mini and white tights. She was the only woman she knew who was trying to write a thesis while she stuffed mashed carrot into a complaining baby. I don't know whether she ever told Dad any of this. All I know is that two years after Maria was born my mother employed a lovely elderly lady called Auntie Beryl to look after the children while she went back to work.

She taught history at the university. When I came along, I was off to Auntie Beryl's as soon as possible and my mother was back at work, driving off happily every morning in her stripy tights. My earliest memories are of going to meet Mum at the university and playing in the grounds, with their exciting glass walls, sculpted lawns and covered pathways. I loved it. When I got older, I loved having a working mother. Of course, it was not as if she worked in a factory. I didn't (to my secret disappointment) have my own front-door key. My mother's job was flexible enough to allow her to pick me up from school most days and on other days I had Auntie Beryl with her endless supply of Quality Street and her forbidden doses of ITV.

I loved the fact that my mother had a life outside the home, outside us. I loved the way she read enormous dusty books instead of magazines about how to knit yourself a new husband. I loved the incomprehensible arguments she used to have with my father, about Marx and Proudhon and someone slimy-sounding called Neecher. When my mother got her PhD, I was proud that we were the only children at school to have two parents who were doctors.

'Mummies can't be doctors,' said Maisie White at my primary school, damningly.

'Yes, they can,' I said, equally firmly. 'She's a doctor of *books*, not people.'

As I sat on my parents' bed, watching Kitty asleep, I thought, for the first time, Did my mother even want a third baby?

'Gaby?' Someone was at the door. It was Bob, with a cup of tea. 'All I seem to do is make you cups of tea,' he said. 'No one can say I'm not a hands-on father.'

'You are hands-on,' I said humourlessly. 'It's just that only I can feed her.'

This is another truth about the great breastfeeding mystery. Once you get good at it, you're trapped. At first Bob was as good with Kitty as I was, if not better. He could pick her up and comfort her. I loved to see his big hands holding her tiny body, just like an Athena poster. But I was always having to take her back to try to get some food inside her. She would struggle hotly against me, taking hours to ingest a tiny drop of milk. But now, after the miracle of Dad's funeral, I foresaw that I would become The One and no one else would do. It made me feel triumphant – and a bit scared.

I took a gulp of tea. 'Are Anna and Maria still arguing?' I asked.

'Yes. They've got on to the role of women in the death process. Maria says that women used to lay out bodies and now male undertakers have usurped them.'

'Christ. Imagine Maria as an undertaker.'

'Lots of black velvet and candles.'

'Her house is already like that.'

'There you are. A ready-made business. Working from home and everything.'

We were sitting on the bed. Kitty was on my dad's pillow, both arms above her head in an attitude of complete surrender. The traitorous clock ticked on.

'I can't believe he's dead,' I said.

'No,' says Bob, looking at Kitty. 'I keep expecting him to come in and say, "*Basta*. Enough with all this sitting around looking gloomy."'

Bob's impression of Dad made me laugh, but, as always these days, tears promptly followed.

'Bloody hell,' I said, wiping my eyes on the counterpane. 'What's the matter with me?'

'You've just lost your dad,' said Bob gently.

'Yes, but it's the same for everyone, isn't it? Mum and Anna and Maria don't keep bursting into tears every few minutes.'

'Your hormones are in a whirl,' said Bob, smiling.

'God, you sound like one of the midwives.'

'Perhaps I should become a midwife. That would be one in the eye for Maria. Another role usurped by men.'

'No, women get birth and men get death. Sounds fair to me.'

Bob put his arm round me. 'Are you upset about this ashes thing?'

I shook my head. 'No. Yes. I don't know. I just don't want to trail round Rome looking for a place that's Christian enough for Anna and pagan enough for Maria.'

'What do *you* want?' Bob asked me.

'I want to put his ashes in the Tiber,' I said.

'In the river?'

'Yes, the river,' I said irritably. 'Is that so hard to understand?'

Bob didn't rise. That's another annoying thing about the days after you've had a baby: no one gets cross with you. They look understanding and blame the mysterious hormones. It's so frustrating to have everyone understanding you all the time. You long for some misunderstanding and a good old-fashioned argument.

'What does your mum think?' asked Bob.

'What about?'

'Where does she want your dad's ashes scattered?'

'I don't know.' I picked up the wedding photo again. Mum was looking straight at the camera, but Dad was half turned towards her, smiling down at her. They were married for forty-three years.

Bob was studying the picture too. 'Must be hard for her. How old was she when they got married?'

'Twenty-five.'

'Same age as you when we got married.'

'Yes.' Suddenly I didn't want to talk about me or our marriage. I got up. 'I'd better go downstairs. See which crazy venue they've decided on.'

Bob grinned. 'When I left, Marco was saying that Enzo told him he wanted his ashes scattered at the Stadio Olimpico.'

CHAPTER FOUR

September

Bob and I are standing at the Alitalia check-in desk. I am carrying a handbag (pre-Kitty and rather smart) and a huge, stained backpack, smelling strongly of nappy bags (a peculiar blend of apricot and plastic). Bob is carrying Kitty in a baby sling and holding our passports. Even Kitty has one: the picture shows a howling orange face and my frantically clasping arms. Next to us are two battered suitcases containing our luggage.

My suitcase contains:

- seven Babygros in various shades
- seven baby vests in ditto
- seven sleepsuits
- one snowsuit with feet (in case the weather turns cold)

- three short-sleeved Babygros (in case it turns hot)
- mobile with soothing music to send Kitty to sleep
- hairdryer (because this sometimes works better)
- two pairs of black trousers (elasticated)
- one pair of jeans
- three long, loose shirts, front-opening for easy access
- three T-shirts (large)
- two baggy jumpers
- one black dress (tight)
- one pair of flip-flops
- seven pairs of knickers
- two nightdresses
- spare maternity bra
- green plastic box containing my father's ashes.

When we discovered that, one way or another, we had to take Dad's ashes to Rome, my mother called in the funeral director. I had been too overwrought to notice this character at Dad's funeral so I had imagined a sinister Dickensian figure, probably wearing a top coat in greenish black. Instead he turned out to be a cheerful, pink-faced Geordie in a grey woolly jumper.

My mother introduced us: 'My daughters, Mrs Blackstock, Mrs Golding, Mrs Duncan.' When she said this I saw how effectively our marriages have anglicised us. As Anna de Angelis, Maria de Angelis, Gabriella de Angelis, we sound interesting, even exotic. As Mrs Blackstock and Co. we sound like three housewives queuing at the fishmonger's. I still use the name Gabriella de Angelis at work. Mrs Duncan sounds like someone else. Bob's mother, perhaps.

The funeral director ('Call me Derek') smiled engagingly and accepted an offer of tea. Anna went to make it. Since Dad died, she has been acting as if my mother is incapable of doing anything. Mum explained our problem to Derek. 'So, we wondered, how do we go about taking his ashes home? To Italy?'

Derek heaved a sigh. 'It's very difficult, Mrs de Angelis.' (It's not fair: my mother, the only non-Italian, is now the only one left with an Italian name.) 'The Italians, now, they're very keen on bureaucracy. In order to repatriate Mr de Angelis . . .' We looked at each other. Repatriate. It sounded very final, somehow. ' . . . you will need to get the correct forms from the Italian Embassy. The casket containing the ashes will then have to be sealed with the official seal and transported with the relevant papers.'

Maria shifted impatiently. 'How long will this take?'

Derek smiled apologetically. 'I'd say anything from six months to a year, Mrs Golding.'

When Derek left, Maria turned to us and said decisively, 'We'll have to smuggle him in.'

'*What?*' said Anna, in her best teacher's voice.

Maria looked at her impassively. She was wearing jeans and a long green velvet coat. Now she drew it round her like a witch's cloak. 'We'll have to smuggle him in. We can't wait a year. Besides, it would be bad for us not to have closure.' Anna winced at the psychobabble, but Maria ignored her. 'We need to do it as soon as possible. It'll be easy. Gaby can do it. They never search mothers with children.'

'What?' I said. Kitty, who had been sleeping in my lap, woke up and cried. I rocked her ineffectually. Bob had gone back to work that morning and it was my first day alone with her. I had felt ridiculously nervous driving to Lewes, with Kitty beside me in her baby seat, like an unstable chemical, liable to explode at any moment.

'You can take the ashes in your luggage,' repeated

Maria kindly. 'If they want to search your suitcase, pinch Kitty to make her cry. The Italians would never upset a mother with a crying baby.'

'You seem to know all about it,' said Anna nastily.

Maria smiled enigmatically. We all knew that she and Ray liked the occasional recreational drug; we didn't want to enquire too deeply into her experience of getting illegal goods through Customs.

'What if we were caught?' persisted Anna.

'What if *I* were caught,' I corrected her, struggling to undo my blouse.

'You won't be,' said Maria. 'Just think about Dad.'

'What do you mean?' asked Anna.

'Would he have wanted to go by the rules or would he have wanted to be a bit daring, take a few risks?' said Maria.

We looked at each other. Put like that, there was no choice.

Now we edge closer to the check-in desk. The formidably good-looking Alitalia girl looks sternly at me. 'Did you pack all your bags yourself?'

'Yes,' I squeak.

'Do you have any electrical items packed in your bags?'

'No.'

'Has anyone asked you to carry anything in your bags for them?'

'No.'

'Have the bags been with you at all times since they were packed?'

'Yes.'

A contemptuous swirl of the hair, a swift tying on of a label, a rubber stamp, and Dad is off on his final journey. Repatriated. Bob and I walk off quickly to join another queue.

'Over the first hurdle,' says Bob.

'She looked like Sophia Loren, didn't she?'

'Who?'

'The check-in girl.'

'I didn't notice.'

I sigh. In my maternity jeans and one of Bob's rugby shirts I do not feel like Sophia Loren. I don't even feel like myself. Who is this fat, weepy woman with horrid stains on the front of her shirt? If I sat next to myself on a plane, I would move.

'Gaby!'

'What?'

'Passports.' Somehow we have found ourselves next to the

departures gate. I show our passports. Bob stalks off towards the X-ray machine, leaving me to carry the nappy bag. I feel like a Sherpa. In Bob's arms, Kitty smiles and chirrups. Even the stony-faced X-ray men look at her fondly; one of the women looks ready to marry Bob on the spot.

'Give her to me,' I say, as we reach another circle of shops and cafés.

'What?'

'Give Kitty to me.'

Without a word Bob hands her over and we perform the complicated procedure of putting the sling on to me. All those buckles and straps you have to manage as a parent – it's wonderful for your hand–eye coordination, if nothing else. Kitty starts to cry.

In the departure lounge, we meet up with the rest of my family. Maria, in floor-length denim, holding Kyle's hand. Ray, also in denim (slightly too tight), trying to bribe Mosaic with sweets. Anna hovering round my mother. Marco and Sergio grimly plugged into headsets. David, with his ever-present smile, offering to hold Kitty.

'No, thanks,' I say ungraciously. 'I've only just got the sling on.'

'Does she want a feed?' asks Ray, with what, to me, sounds like gratuitous interest in my breasts.

'No,' I say.

'You should feed on demand,' says Maria. 'I did with all mine.' Now, I know this isn't true. She may have breastfed Kyle until he was ready for school, but Tara was on the bottle as soon as she got her home (to our parents' house, that is).

'Gaby needs to establish her own routine,' says Anna. She loves words like 'routine'.

'I'm going for a walk,' I say. 'It may settle her a bit.'

'Don't go far,' says my mother, as if I were ten.

I walk round the shops. Cameras, stuffed toys, huge packets of Toblerone, suitcases. Who on earth gets this far without a suitcase? At the thought of my own suitcase, with its unconventional cargo, I grasp Kitty tighter and walk faster. I never saw my dad's dead body. The last time I saw him was two days before I went into hospital. He and Mum came up to London for the day, bringing the knitted cardigan and hat as well as a vast quantity of food. 'You won't feel like cooking for a bit,' said my mother.

'That will make a change,' teased Dad. He knew I wasn't

the world's greatest cook. I was the third daughter: Mum had got bored with making pastry animals by the time I came along, and she was not that keen a chef herself.

'I still feel like eating, though,' I said. At that stage, I was hungry all the time.

'Look in my pocket,' said Dad, as if I were a child. I looked. There was the red-and-white packet, with all its childhood associations: stability, treats after swimming. KitKat. Kitty Kat. Maybe that's why I called her Kitty.

'Gaby!' Bob is running towards me. 'Our departure gate's up.'

'Do we have to go this minute?'

He grins. 'Anna's practically got us in a line.'

'Christ! As long as we don't have to hold hands.'

On the plane Bob and I sit in a row of three with fourteen-year-old Sergio. 'You've drawn the short straw,' I say to him.

He eyes Kitty nervously. 'She's not going to cry, is she?'

'If she does, I'll feed her,' I promise. Hastily, he averts his eyes and plugs himself into his headphones.

Behind us, Maria is reading to Mosaic and Kyle in a loud, good-with-children voice that sets my teeth on edge: '"So Teeny Rabbit tucked herself into bed for the winter." What do we call it when animals go to sleep for the winter? You know, Mosaic. It starts with a huh . . .'

'Huh. Who cares?' mutters Bob.

As the plane takes off, Kitty wails. I put her to my breast. Sergio shuts his eyes. I can hear Marco telling Mum the plot of a film he saw where the plane crashed horribly: 'And then the survivors, like, had to start eating each other. And the guy, the one with the gun, goes . . .' I look at Bob, sitting beside me, his eyes shut. Although he has to fly a lot for work, he doesn't like it. I used to love it: that swooping feeling of takeoff, the little trays with inedible meals in plastic compartments, the refreshing towelettes, the minia-ture bottles of wine that you regret as soon as you land. But now, for the first time, I am nervous. My whole family is on this plane (including, of course, my dad) and I understand why the royal family never travels together. If this plane were to crash, like the one in Marco's favourite film, the de Angelis family would be wiped out. The world would lose Anna's teaching skills and Maria's recipe for hash brownies. It might lose a future rock star in Sergio and a prime minister in Mosaic. Except, of course, Maria has given her a name that precludes her ever having a serious job. Dr Mosaic Golding?

Mosaic Golding, MP? I don't think so. What about Kitty? She'd probably survive – babies often do. I imagine her little body in its pink sleepsuit, lying amid the wreckage, and clutch her convulsively.

'Gaby!' Bob nudges me. 'Are you all right?'

'Yes.' I loosen my hold. Despite everything, not knowing that she has narrowly escaped being the only survivor of a plane crash, Kitty has fallen asleep.

We land in Rome at five o'clock in the afternoon. The shadows are lengthening but the sun is still warm as we walk into the terminal. It is only four years since I was last here at Fiumicino airport but I can't believe how much it has changed. Endless moving walkways, driverless trains that circle overhead like something from *Blade Runner*, mile upon mile of concrete, chrome and glass. 'This is how Rome celebrated the millennium,' says Bob, 'expanding the airport, improving public transport, cleaning up the tourist attractions. I'm sure they would have built a Dome instead if they'd thought of it.'

Despite the impressiveness of the terminal, I am exhausted by the time we reach the baggage-collection area. We have checked in the pushchair with the suitcases so I have to carry Kitty all the way. When we get to the carousels, we find that you need a euro for a trolley and, of course, no one has one. Mosaic and Kyle run around screaming excitedly. Marco and Sergio stand side by side, headphones on, incommunicado. Mum, Anna, Maria and I sit down, leaving the men to reclaim the bags.

I look across at the three husbands. David, with his little gold-rimmed glasses and creased linen jacket, could have a sign round his neck saying 'Teacher on Holiday'. Ray, the oldest of the three, is the most macho about heaving his suitcases off the carousel. Despite this, he is sweating profusely. By contrast, Bob lifts off ours easily, without feeling it necessary to hoist the cases shoulder-high or jog importantly towards the exit, leaving me to run behind. With his red-gold hair and long legs, he looks like Boris Becker on his day off.

I put Kitty into the pushchair and follow Bob through the arrivals door. All around us Italians are exclaiming excitedly at the sight of their loved ones. Next to me a beautiful girl with Gucci luggage is forcibly dragged into an embrace by her weeping family. Then I hear Mum give a little squeak of delight. 'Tara!' she says, and there, standing beside the bored taxi men with signs round their necks, is Tara, Maria's eldest child, who is spending her gap year in Italy. Mum, who has always had a special thing for Tara, runs towards her, tears pouring down her face. In the excitement, I hardly notice Franco waiting beside Tara or the fact that, standing slightly to one side, as incongruous in this setting as the Grim Reaper complete with scythe, is a dark-suited clergyman.

Jonathan.

CHAPTER FIVE

I met Jonathan at university. That much is cliché. I had a steady boyfriend at home, to whom I had promised undying love. He lasted three days into freshers' week. Then, in rapid succession, I went out with Seth (a long-haired English postgraduate), Martin (a left-wing law student with a Che Guevara hat), Miles (a posh geography student) and Findlay (a Scottish medical student). Coming from a school at which I had always been overshadowed by my sisters, I was overwhelmed by my popularity at university. It helped that I was doing a subject (maths) where there weren't many girls, that I had unaccountably lost half a stone in the summer holidays and had taken to wearing very short skirts. But there was no getting away from it: I was flavour of the month. I came top in the 'Sexiest Fresher' competition, run by the college magazine. 'Sexist and degrading,' said my friend Mel. Well, obviously. Quite flattering, though.

So, I went out with lots of boys, but didn't sleep with any of them. I was aware that people assumed I did, that I was, in one rugby student's phrase, 'a bit of a goer'. When the same magazine had a competition to find songs to fit different students, mine was 'Too Much, Too Young'. I didn't mind. I liked the thought of seeming slightly wicked, the sort of girl who kept her contraceptive pills next to her cigarettes and a copy of *The Brothers Karamazov* in her handbag. But I was, secretly, a virgin at eighteen.

Why? Well, partly Catholic conditioning, although there wasn't much of it about at a Catholic comprehensive in the eighties. I know for a fact that both Anna and Maria slept with their boyfriends. Maria, of course, had a baby to prove it, but even Anna, good, holy Anna, disappeared for hours into her bedroom with Stuart Wilkins and bribed me with Bailey's Irish Cream not to disturb them. Why was I different? Why did I start to get panicky when a boy's hands left the comfort zone of my breasts and moved, inexorably, downwards? Well, I suppose my sisters hadn't given sexual freedom a very good press: there was Maria, pregnant at nineteen, and Anna, married at twenty-two and immured in Forest Hill. Staying a virgin was safer, somehow. I don't know. I liked the 'going out': the love letters, the angst, the accidental bumping into someone in the corridor, the slow dances, the first kiss. It was just that when things got more serious ('It won't be tacky,' promised Seth, breathily, 'it'll be beautiful') I tended to dump the boyfriend and move on to the next. On second thoughts, this was probably why I was so popular.

Anyway, I was going out with Findlay the medic ('Sex is a necessary biological process') when I met Jonathan. We were at a party given by some law students and I spotted him instantly. He had long black hair, a leather jacket and was smoking a roll-up. 'Who's that?' I asked Mel.

'Jonathan Casey,' she told me, 'third-year law student. Apparently he's got a terrible reputation. A first-year tried to commit suicide over him last year.'

I looked up to find Jonathan staring at me. He had the bluest eyes I had ever seen.

'Oh, God,' said Mel. 'Looks like you're next.'

He left it until the end of the party and then he walked over, put his hand on my back and said, in a soft voice, 'Would you like to go for a walk?'

'No,' I said stupidly. 'I've got a boyfriend.' Jonathan glanced across at Findlay, who, with a group of other medics, was trying to balance a pint of beer on his head, and grinned. 'I can see that. Lucky you. But I'm not asking you to marry me, just to go for a walk.'

We walked. The party was in a run-down area of Paddington and the streets were full of rubbish and syringes. Beside a boarded-up newsagent's, Jonathan pushed me against a wall and kissed me hard. His body felt dangerous against mine; one hand forced my head back, the other plunged into the waistband of my jeans. 'No,' I said weakly.

Jonathan let go instantly. 'No?' he said, smiling, his teeth very white in the darkness.

In answer, I pulled his head back down to mine.

We slept together a week later. Not without tears, soul-searching and frantic delaying action on my part. Jonathan listened to all of it with a polite, quizzical expression on his face. It was just that it seemed inevitable somehow. From the moment he had kissed me, we were trapped on a course that could lead only one way. It was as if I were hurtling along a four-lane motorway. I could go slow, put on my hazard lights, even stop at the service station for a while, but I knew that, one way or another, I had to get back on the road. Eventually, in my room at halls, under the baleful stare of Humphrey Bogart, the deed was done. 'How does it feel not to be a virgin any more?' asked Jonathan.

'Restful,' I said.

To everyone's surprise, Jonathan didn't dump me after I had slept with him. We started going out together in earnest. After he left university and went to law school, we became closer. When he got a job with a firm of City solicitors, we moved into a tiny flat in Hackney. We were in love. Nothing I achieved at university, even my surprisingly good degree, compared to this. I loved Jonathan Casey and he loved me.

Then came the day, four years later, when Jonathan met me from work for lunch (I was a trainee with a firm of accountants) and suggested, once again, that we 'go for a walk'. There, in Bedford Square, he told me he thought we should 'give it a rest for a while'. 'Why?' I asked wildly. We were happy, I'd thought. We had our flat. We had talked about getting a cat. We went on holiday together. People at work talked about Jonathan as 'your partner'. I liked that, although I hoped it might be replaced in time with something a little more traditional.

'Why?' I asked again.

Jonathan turned to me. He looked wild, haunted, his eyes dark in a deathly pale face. 'I want to become a priest,' he said.

I don't think I have ever been so shocked, so *dumbfounded*, as I was at that moment. Jonathan, my wicked blue-eyed Jonathan, was leaving me to become a priest. It was unthinkable and, literally, I couldn't think about it. My mind could not take in the enormity of what he had said. I stared at him. 'What?'

'I've decided to enter the priesthood.'

Enter the priesthood. That phrase, with all its associations of smug Sunday sermons, silenced me. Jonathan stood there, in the sad green square while office workers ate their sandwiches all round him. Just stood there, in his smart lawyer's suit, gazing at me anxiously.

'You're joking, aren't you?' I whispered at last.

'No,' said Jonathan, with a heavy sigh that nevertheless sounded partly proud. 'I've never been more serious in my life.'

There followed a few horrible days of talking, crying (me) and praying (him). The idea of Jonathan praying was, oddly enough, the final straw. It seemed so alien, so craven, so *effeminate*. I suppose that somewhere, deep down, I consider that religion is only for women. Certainly in my life it was Anna and the nuns at school who figured largely as icons of Catholicism. My dad was a Catholic but, like a lot of Italian men, he considered that *going* to church was enough. He did not actually have to enter the building, much less sit down and certainly never kneel. I remember him taking us to church when we were children. He would lead us into the little lobby full of posters about the Society for the Protection of Unborn Children and Pilgrimages to Lourdes ('Sign here'), then usher us in with exhortations to good behaviour. He would stay where he was, behind the glass doors. During mass, I would often turn round to look for him and he would be standing beside the holy water, hands behind his back, with a respectful, if amused, expression on his face. I never saw him go to communion and I certainly never saw him praying. It would have been unthinkable, cringe-making, deeply disturbing. My father believed in the dignity of mankind: he bowed to nobody. So, when Jonathan knelt despairingly by the bed that first night, I hissed at him: 'What are you *doing*?'

'Praying,' he said. 'Praying for guidance.'

I could not have been more disgusted if I had caught him with a pornographic magazine.

I had known Jonathan was a Catholic, of course. At first this only added a delicious sense of danger to the already fraught process of losing my virginity. Only a Catholic would have whispered thrillingly into my ear, that first night, 'And how's your immortal soul?'

'In danger,' I replied, and muffled my laughter in the pillow.

But that was it. We never went to mass together, never discussed religion, never, to my knowledge, saw Catholicism as anything other than a rather picturesque background to our all-consuming passion.

'How can you want to be a priest?' I said. 'You never even go to church.'

'Well, not here,' he said, in an odd, embarrassed voice, 'but I do at home.'

Jonathan moved out a week later. I left the flat soon afterwards and moved in with Mel. For a while, Jonathan rang occasionally to tell me his news (he was going on retreat, to a seminary, to the English college in Rome), but his voice made me so bitter and angry that it was a relief when the calls ended. Gradually, I stopped thinking about him; the sound of an Irish voice no longer made me feel sick with longing; I could watch the *Eurovision Song Contest* without bursting into tears. I threw myself into work: there were a lot of other trainees at the firm and we had a fairly hectic social life. Jonathan sent me an invitation to his ordination, but I didn't go.

Home. I think that was what really got me. All our plans for that little flat, all our evenings together watching TV and shutting out the world, and Jonathan still did not think of it as home. Home was Ireland. Home was the mother who never once pronounced my name correctly.

Jonathan had the standard-issue saintly Irish mother: he was always sending her big, sloppy Mother's Day cards, the kind with quilting and pictures of kittens. My cards to my mother were always the sort whose jokes are vaguely to the sender's benefit: 'And most of all – you've got me', that sort of thing. So, I knew that Jonathan adored his Irish mother and I imagined that they might go to mass together, but other than that, they didn't seem a particularly religious family. I had visited Jonathan's home in Ireland only twice in four years. Jonathan's mother was always very nice to me ('Would you look at the size of her? She's as thin as a stick!') while leaving me in no doubt that I was not nearly good enough for her darling boy. Jonathan, her only child, was clearly the light of her life.

My parents were always ambivalent about Jonathan. He made the mistake of being too charming to my mother – 'You're Gaby's *mother*? You look more like her sister' – and she distrusted him ever afterwards.

Dad distrusted him, too, for different reasons. Once he asked me, only half joking, 'Shall I ask him about his intentions?' Of course, I laughed scornfully, telling him that he sounded like the Godfather: '"You come to me, on my daughter's wedding day ..."' But he had seen something I had missed: in his atavistic, Italian-father way, he had realised that Jonathan never had any intention of staying with me. After all, hadn't his first words to me been 'I'm not asking you to marry me'?

Maria and Anna liked him, Anna especially. She was uncharacteristically skittish in his presence. When I met Jonathan, she had just had Marco and was at home in her little, educationally sound house in Forest Hill. Jonathan and

I used to go round quite often and I think Anna must have enjoyed flirting with this handsome, admiring twenty year old. It was a change from reading Dr Seuss books to baby Marco ('It's never too early to introduce them to books') and doing good works about her parish. She was on maternity leave and was dreadfully bored. Anyway, she liked Jonathan and laughed at his jokes and sided with him against me. Once when we arrived at her house, she met us with Marco in her arms and I noticed that there was something odd about her appearance. She looked strangely lopsided. It was only when we were sitting down with cups of tea and home-made cake (of course) that I realised what it was: she had made up only one eye. She must have been distracted by the baby when she was putting on her mascara. Even at the time I knew that the makeup wasn't for my benefit.

When Jonathan and I split up, Anna wouldn't hear a word against him. Dad was satisfyingly dogmatic: 'Bastard. I never liked him.' Mum was typically calm and rational: 'Well, it was a good thing he discovered this God fixation now, before it was too late.' I sobbed that I wished it had been too late, I wished we were married with three children and then he *couldn't* leave me, could he? 'Oh, couldn't he?' murmured

Maria. But, for Anna, the fact that Jonathan had discovered he loved God more than me was only another example of his superiority. 'He must have suffered,' she said to me, eyes huge and glittery. 'He must have had a dark night of the soul.'

'He made me suffer,' I said sulkily. 'I don't see anything saintly about that.'

'Of course not, *bambina*,' said Dad soothingly. 'Man's a self-dramatising fool. He'll make an excellent priest.'

CHAPTER SIX

Rome. I've been here many times before, of course. As a child we had holidays in Rome every year: winters in the city and summers in Ostia Lido, the nearest seaside resort. We went to other places in Italy, too, Sorrento, Tuscany, the lakes, but Rome was special because it was Dad's place. I remember Sister Immaculata asking one day in class, 'Now, can anyone tell me what is so special about Rome?' and me answering, 'It's where my dad comes from.'

Dad was born in the centre of Rome, at Campo de' Fiori. The Field of Flowers. As a child I loved this name. I imagined Dad running through a perpetually sunlit field, full of daffodils and bluebells (rather English flowers, true, but a nice idea). It was a disappointment when I first saw the place for myself. Campo de' Fiori is where the fish and vegetable markets take place: old ladies on Vespas roaring around with bags of tomatoes on the handlebars, middle-class Romans in fitted tweed jackets poring over the aubergines.

I remember Dad's father, Ferdinando de Angelis, as a lovely, twinkly old man with sugared almonds in his pocket, although he was a brilliant doctor. I don't remember Nonna Attilia, but apparently she was formidable. When she was young she was supposed to have been a great beauty, but Mum remembers her as an old woman with too much make-up, barking orders at her husband and sons. Dad was the oldest son; Uncle Bruno is two years younger. There was another, Armando, but he died when he was a child.

My father and Uncle Bruno were both very clever. They studied together at Rome University before Dad left for the LSE and Uncle Bruno went to Padua to study medicine. They were always close – 'Like twins,' said Dad. 'Romulus and Remus. Rome is the city of twins.' However, unlike Romulus and Remus, they refrained from murdering each other and were, apparently, inseparable. Dad never talked about Armando, who died of pneumonia aged eight, but I knew he kept a picture of him (dark-eyed and serious in a sailor suit) in his wallet. Bruno was still his closest friend. They spoke to each other on the phone every week, always at the same time, on Sunday mornings after mass, Dad holding the phone under his chin so that he could wave his arms about as he spoke.

Now we are on our way to see Uncle Bruno, carrying his beloved brother's ashes. For a moment we are all overcome by emotion. Mum sobs in the arms of Bruno's son, Franco. Maria weeps into Tara's hair. Both Kyle and Mosaic burst into tears and I am left facing Jonathan.

'Gaby.'

'Jonathan.'

He doesn't kiss or even touch me. He has lost weight and looks remote and ascetic in his black suit. But his eyes are the same.

I am aware of Bob at my shoulder, carrying Kitty.

'Bob.' Jonathan extends his hand. It's a real priest's hand-shake, hearty but brief. I'm relieved that he doesn't do the two-handed 'sign of peace' special.

'Hello,' says Bob. He knows all about Jonathan, of course, but it doesn't bother him. As he once said to my dad, 'How could I be jealous of a man who wears a dress?' Dad, who adored Bob, roared with laughter. I remember being a little offended. It was all right, praiseworthy, even, for Bob not to be jealous, but did he have to take it quite so far?

Suddenly Franco is beside me, exclaiming over Kitty. 'Franco,' I hiss, 'what's Jonathan doing here?'

He looks surprised. 'He rang me yesterday and said that Anna asked him to come. He's going to conduct the service, apparently. Seems a nice enough chap. Says he knew you at university.'

The last time I saw Jonathan was five years ago at a friend's wedding. The friend was a Catholic (unsuspected by me) and the church was the English Martyrs in Streatham, near where Bob and I now live. The church stands on its own in a sort of island in the middle of the high street, like a baroque ship that has somehow sailed its way past Lidl, KFC and the Carphone Warehouse. Inside, it is a typical old-style Catholic church, full of paintings with gold haloes and bleeding hands. Sitting waiting for the service to begin, self-conscious in my hat, I heard a soft voice at my side. 'Gaby? Is it you?' It was Jonathan, wearing the dress.

'Jonathan!' It was the first time I had seen him in his priest's get-up. The vestments, purple and white for a special occasion, took me back to my childhood. For a second, standing there in the dark church, Jonathan had been like any other priest: anonymous, sexless, mildly benevolent. But his face was the same as ever, dark and dangerous above the purple robes. I kept looking at his hand, resting on the pew in front, at the square fingernails and black hairs on the fingers and remembering its touch on my body.

'Are you the priest here?' I asked.

'Assistant priest. I don't normally do weddings but Father O'Brien is sick.'

'So it's the understudy's big day.'

He had laughed, rather too heartily. A priest's laugh. I had introduced him to Bob, who leaned forward to shake hands. The words 'my husband' echoed loudly in the air. I was excessively proud that I had this prize to show to Jonathan. A husband, a good-looking, tall husband who had all his own hair (even if it was red) and could shake hands and smile as if he were anybody.

'Yes, Anna told me you'd married.' Anna kept in touch with Jonathan. She had started to write to him when he was at the seminary in Rome. 'You don't mind, do you, Gaby?' she said once, seeing me looking at a Christmas card in her house, a tasteful etching of the seminary, black lines on white paper, wildly out-of-place among the cheery Santas and laughing reindeer. 'Of course not,' I had said.

Just then there was the bustle peculiar to weddings at the back of the church and Jonathan had straightened. 'I've got to go.'

'Yes, they'll be playing your tune in a minute,' I said.

All through the wedding, the hymns, Jonathan's brief, eloquent sermon, I kept thinking, This could have been me, once I wished it was me. Once, although I am ashamed to admit it, I had wanted to marry Jonathan more than anything in the world. Once the idea that he would one day marry someone else was the most painful idea possible. Now I knew that it wasn't.

Jonathan glides easily around the arrivals lounge like a ghost, organising luggage, greeting my mother, expressing commiseration – all without making any real physical contact. Anna is beside herself with pleasure. 'Isn't it wonderful that Jonathan is here?' she keeps saying. 'Isn't it good of him?' No one knows quite how to answer this. Maria is keeping a proprietorial arm around Tara, Ray is comforting Kyle who is still crying, my mother has gone back into her trance, Bob and David are piling cases on to the trolleys conjured up by

Jonathan (possibly by divine intervention). I turn round and find myself looking into the most amazing eyes I have ever seen. They are golden, like a lion's, flecked with brownish lights and fringed with dense black lashes.

'Gabriella?' says the owner of the eyes. '*Come sta?*'

Now, I have a bit of a problem with Italian. Dad tried to teach us all to speak it but we were all, even the studious Anna, astonishingly lazy and slow to learn. His attempt to get us all singing a jolly Italian song about a cuckoo had us running for cover. Christmas Day telephone conversations with Uncle Bruno were the cue for terrible tantrums as we all refused to come to the phone and had to be dragged there screaming.

'*Buon Natale, bella.*'

'*Buon Natale, Zio Bruno.* Dad, can I stop now?'

Eventually, we learned the basics of the language and became slightly more fluent when we were in Italy. But I have always found Italian an embarrassing language. I don't like the way it swoops and curls. I don't like the way you have to pronounce every letter, rolling the Rs like a demented animal impersonator. It's not too bad listening to real Italians like Dad and Uncle Bruno: they can get away with it – they do it with a nonchalant brilliance. It is listening to English people speaking Italian that I find so excruciating. Especially English people who think they're good at it. It makes me cringe. It's like watching Anna praying – too horribly heartfelt.

So I look at the Lion Man and mutter, '*Bene, grazie,*' in an embarrassed English whisper, though I'm not really. He smiles at me as if he understands everything: about the flight, about Kitty (now sleeping peacefully but heavily on my chest), about Jonathan, about Dad dying, about the little green package in my suitcase, everything.

'Gabriella.' Franco has appeared, with his arm round my mother. 'This is Luca, our driver.'

Driver? Since when have we had a driver? I am saved from answering by Jonathan, who materialises again at my shoulder. He is so close that I can see the little flecks of grey in his hair and smell his aftershave. Are priests allowed to wear aftershave? 'Gaby,' he says.

'What are you doing here?' I blurt out. I can sense Bob, Franco and the lion-eyed Luca all staring at me.

Instead of answering, Jonathan leans forward and kisses my cheek. His lips are icy cold. 'I'll be in touch,' he says.

For a second, I just stare after his departing black back,

then Franco takes my arm and gently pulls me away. As he has my mother on the other side, we walk awkwardly three abreast towards yet another moving walkway, which leads to the car park. Bob follows with Kitty. Nobody speaks.

In the underground car park, Franco organises us briskly. He will take my mother, Anna, David and the boys. The rest of us will go in Luca's people-carrier, 'the MPV', he calls it importantly. We will meet at his parents' apartment. *Bene? Bene.* Luca helps me tenderly up the steps and arranges Kitty in my lap. Bob sits next to me, then Ray and Kyle. Maria, Mosaic and Tara sit in the row in front. I feel confused and disorientated. Was Jonathan really here? Will I see him again?

We drive crazily through the Roman evening. The people-carrier is air-conditioned but I can tell that outside it is still hot. The Italian flags flanking the entrance to the airport hang limply in the heat. Luca steers the monstrous vehicle as if it were a tiny Fiat, emerging from the underpass into a blaze of headlights, veering diagonally through lines of traffic, ignoring the horns blaring around him. He steers with one huge hand on the wheel, the other resting on the gear-lever. He does not speak and we are all stunned into silence. Kyle is asleep on Ray's lap. Maria is playing with Tara's hair.

I haven't spoken to her yet but she looks amazing. The ash-blonde hair she inherited from Lee is now an expensive gold, cut into flattering layers that look as if she has just run her hand through it. She is wearing blue jeans and a tiny pink sequined top. She makes me feel a hundred years old. Kitty whimpers and I shove her under the rugby shirt.

Luca drives us through the centre of Rome (archways, fountains, floodlit churches) to Uncle Bruno and Auntie Carla's apartment. It is the first time I have been to this one but driving through Rome to visit Uncle Bruno was so much a part of my childhood that I keep getting lost in a maze of past and present. Is that me standing beside that grim-looking church, holding Dad's hand and nagging for an ice cream? Are those two girls Anna and Maria, sitting with their feet in a fountain, hoping that the boys opposite are looking at them? Surely, as the shadows darken and the Romans come out on to the streets, shouting, gesticulating, roaring with the sheer joy of being alive in Rome on a September night, Dad is here somewhere?

Bruno and Carla's apartment is in a smart suburb. Like many middle-class Italians, they have several apartments rather than one large house. As well as this place in Rome, they have a seaside apartment in Ostia and another in the mountains, near Lucca. There is something in the Italian psyche that likes apartments. I remember thinking this when I first saw Pompeii and heard the guide say that the original Roman town contained three-storey apartment blocks. Apart from this being a spectacular building feat, it seems to confirm an age-old Italian liking for living close to other people. Not for them the detached house, with its own neat little garden, fenced off from the neighbours. In Tuscany, remote farmhouses are bought by expatriate English families while the farmers retire to modern flats in Milan. Italians like communal spaces, shared living: the old people like to sit on chairs by the side of the street and watch the world go by; the young move in packs like well-dressed wolves.

The apartment is reached through an underground car park. Luca punches in a number and the doors open to admit us. Before we vanish underground, I catch a glimpse of tennis courts and a sprinkler watering banks of flowers. As apartments go, this is fairly swish. A lift takes us upstairs and I am smothered by Auntie Carla's tearful embrace. 'The little *bambina*. So beautiful. How Enzo would have loved her. Ah, *che peccato!*'

The apartment has marble floors, huge dark-wood furniture, which reminds me morbidly of coffins, and lots of photographs in silver frames. There is also a giant widescreen television and (thank God) a table laid for a substantial meal.

I put Kitty on the sofa where Auntie Carla carefully arranges a barricade of cushions. '*Che carina*. The little Caterina.'

'Her name's Kitty.'

'Keety? Caterina?'

We have been here before, of course. 'Kitty?' said Anna scornfully, as soon as Bob told her the name. 'That's not a name. There's not a Saint Kitty.' Auntie Carla, Uncle Bruno, Franco and Franco's wife Paola are looking at me expectantly. My face goes red: I don't feel equal to the challenge of explaining Kitty's name. Kitty. Kitty Kat. I miss my dad.

'It's after my mother,' lies Bob, whose mother is called Doreen.

'Ah, *capito*.' Everyone relaxes.

There are two dining tables, one for children and one for adults. Marco and Sergio are sulking at being relegated to the children's table, Kyle and Mosaic are whining for crisps. Ray nobly offers to eat with them, and I sit gratefully at the adult table, with Luca next to me. Clearly he is a driver who eats with the family. Auntie Carla puts her hands on his shoulders affectionately and speaks to him in rapid Italian. I don't catch all of it but hear the word '*moglie*', wife. Does the lion-eyed Luca have a wife? A domestic lioness?

The food is wonderful: pasta in creamy sauce, veal with lemon and asparagus. As Mum was never keen on cooking and Dad's idea of Italian cuisine was frozen pizza, I feel I've missed out on the Italian food thing. Bob always says he only married me because he believed I could make my own ravioli. I think he's joking, but I have noticed that people expect me to know about sun-dried tomatoes and extra-virgin olive oil. What with that and not speaking Italian, I'm a severe disappointment in the ethnicity stakes.

Over dinner, we discuss the next day's trip. Luca is to take us to the Forum to see Maria's proposed pagan scattering site. Maria adjusts her sequined scarf and gives Luca a hot look. He smiles into his Chianti. Anna huffs with disapproval.

I am aware that Uncle Bruno and Auntie Carla are anxious. Auntie Carla gets out a small, lace-trimmed handkerchief and dabs her eyes. Franco leans towards us and says, 'This is difficult for my parents. The Italian people, they like to know where their dead are. In a tomb. In a graveyard. Not scattered around the city.' He uses the phrase '*i morticelli*', literally, 'the little dead'. It sends shivers down my spine.

'Is it illegal in Italy,' asks Bob, 'to do what we're doing?'

Franco answers in English: 'Yes, it is illegal, but they don't mind that so much. It is . . .' He pauses for the word. 'It is God's law that matters.'

Anna nods vigorously and I wonder if that is what Jonathan is for: to give legitimacy to the proceedings, in God's eyes if not the state's. It still amazes me that Jonathan is the real thing. A priest, entitled to speak for God.

The meal seems to take for ever. I have had two glasses of wine and feel light-headed. I haven't been drinking much because of the breastfeeding. Kitty is going to be high as a kite. Auntie Carla brings in cheese, Amaretto and little almond biscuits. Suddenly the lavish meal feels like torture and I hear with dread the tap of her high-heeled shoes coming from the kitchen. Next to me Paola, as thin as a rake in designer casual, takes a second slice of dolcelatte. To escape, I get up to check on Kitty. She is awake but quiet, gazing up happily at Auntie Carla's elaborate chandelier. I put her on my lap and let the conversation flow over me.

'Unique energies coming from a pagan burial place . . .'

'Great devotion to Our Blessed Lady. Said the rosary every day.'

'Sacrifice a few goats, he said . . .'

'Impossible to buy size six clothes in London.'

'No way should Cassano be playing. Totti is well better.'

'Just try the pasta, Kyle. Look, Daddy's eating it. Yum-yum.'

I let my head fall back against the brocade sofa. I think of the moving pavements at the airport. I feel as if I'm on one now, powerless to change direction, not sure if I care where I'm going. I don't feel as if I could care about anything ever again. I think of Jonathan's kiss at the airport. As cold as Judas's.

'Is she asleep?' Bob sits down beside me. It seems weeks since we said anything to each other that was not concerned with the all-powerful 'she'. She who must be obeyed.

'Yes.'

'We're leaving in a minute. That chap Luca's going to drive us.'

Mum and Anna's family are staying with Auntie Carla. Maria and Co. are staying with Franco and Paola. Bob and I have been awarded a one-bedroomed flat that Uncle Bruno normally lets to tourists. It's in a wonderful location, right by the Trevi Fountain, but I know from past experience that it is tiny and uncomfortable. Ungratefully, I wonder if we have been put there so Kitty doesn't keep everyone awake at night.

'I'm exhausted,' I say. 'Aren't you?'

'Yes. I feel like I've had enough food to last me a lifetime.' Bob runs his hand through his hair, leaving it standing up in a crest.

'Are you having a terrible time?' I ask.

'No. I just feel that I've had enough sermons from Anna and mystic revelations from Maria for a bit.'

'Me too,' I say, with feeling. 'Me too.'

Bob is about to speak again but Mosaic knocks over her lemonade and starts to cry. Kitty wakes up and joins in, and Luca, with impressive timing, stands up, jangling his car keys. It is time to go.

I sit in the back with Kitty as Luca drives us through Rome at midnight. The famous buildings loom up, floodlit and wonderful. The tail-lights of Vespas lead the way along the Corso Vittorio Emanuele. In the Piazza di Trevi, the sea gods of the fountain are lit with an unearthly green light. The two tritons blow their conches and the water is silver in the moonlight.

I think of a Wordsworth quotation, one that would gladden Maria's heart:

> Great God! I'd rather be
> A pagan suckled in a creed outworn . . .
> Or hear old Triton blow his wreathed horn . . .

Luca stops the car, turns to me and speaks his first sentence in English: 'Welcome,' he says, 'to the eternal city.'

CHAPTER SEVEN

The first holiday in Rome that I remember clearly was when I was eight, Maria eleven and Anna thirteen. It was unusual because we were there in the middle of August. Usually we went to Ostia Lido in the summer because in August Rome is stifling. The streets throng with tourists and huge coaches and the Italians disappear for holiday homes in the mountains or by the sea. Summer in Rome consists of edging along pavements, dodging from shade to shade, avoiding the sweaty hordes, then buying a can of Coke for two million lire.

Dad must have been attending a conference at the university. Certainly he wasn't around much. We were staying with Auntie Carla and Uncle Bruno and my mother spent a lot of time shopping with Auntie Carla or sitting on the balcony fanning herself with Dad's lecture notes. We three girls were thrown together as we never were at home. In Lewes, we had our separate friends and did our own thing. Anna played the violin and collected for CAFOD; Maria went swimming and giggled with her friends (hours shut in her bedroom, writing each other little notes, which then had to be destroyed before I could read them); I went horse-riding and watched football with Dad. But here we were in Rome, in August, with no entertainment but each other. And Franco.

Franco was exactly my age but, as is often the case with boys, he seemed a lot younger. He collected toy cars and pretended to be Batman. I liked to read and told myself long stories about horses that talked. Dad, who always thought of me as younger than I was, used to say dotingly, 'The two little ones can play together,' but we had nothing in common. We spent one whole day playing battleships but mostly we ignored each other. I would lie on my bed reading, with the blinds closed, while Franco raced his toy cars up and down the balcony.

Uncle Bruno and Auntie Carla had a different apartment then. It was on the outskirts of Rome, with a railway line that ran through the gardens. There was a fantastic restaurant right next to the railway and you could be savouring your *risotto ai funghi* when the 19.00 to Rome Termini blasted past your ear. It wasn't a salubrious location but the apartment was huge: five bedrooms, two bathrooms and a massive balcony. It is the balcony that I remember best: it ran the length of the apartment. The large table where we had our evening meal stood at one end, shaded by a green awning, which gave a rather restful, underwater feel. A forest of plants, olive trees in pots, tomato plants, a vine as thick as a man's arm, was arranged in the middle, with a hammock and a selection of Franco's toys, cars, tractors, table football and a scale model of a Ferrari, at the far end.

Anna and Maria immediately made the balcony their place. They would sit for hours, lounging in the hammock, talking softly and breaking off if Franco or I came into sight. They would lie sunbathing among the tomato plants, obsessively comparing the white marks left by their watch straps. They would play table football, not as I would have played it (competitively, using proper FA rules) but annoyingly, giving the footballers the names of pop stars they fancied and not keeping score. Sometimes, if I approached them slowly, stalking them through the vine leaves, they would deign to let me stay with them, mainly so that they could get me to run to and fro with cans of lemon soda and Auntie Carla's almond biscuits, but eventually they would say, 'Haven't you got anything else to do? Why don't you play with Franco?' and finally, 'Mum! Gaby's annoying us!'

It was on one of these hot, fraught afternoons on the balcony that we first saw the Golden Boys. Anna and Maria were lying top to tail in the hammock and I was sprawled at their feet drawing horses. Mum and Auntie Carla were having a siesta, and Franco was watching television. I lay on my tummy, carefully sketching in horses' manes and tails. I couldn't do the legs very well so I left these as an impressionistic blur. From my position I had a perfect view of the balcony of the adjoining block of flats. Until now, it had been empty, apart from a plastic table and a dead Christmas tree, but now I saw people on it, two boys sitting at the plastic table and playing *scopa*, a fiendish Italian card game. I could see the tops of their heads, one black and one dark blond, their brown hands and arms. One wore a leather wristband, the other a complicated-looking watch. 'Hey!' I hissed at my sisters. 'There are *boys* on the next-door balcony.'

Anna and Maria joined me on the floor. They gazed,

entranced, at the card-playing hands, breathing in the details of the leather band and the diver's watch.

'Boys!' breathed Maria.

'At least sixteen,' whispered Anna.

'Two of them. Just right for us.'

'What about me?' I protested.

Maria giggled. 'Maybe they've got a baby brother.'

For days we stalked the Golden Boys, as Anna named them. 'Their skin,' she said – on the day before, we had seen them, thrillingly, without their tops – 'it's not exactly brown, more a sort of golden colour.'

'I'm going to call mine Romeo,' said Maria.

'Yours?' said Anna. 'Which one's yours?'

'The blond one.'

'Oh, that's OK. I like the dark one. I'm going to call him Ferdinand.'

I think Anna and Maria would have been happy to go on like this indefinitely, arguing over Romeo and Ferdinand, making up elaborate stories about them, imagining what it would be like to kiss them, but something happened that turned the game into scary reality. Anna, visiting the market with Auntie Carla, had suddenly come face to face with them.

Auntie Carla had said casually, in rapid Italian, 'Oh, hello, boys. Have you met my niece, Anna? Anna, this is Giancarlo and Massimo. Our neighbours.'

'It was terrible,' said Anna later, during a whispered conference on the balcony. 'I didn't know where to look. And then Ferdinand – I mean Giancarlo – put out his hand and said, "*Piacere*." I didn't know where to look! I couldn't say a word, just took his hand – it was lovely and warm – and sort of smiled. And then Auntie Carla – can you imagine it? – said, "You young people must get together one day."'

'She didn't!' gasped Maria.

'She did! It was so embarrassing. My face literally *burned*.'

The golden boys didn't wait for Auntie Carla, though. That very evening, as we sat on the balcony after supper, we heard a soft voice calling, 'Anna! An-na!' It was Giancarlo. He was leaning out over the side of his balcony and looking up at us. It was, as Anna said later, just like Romeo and Juliet.

'Hello,' said Anna.

'Hello. Who are your friends?' said Giancarlo, in English.

'They're not my friends.' Anna disowned us. 'They're my sisters.'

'I'm Maria,' said Maria, giving them her best smile, all eyes and teeth.

'I'm Gaby,' I said.

'Gaby?'

'Gabriella.'

'So, Anna, Maria and Gabriella, would you like to come over and play cards with us?'

Dad said no, of course, but Auntie Carla overruled him. They were nice boys, their mother (a most respectable woman) would be there and, besides, he would be able to see us plainly from the balcony. So, quivering with excitement and smelling strongly of Anna's Floral Notes Rose perfume, we made our way to the Golden Boys' apartment.

Their mother met us at the door. She was, indeed, the epitome of respectability, wearing a flowered summer dress, low-heeled sandals and tights (in August!). She irritated me, though, by calling me *piccolina*, little one, just when I was hoping to look ten, at least.

The boys were waiting by the balcony. They were every bit as glorious close up. Giancarlo, the elder, was fifteen, and he had an assured swagger that made us all feel weak at the knees. Massimo was thirteen, quieter and more smiley, but he too had that Italian-male confidence. You could see it in the way they shuffled the cards, in the way they yelled at their mother for refreshments, in the way that Giancarlo spread his arm across the back of Anna's chair and said, 'So, Anna, are you a nice little English girl?'

I don't remember much of the card game. I couldn't understand the rules and the drink the boys' mother brought was so sweet it made my teeth ache. My sisters ignored me, and although the boys smiled at me from time to time and Massimo said I had pretty hair, they were concentrating on flirting with Anna and Maria. Eventually I wandered away and waved at Dad, who was sitting on our balcony, watching the Golden Boys' every move.

It was two days after that first card game that Giancarlo and Massimo asked if they could take Anna and Maria out for an ice cream, and not just any ice cream: they wanted to take them to the Piazza di Spagna, right in the heart of Rome. 'And how would they get there?' asked Dad, dangerously calm.

'By motorbike, of course,' said Auntie Carla.

'No,' said Dad. 'No, no, no, no, no.' It was impossible, he said. They were children – Maria was just eleven, for heaven's sake. He would not let them gallivant over the city at night with two unknown boys – and as for riding on the back of motorbikes, *Dio ce ne scampi e liberi!* God forbid. He would not allow it. No. *Basta. Finito.* Anna and Maria cried and pleaded. Anna said that she could go alone – she was thirteen, after all. 'They want me as well,' said Maria, sulkily. And that was a sore point with Anna: the Golden Boys shared their favours equally between her and Maria, although Maria had only just finished primary school. In fact Massimo, who was exactly Anna's age, seemed to prefer Maria.

Eventually, Auntie Carla secured a compromise. Dad would drive Anna and Maria to the Piazza di Spagna. He would leave them there to have an ice cream with the boys and collect them an hour later. They accepted this reluctantly. 'But go right away,' Maria insisted. 'Don't hang around glowering like a Mafia leader.'

'I won't,' Dad promised mildly.

I went along for the ride. I had not been included in the invitation even though, the day before, Giancarlo had called me '*bella*' when he met me in the apartment gardens. I didn't mind: I knew my limitations, and going out at night with teenage Italian boys was one of them.

We drove to the Piazza di Spagna in tense, excited silence.

After a lot of discussion and discarded dresses, Anna and Maria were both wearing jeans and the smallest tops they could find. Anna's was pink with thin little straps that kept falling over her shoulders; Maria's was white with 'angel' written in red across her developing bosom. I saw Dad looking at it dubiously.

There were so many young people at the Piazza di Spagna that, at first, we couldn't see the Golden Boys. 'Perhaps they aren't here,' said Maria.

'Oh, shut up!' snapped Anna, furious with Maria for saying what she was thinking.

'There they are!' said Maria, and sure enough, Giancarlo and Massimo were extracting themselves from a crowd of laughing, chattering teenagers. Anna and Maria were out of the car so quickly that Dad's parting admonition to be back promptly in an hour's time was shouted at the backs of their heads.

As we watched them go, Dad turned to me and said, with a guilty smile, 'Shall we go somewhere where we can see them?'

'Oh, yes!' I agreed. I don't think I had ever doubted that this had been his plan all along.

Dad took me to a café around the corner from the piazza.

We sat on spindly chrome chairs, Dad had an espresso and I had a delicious ice cream in a long, frosted glass. Cars, bicycles and mopeds passed us in a steady stream, so close that we could feel their hot breath on our faces. The tables were filling with people: couples engrossed in each other, shouting groups of teenagers, elderly men with tiny glasses of grappa watching impassively as the evening unfolded in front of them. I sat up straight and imagined myself grown-up, twelve at least. I was alone with my dad, in Rome, the best city in the world. A burst of pop music came from inside the café and I heard it as the soundtrack to my fabulous life: 'Gabriella de Angelis, youngest and most beautiful daughter of Enzo de Angelis, sits outside a café in Rome, enjoying an ice cream. Gabriella, the famous . . .' Famous what? Actress? Singer? Writer? The choices were endless . . .

'Gaby?' It was Dad, breaking into his beautiful youngest daughter's fantasy.

'What?'

'Can you see them?'

'Who?'

'Anna and Maria.'

Reluctantly, I twisted round. I could just see Maria's

shoulder in the white T-shirt as she sat at a café across the road. Massimo's arm was draped over the back of her chair.

'Yes. Just,' I said.

'What are they doing?'

'Talking.'

'Oh.'

Dad said nothing for a while and I ate my ice cream and returned to my jet-set lifestyle. 'Gabriella de Angelis can stay out all night if she wants. She has hundreds of boyfriends and they all want to marry her . . .'

'Gaby?'

'What?' I picked up the glass and drained the last of my ice cream with a disgusting gurgle.

'Are you finished? Let's go for a walk.'

We walked past the Golden Boys' café, which was now teeming with desperately cool youngsters making that peculiarly Italian noise of high-pitched excitement punctuated with hoarse cries of '*Eh, Mario! Ciao, Andrea! Cosa fai?*' Anna looked up as we passed and made a don't-embarrass-us face. Maria was too busy tossing her hair to notice us. Dad smiled grimly but said nothing.

Dad and I wove our way slowly though the crowds and

began to walk up the Spanish Steps. This was a difficult feat as each step was full of hot German tourists, comparing blisters and taking water-bottles out of vast fluorescent backpacks. But we persevered, not speaking but climbing steadily. The night air was as hot as breath.

When we reached the top, the chattering tourists were below us and the gardens of the Villa Medici stretched behind us, calm and mysterious. I'll always remember how my dad looked, with the dark trees behind him, gazing down on the lights of the piazza. He put his hand on my shoulder and, for a moment, we stood there in silence. Then he said, 'Never forget. This is my city.'

Later, we collected a giggly Anna and Maria and drove back to the apartment. As we crossed the garden a small figure jumped in front of us. It was a boy, of about my age, and now I remember that he had curious yellow-brown eyes. 'Ha!' he said exultantly, then soaked us with an extremely efficient water pistol.

When we got up to the apartment, Dad related the incident to Auntie Carla. 'Oh, that Luca,' she said, with irritated affection. 'He is such a naughty boy.'

CHAPTER EIGHT

'The Vestal Virgins were forbidden to see any men but the Pontifex Maximus. They had to cut off their hair when they entered the house and they wore long robes and veils.'

'They sound like the Sisters of Mercy, don't they, Anna?' says Maria, adjusting her sandal strap. Anna ignores her.

'Who the hell was Pontifex Maximus?' whispers Marco to Sergio. 'Sounds like a bloody good job.' They snigger.

Franco continues his spiel: he has a guidebook in his hand but is not referring to it. He is staring at the sky, rapt with the joy of imparting information. I find him incredibly annoying.

'The Vestals spent thirty years in this cloister, ten years learning the rites, ten years practising them and ten years teaching the novices . . .'

'After which they died of boredom,' suggests Maria.

Franco smiles calmly. 'After which they were free to leave, Maria.'

'Can't have had much to look forward to, though,' says Maria. 'Who would want a forty-year-old virgin with no skills apart from some stupid rites?'

'On the contrary,' says Franco smoothly, 'Vestal Virgins had great honour and privileges. They were second only to the Empress. They could stay a prisoner's execution, they had front-row seats at the Colosseum, and were in charge of all wills and treaties.'

'You see, Maria,' says Anna sweetly, 'a celibate's life is not all bad. There are rewards for forsaking a worldly existence.'

'I bet they were punished if they broke their vows, though.'

'They were buried alive,' admits Franco, 'under the Piazza Indipendenza.'

We are in the Forum, at the Temple of the Vestals. It is a perfect day, bright blue skies and light breezes; hot enough for shirtsleeves but without the awful, enervating heat of Rome in August. Kitty is wearing one of her lightweight Babygros and a rather cute sunhat. I don't have to feel that I'm a terrible mother if I don't smother her with factor forty-five every ten minutes.

Although I have been to Rome many times, this is only the second time that I have visited the Forum. We usually avoid tourist places; for us the Forum, the Colosseum and the Pantheon are usually a backdrop to an endless round of visiting relatives and drinking tiny cups of coffee while we look at family photos in fat velvet albums. The only other time I have been to the Forum was, oddly enough, with the Golden Boys.

It was a boiling hot day. Having suggested the trip for educational reasons (Anna was studying *Julius Caesar* at school) Auntie Carla relented and asked Giancarlo and Massimo to accompany us. That sent Anna and Maria into a frenzy of hair-curling and clothes analysis. When the day dawned, Anna was in her highest-heeled sandals, teetering over the uneven ground of the Forum – where it feels as though all the buried dead of Rome are about to rise up under your feet – and once, gloriously, falling headlong over a broken pillar. Maria wore her sundress and piled her hair on top of her head. The next day she had terrible sunburn on the back of her neck and Mum made her stay in bed all day.

Now we are standing by the curved wall of the temple. The sun is warm on my hair and I had five hours of uninterrupted sleep last night. I feel as if I'm emerging slowly from a long, dark tunnel. I hear Franco's monologue through a dreamlike haze, shutting my eyes so the sun beats red on the lids. The temple was round, Franco tells us, to symbolise the earth from which all life springs. Maria says this is an admirably pagan idea. I sit on a nearby stone, smooth and worn with age. Nearby, a bee buzzes loudly. Franco and Maria's voices fade into a pleasant insect drone. I look across at Bob, who is holding Kitty. He smiles at me and I smile back.

We leave the Temple of the Vestals to look over the wall of the Vestals' house. Headless marble statues flank an overgrown rose garden. Down more steps and across the Via Sacra, the sacred way. Below us are the remains of a row of buildings. Maria asks Franco what they are. 'It's believed to be a brothel,' says Franco, 'from the Republican era.'

'Those women really did lead useful lives,' says Maria.

'I'm sure old Pontifex Maximus was a frequent visitor,' whispers Marco to Sergio.

It is weird to see all the different layers of buildings, like the strata of a cliff. All the walls, columns and steps climbing crazily on top of one another. Despite Franco's best efforts, I find it impossible to imagine the Forum of Roman times, the

shops, marketplaces, law courts and temples. This stone landscape of pillars and columns seems right to me. The ruin
has become a place in its own right, with cypress trees and
statues rising side by side. It's hard to imagine the stark white
stone covered with gaudy marble or the beautiful faded
frescos bright and new. Ruins are more tasteful, somehow.

On the day with the Golden Boys, Anna and Maria had a
psychic experience. Anna denies it now as, to her, belief in
ghosts ranks, along with reading your horoscope and having
a dream-catcher over your bed, as dangerously pagan behaviour. 'How can you not believe in God yet believe in all that
rubbish?' she once yelled exasperatedly at Maria.

'How can you believe in bread and wine turning into
someone's body and blood and dismiss horoscopes as fantasy?' countered Maria. She, of course, believes passionately
in ghosts. Her Brighton house is haunted by a benign spirit
called Arnold, who sometimes helps with the washing-up.

Anyway, on that hot August day, as Franco and I trailed
behind a giggling Anna and Maria and a rather distant
Giancarlo and Massimo, Anna stopped because her shoes
were hurting. '*E vero*, I told you to wear trainers,' said Auntie
Carla. Anna ignored her. The *idea* of wearing something as

utilitarian and ugly as trainers in front of the Golden Boys! Although Anna was in the school netball team and Maria swam well, they loathed the idea of seeming sporty, especially in Italy where the women look as if they would faint if a ball came too close. So Anna sat down in front of a temple, Maria loyally stayed with her, the Golden Boys wandered off, bored, and Franco and I went to nag Auntie Carla for Coca-Cola.

Suddenly Anna gave a loud scream. Auntie Carla rushed over to her, by which time Maria was screaming too, obviously enjoying herself. Anna was pointing to the temple, which had steps that stopped, weirdly, in mid-air, with a headless, seated statue at the top.

'I saw someone coming down the steps!' shrieked Anna.

'What do you mean, *cara*?' said Auntie Carla. 'The steps are broken.'

'That's just it! I saw someone coming down the steps – the *steps that aren't there*.' And she was off again.

Maria joined in. They had seen two men in full Roman dress ('togas and everything') gliding down the invisible steps to disappear on the Via Sacra. Auntie Carla was half inclined to believe them: she was interested in the paranormal and saw no contradiction between being a devout Catholic and believing that the spirit of her dead father sometimes visited her in the form of a large white pigeon. Giancarlo and Massimo obviously found it all embarrassing: they walked away from us and sat on the steps of the Curia, talking in low voices.

When we told Dad the story, he thought it hilarious. 'It's a monastery now, that temple,' he said. 'Maybe you saw a monk. Maybe it's a sign that you will be a saint, Anna.'

My mother was more dismissive still: 'Teenage girls,' she said. 'You know what they're like.'

Today I wander over to the temple for nostalgic reasons. The broken steps are still there but I notice that there is also a door, half-way up the wall, with pillars directly in front of it, opening on to a sheer drop. At the time, I thought that Anna's ghost was nothing more than a ruse to get the Golden Boys' attention (a ruse that failed spectacularly) but today the temple, with the headless statue, the blocked doorway and the steps leading nowhere gives me a jolted, nightmarish sensation. Perhaps Anna really did see a Roman ghost – the place must be teeming with them. You can't move in Rome without falling over a grave or a monument to the dead. City of the soul, Byron called it, but sometimes it seems more like the city of the dead. I shiver and glance back to the others. As Bob lifts Kitty into the air, I can see her red-gold hair glinting in the sun. Her black baby hair has gone and she is now, like Bob, a redhead. I hurry over to join them.

We reach the end of the Via Sacra. In front of us a squat white arch stands on its own. 'The Arch of Titus,' says Franco, impressively. Mum sits down on a low wall and fans herself with her hat.

'Are you all right, Mummy?' asks Anna solicitously.

Marco and Sergio chase Kyle and Mosaic through the maze of broken columns.

'It is believed,' says Franco, 'that it is impossible for a true Jew to pass through the Arch of Titus.'

We all look at Ray, who is Jewish. He grins and says, 'Shall I give it a try?'

Mosaic screams. 'Don't, Daddy! You might die!'

'Don't be silly, Mosaic,' snaps Maria. 'It's only a superstition.'

'And you never believe in those,' says Anna, getting her own back about the Vestals. I'm tempted to remind her about her ghost, but I don't. Somehow it is hard to remind Anna about her childhood: it is almost as if she didn't live it at all.

Ray squares his shoulders, takes Mosaic's hand and walks through the arch. We all cheer.

'Another triumph for reason,' mutters Bob, holding Kitty above his head so that she can see. She loves the cheering and claps her hands frantically.

'Why aren't Jews meant to pass through?' Ray asks Franco, as Mosaic and Kyle run to and fro under the arch.

'The arch was erected to celebrate Titus's victory over the rebellious Jews,' says Franco. 'The frescos inside show the victors carrying away the treasure from the Temple in Jerusalem.'

We crane our heads upwards and see a series of little frescos under the archway, like an Ancient Roman comic.

'How horrible,' says Marco, shocked. 'What happened to the treasure?'

Franco shrugs. 'No one knows. Some people believe it was thrown into the Tiber.'

We make our way back through the Forum, past the headless statue and the Vestals' rose garden, up another endless flight of steps (impossible to bring the buggy) into the square of the Campidoglio. The statue of Marcus Aurelius gleams bronze in the sun, a pigeon perched on its shoulder.

A barefoot monk in a brown habit passes a flock of Japanese tourists. Anna takes pictures of Marco and Sergio by the statue. Dad used to claim Marcus Aurelius as a first cousin.

Down more steps, shallow and traitorous, to the Piazza Venezia and the massive tiered wedding-cake monument to Vittorio Emanuele. We cross the piazza, flagging a little in the heat. Bob carries Kitty; Mosaic and Kyle hang on to Ray's hands. I trail behind with Mum. A fat man dressed as a legionary comes up to us and offers to have his photo taken with us. '*Una bella fotografia*,' he says engagingly and unconvincingly. He is wearing socks and slip-on sandals.

'He wouldn't last a minute in a Roman legion,' says Marco, as Franco hurries us past. 'You had to be over six feet tall.'

'Really?' says David, surprised. 'You wouldn't think many Italians were that tall.'

Franco, who is a good few inches taller than him, snorts contemptuously.

At the other side of the square stand several *carrozze* pulled by dispirited horses. Mosaic starts crying and says she wants to go in one. 'No, no,' says Franco. 'They are for tourists.' Tara says that if no one uses the *carrozze*, the horses will starve. Mosaic howls in earnest. Franco hurries us on.

Trajan's Column is hidden in a corner between two domed churches. It is a curiously desolate spot, even though it is only a few yards away from the gleaming splendour of Vittorio Emanuele. One of the churches even has grass growing on its roof. Trajan's Column is covered with scaffolding and the whole thing is fenced off with a kind of pit around it. If we scatter Dad here, it will mean leaning over the side and tipping him over the wall. Not, I fear, the mystic, romantic ceremony that Maria had in mind.

We gaze in silence at the column. In front of us, on yet another level, are the ruins of Trajan's Forum, where a black cat picks its way delicately through the stones. The column is amazingly high, pockmarked with sculptures, and there are tiny windows, like arrow slits, all the way up. At the top there is a bronze statue surrounded by a railing, but it is impossible to imagine anyone ever being allowed up there. I gaze upwards: the clouds scudding past make me feel dizzy.

'Could people ever get up there?' I ask Franco.

'Yes. There is a spiral staircase inside. There used to be two big buildings, libraries, on either side with balconies where you could see the sculptures.'

'What do the sculptures show?'

Franco shrugs. 'The works of the Emperor Trajan, I think.'

Now the libraries have been replaced with churches: Santa Maria di Loreto and Santo Nome di Maria. Our Santa Maria makes three. She gazes up grumpily at the column. 'Can't think what Dad saw in the place,' she says at last, denying all responsibility.

'It might have been the legend of Pope Gregory,' offers Franco.

No one asks, 'What legend?' but Franco tells us anyway. Apparently one day, Gregory (who presumably had a better view than us) saw that one of the sculptures showed Trajan dispensing justice to a poor widow. He wept to think that this good man was now condemned to eternal hellfire for being a pagan. As he wept, the voice of St Peter was heard in the clouds, announcing that Trajan was saved and could go to heaven. However, St Peter warned the Pope, in a rather bad-tempered aside, not to make a habit of such requests or there would be no one left in hell. The area around the column was duly consecrated and became a Christian cemetery. As a finishing touch, a statue of St Peter was placed on top of the column.

We are all silent. I look sideways at Maria, who is gazing

up at the column, probably trying to see the interfering saint. I wonder if she feels that Dad has somehow stolen a march on her by choosing a pagan burial place that turns out to be a Christian cemetery. Before Anna can point this out, a voice is heard behind us. Not St Peter this time but someone equally welcome.

'Trajan himself is buried here,' says the voice. It is Luca. Earlier that morning he had collected us in the MPV and deposited us at the Forum, then disappeared on unnamed business of his own. Now he is back, having apparently driven straight through the piazza, scattering the fake legionaries and the *carrozze* alike.

'Hadrian, Trajan's successor, insisted that he be buried here,' he says, in his accented but fluent English. 'People protested that it was sacrilege to be buried within the *pomerium* but Hadrian replied that Trajan was not a mortal but a god.'

By now we are all in a state of numb acquiescence, and obediently allow Luca to install us in his car and drive us, at breakneck speed, towards the restaurant of his choice. He has even found a baby seat from somewhere and Kitty is installed in the back. Bob gets in beside her and I realise that the only seat left is in the front, next to Luca. It is terrifying because, as I'm on the right, I feel as if I'm driving. My whole body is clenched in fear as motorcycles, pedestrians, ancient monuments rear up in front of me. Eventually, though, as the ugly suburbs give way to countryside, I can talk to Luca in an almost normal voice. I tell him that I think I remember him as a child – I don't mention the water pistol. Yes, he says, he has known Franco for many years. They were at school together, but he was not clever like Franco. He was interested only in having fun. After school he went into the army but, *è vero*, it was a terrible life and he left after three years. Now he is a taxi driver: he has another car and this MPV. He always helps out Franco and his family because they are still friends, after all these years.

I catch Bob's eye in the passenger mirror. He is looking bored and rather distant. I turn back to Luca. Is he married? No, a suppressed laugh, he is not. *Sfortunatamente*.

The restaurant is outside Rome, near Castelgandolfo, the Pope's summer palace. By the time we get there, Kitty, Mosaic and Kyle are all asleep and I feel quite faint with hunger.

It is a lovely place, with huge windows looking out on to

the lake. The owner greets Luca like a long-lost son. It seems that one of his other jobs is arranging wedding receptions, so he knows every possible venue within a ten-mile radius of Rome and is guaranteed gold-plated service at them all. The owner ('Call me Gino') ushers us to a sumptuous table by the window, organising a high chair and ordering sparkling wine on the house. Gorgeous crostini arrive, shiny pieces of olive and liver on garlic-soaked bread. I am desperate to eat, but Kitty is bad-tempered at being woken and will not settle. I shift her from shoulder to shoulder and she still cries piteously. Bob offers to take her but I can see him looking longingly at his bruschetta and I feel the hot embrace of martyrdom. 'No, I'll take her outside and try to get her to sleep. Don't worry about me. Enjoy your meal.' I flash a bright smile round the table and stumble out, clasping my screaming baby.

I walk slowly down to the lake. It is two o'clock and still hot. The shore has black volcanic sand and I walk up and down, rocking Kitty mechanically. Despite the presence of a four-star restaurant fifty yards away, I feel as if I am the only person in the world. The water looks dark and mysterious, fringed by pines and silvery olive trees. Gradually Kitty's sobs become whimpers and I turn her cautiously so that I can see her face. Her eyelids are fluttering. Hardly daring to move, I walk slower and slower. Kitty breathes heavily through her mouth. I stop walking and lower myself carefully on to a rock. Kitty doesn't wake.

As I sit there, I see a wonderful thing, so unexpected that it seems to have been laid on purely for my entertainment. A sea plane comes swooping down and performs a perfect landing on the lake. Ripples turn into water and splash by my feet. The plane glides across the surface, then its engines roar (mercifully Kitty stays asleep) and it takes off again in a sheet of glistening water. The whole thing is over so quickly that I wonder if I have imagined it.

I sit by the lake, holding Kitty and feeling sorry for myself. Suddenly it seems terrifying that I can no longer put myself first. I can't go back into the restaurant and stuff down pasta and red wine. I have to sit outside, starving and light-headed, because Kitty comes first. Even Bob can forget her for a few minutes and laugh and drink, but I never can. I am her mother and also, for the moment, her main source of food, drink, entertainment and comfort. And I know, in a dizzying flash of recognition, that nothing will ever be the same again. True, Kitty won't always need me for food but she will always need me and, almost more terrifyingly, I will always need her. I think of the five or six times a night that I check she is still breathing, hanging low over her cot until my hair touches her face and she wakes up, sneezing. Maria might not do this any more for Tara but I saw the expression in her eyes when she tugged her away from my mother at the airport. Tara may be nineteen and stunningly beautiful but she is still Maria's baby.

'Gaby!'

I twist round and see Tara coming towards me now, carrying a tray with a plate and a glass of wine. She looks like a waitress painted by Botticelli. 'I thought you might be hungry.' She climbs carefully down the bank and places the tray on a rock. 'Shall I hold her while you eat?' I put Kitty into her arms. As she bends her head and says, 'Hello, baby,' I realise that it is the first time that Tara has held my baby and the ever-present tears spring again to my eyes. I adore my nieces and nephews. In some ways my relationship with them seems like the purest one in my life; free from the jealousies and power-plays of my relationships with my sisters or the churning emotions of my feelings for Bob and Kitty. It is just a lovely thing to watch beautiful Tara holding my baby. And, thank God, it means I can eat at last.

As I shovel down the (delicious) pasta, Tara walks along the lake shore, holding Kitty. I sip some wine and enjoy a few moments' freedom. Nothing to hold. Motherhood is all about holding things: carry-cots, changing bags, car seats and, heaviest of all, the baby, deadening my arms and giving me a constant, whingeing backache. How can it be that already I am missing the weight in my arms?

Tara turns and comes back to me. She is holding Kitty like a doll, slightly away from her body. I want to tell her that she won't break.

'I couldn't imagine you with a baby,' says Tara, coming nearer. 'Before I saw you, I mean.'

'Well, you knew I was pregnant at Christmas.'

'Yes, but being pregnant isn't the same thing.'

'One does lead to the other, you know. Didn't you do biology at school?'

Tara laughs. 'It's just . . . It's odd to think of you as a mother.'

'Why?'

'I don't know. I suppose you've always seemed a lot younger than Mum and Auntie Anna. And you've got your job and you go away on exciting holidays. It's just hard to imagine you at home with a baby.'

'It's hard for me too,' I say, scraping up the last of the pasta. 'I'm thirty-five but I still feel too young to have a baby.' This was a great bone of contention between Bob and me. On my thirtieth birthday, Bob asked me if maybe we should think about having children and I replied that it was too soon, I still felt too young. 'You're thirty, for God's sake,' Bob had snapped.

Tara sits down next to me, holding Kitty carefully, like a tray. 'Do you ever forget you've got her?' she asks.

'Once. I left her with Bob's sister and went into the office for a visit. It was wonderful. Seeing everybody, my name on my office door, going out to lunch in a nice restaurant. Feeling important again. Anyway, I got my usual tube home, read the *Standard*, walked my usual walk back to the flat. Got in, put the kettle on and then thought, Have I forgotten something?'

'What happened?' asks Tara.

'I rushed over to Bob's sister's house in a panic. She was

fine about it. She'd hardly noticed – she's got three kids of her own. Kitty took one look at me and started crying. I was . . . Well, when you're breastfeeding you get a bit full if you're away from the baby. I was leaking all over the place. It was a million miles from the office.'

'Will you go back to work?'

'I think so. I really miss it. I know it's hard to believe.'

'Mum always says it must be the most boring job in the world.'

'Well, it's not. It's difficult to explain, but it's not.'

We're silent. I'm thinking of how much I love my job: the deals, the meetings where you have to stop your client saying something too stupid to potential backers, putting together a business plan, the mad panic to have everything done in time, the euphoria when you get a result. Then I look at Kitty, cherubic in Tara's arms and think, I'm never going to be able to leave her.

From a long way off, I hear the restaurant door open. I look round and see Bob come out. For a moment, I am overcome with affection for him: he has come out to see how we are – he hasn't stayed inside, selfishly eating and drinking. But then I see he has his mobile with him and is talking rapidly in a way I associate with work. 'Yeah, OK, I'll let you know,' I hear him say.

He walks slowly towards us. Kitty wakes up and we all stare at him. He spreads out his hands in a curiously Italian gesture of resignation. 'Gaby, I'm sorry. I've got to go home.'

CHAPTER NINE

It's work, of course. Bob is a solicitor and his biggest client has bought a new property portfolio. The deal has to be completed in three weeks and Bob is needed to take charge. Back at the little apartment by the Trevi Fountain, we argue in and out of the four rooms. Rented apartments are not really suited to arguing. This place has just four rooms: a bedroom with a huge gilt double bed, a sitting room with a sofa, apparently stuffed with rocks, and a low table covered with leaflets advertising tourist attractions, a narrow kitchen with a bench seat and peeling Formica table, and a tiny, but luxurious, bathroom. We follow each other in and out of the rooms, snapping and needling, but we can't get far enough away from each other to build up a good head of steam. At our flat in Clapham we can storm in and out of the rooms, crashing doors. Houses with stairs are even better: you can sulk properly by going upstairs, thus putting yourself (literally) on a higher level than your opponent. Here, I can see the whole apartment from our bed. The furthest Bob can go is to the kitchen to make tea. He opens the cupboards, thoughtfully stocked by Auntie Carla, and finds teabags, coffee, almond biscuits, pasta and orange juice, but no milk.

'There's no milk,' he says helpfully.

'Great,' I say, laying Kitty on the bed so I can change her nappy. 'I'm about to be left alone in a foreign country with no milk.'

'I'll go and get some,' says Bob, through gritted teeth.

While he is out, I have a hasty examination of my feelings. I am jealous, of course. I want to have a client who needs my presence urgently. When I went into the office that time, everyone told me what a wonderful job my assistant, Toby, was doing in covering for me. The sight of him sitting behind *my* desk made me feel sick. That night I dreamed I was dead and that Toby had climbed into my coffin. As far as my work is concerned I don't want to be dead and buried, but do I feel it's inevitable? Can I ever go back to being the Gabriella (never 'Gaby' at work) who could work flat out for twenty-four hours on a client presentation? Will I ever be able to take clients out for dinner (laughing uproariously at their jokes and paying discreetly for the meal with my gold card) without leaking milk and longing to be at home with my baby? Will I ever be able to bark self-importantly into a mobile as Bob has been doing for the last two hours – 'No. No. I want it done now. Tomorrow's no bloody good. Just do it'? There is now no one in the world to whom I can say, 'Just do it.'

I feel powerless, unimportant and hard done by. I still feel nervous about looking after Kitty and don't want to be left to do it on my own. It's not that Bob knows any more than I do, but when he's here at least we're in this thing together. True, my mum, Anna and Maria have loads of childcare experience, but Kitty is not their baby. I feel simultaneously that only I know how to take care of her and that I know nothing. Bob is the only other person in the world who loves Kitty as much as I do and he is leaving. Tears of self-pity roll down my cheeks.

And there's something else. Something a bit harder to define. When he first told me the news, Bob suggested I ask Tara or my mum to stay with me at the apartment.

'I don't want a member of my family,' I screamed. 'I want you.'

'I am a member of your family,' replied Bob, with annoying lawyer logic. But he isn't, not really. He isn't part of the whole sick-making, emotional turmoil that is connected in my mind with my dad's death. Bob hasn't lost his father and, although he loved mine, it isn't the same. I've lost count of the times that, over the last few months, I've said to Bob, 'You don't understand.' And he has always agreed humbly that he doesn't: he doesn't know what it's like. His parents are alive and well and living in Thornton Heath. But it is this freedom from unhappiness that I cling to. It is as if Anna, Maria and I are staring into the abyss, but Bob can pull me back from the brink because he isn't suffering as we are. I'm afraid of being left alone with my family. I'm afraid of seeing Jonathan again.

Why did he come to the airport? I knew that Anna had contacted him when Dad died and asked him if he would conduct the 'ceremony' of scattering the ashes, even though most of us don't consider a ceremony essential. That much, I suppose, is logical. Jonathan is in Rome; we are in Rome. He is a priest; Anna thinks we need a priest. But why did he come to the airport? Was it for Anna? Was it for me? Is he so bored that he'll do anything for a diversion? Does he have so few friends that even patting the air behind someone's back seems like meaningful contact?

Jonathan never had many friends. I didn't notice it at first because he was always surrounded by a loud group of baying law students. He was always in a crowd but he didn't have any close male friends. Girlfriends, yes – and ex-girlfriends were legion. But male friends, no. At the time, I thought this was rather romantic. We didn't need other people: we had each other. By the time we moved in together, we had severed practically all ties with the outside world. My closest friends, like Mel, hung on grimly, but it was hard work. When they did lure me out for the evening, I spent half of it on the phone to Jonathan. I would tell him where we were and then, at the end of the night, he would suddenly appear, handsome and smiling, through the beaded curtains of a Chinese restaurant. 'I missed you,' he would say. 'I thought I'd surprise you.' Then I would throw myself into his arms and the evening would be over. Jonathan would join our table, charming my friends and ordering more wine, but the giggly girls' night out was finished. It's surprising, really, in retrospect, that my friends tried as hard as they did.

When I first met Bob he was on holiday with two friends, Matt and Santa. He has no idea how much that circumstance prejudiced me in his favour. Even the jokey, laddish nickname Santa (because his real name was Nick Christmas) seemed endearing. Bob, Matt and Santa joked about who snored at night, about which of them the emaciated holiday rep fancied, about what had happened on their last holiday and the one before. They had a genuine bond; they had history. I thought it was wonderful.

I was on holiday with Mel and we had picked Crete because we couldn't decide between Sardinia and Corsica and were too chicken to try Club 18–30. We had ended up in a tiny apartment that flooded when you used the shower and was plunged into darkness if you turned on the ceiling fan. There was a little balcony that we festooned with wet swimming costumes and from which we could see the puddle-shaped swimming pool. From above, especially at night when it was floodlit and empty, it looked inviting; close up, surrounded by sunbeds and spilled drinks, it was too small to swim in and smelt unpleasantly of chlorine.

Every morning, Mel and I set out on the ten-minute walk to the beach – the brochure had, of course, promised 'sea views'. We didn't mind any of that, though: we were on holiday, we were going brown, we knew each other well enough not to have to chat all the time.

It was a year after my break-up with Jonathan, but I was still rather brittle, wary of new men. I had quite a few male friends at work but I deliberately kept those relationships on a rather superficial let's-go-out-for-a-drink basis. I had been on only two dates since Jonathan (I still thought of my life as pre-Jonathan, Jonathan and post-Jonathan). The first was with someone I had known at university. We had a wonderful evening of nostalgia and drunken reminiscence, but in the tube on the way home he jumped on me with such single-minded intent that I was terrified. All our talk of rag week and the freshers' ball vanished as if it had never been, to be replaced by something grim and adult. I pushed him away and got off the train two stops early. The second date was with the brother of someone from work. 'You'll love Vince,' Emma had said. 'He's just your type.' The night after my date with him I sat up for a long time, staring at myself in the mirror and wondering if it could be true that

Vince was my type and, if so, how long it took to slit your wrists with a Ladyshave razor.

So, all things considered, I was quite happy to be walking along a dusty road in Crete, swinging my beach-bag and towel with Mel for company. She was taking a break from her uxorious boyfriend, Peter. We avoided the subject of men and talked instead about where we would go that night and whether we would ever have the nerve to go anywhere that advertised 'karaoke'.

'Can we offer you ladies a lift?'

We swung round and saw three youngish men on mopeds. They were all bright pink and one of them (Matt) wore an England T-shirt, but they smiled nicely and didn't seem to be demonic teenagers on a wild mission to shag as many girls as possible before throwing up into the gutter. They seemed older than most of the other holidaymakers, about our age in fact, and their middle-class vowels soothed us. We were tired and the sun was hot. Bob was wearing a Bart Simpson top. No one with a *Simpsons* top can be a rapist, I thought, as I climbed on to the back of his moped. It was bad move because, although he wasn't a rapist, he was a terrible driver.

In the few moments of post-Jonathan optimism, I made a mental list of the qualities I wanted in a man:

- black hair
- blue eyes
- committed left-wing politics
- not a lawyer
- likes the arts
- Catholic

It's fair to say that Bob scored only one point, for his blue eyes, but somehow, as I clung to his waist on that first terrifying ride to the sea, I felt wildly, unaccountably happy. It seemed so easy, somehow, careering madly over the scorched countryside with the sun hot on my back. I wanted that ride to go on for ever.

When we got to the beach, we spread out our towels side by side. Suddenly embarrassed by my attraction to Bob, I ran into the sea. The water felt cool and silky as I floated on my back and stared up at the sky. I've lost the love of my life, I reminded myself, I'll never be happy again. I could hear Mel and the boys laughing on the beach. Someone had switched on a radio and it was playing a silly, sexy summer tune. I felt my mouth stretch into an unaccustomed grin.

When I came out of the sea, only Bob was by the towels. Mel and the others had gone to the beach-front bar and could be heard arguing the merits of bottled versus draught beers.

'Good swim?' asked Bob.

'Lovely.'

'You looked like a fish,' said Bob. 'Happy in the water, I mean,' he added hastily, perhaps realising that it wasn't the most attractive image.

'I'm not sure I want to look like a fish,' I said.

'Dolphin?' offered Bob hopefully.

'Too sinister.'

'I know what you mean. All that smiling.'

'And jumping through hoops.'

'And giving out-of-body experiences to American tourists.'

'Exactly.' I smiled at him and he smiled at me. The sun beat down and the sea did its blue, sparkling thing. It was one of the happiest moments of my life.

That night we gave the karaoke a miss and went to a seafront restaurant. Bob's skin had turned dark brown and he wore a crisp white shirt. He told me later he'd had to borrow a travel iron from the middle-aged couple in the next-door apartment. I was touched that he had gone to so much trouble. We all ate and drank and laughed a lot. Later, Mel got off with Santa (she never did marry Peter) and Bob and I walked on the beach and talked and talked. Two days later we made love for the first time and it was wonderful, but by then I'd known that even if it hadn't been it wouldn't have mattered. We were married a year later.

I didn't fall in love with Bob because he wasn't Jonathan, but it did help. With Bob everything was fun, nothing too serious. Even before God got involved, Jonathan and I had had a tortured, agonised relationship. All that worry about our immortal souls. All that time spent on our own together. All those declarations of undying love. All those discussions about what we would do if the other died ('I'd kill myself,' 'I'd never smile again,' 'I'd go into a convent'). I can count on the fingers of one hand the times that Bob has told me he loves me but I know he does. Or I did know it. I'm not sure of anything any more.

The front door crashes and Bob comes in, sheepish and irritated. 'All the shops are shut. They don't open until the evening.'

'Bloody foreigners.'

'Yes. Can't even get a nice cup o' tea.' Bob glances at me sideways, trying to gauge whether my mood has lightened.

'Have you booked your flight?' I ask abruptly.

He nods. 'Tomorrow at nine.'

'That was quick.'

'Anita fixed it.'

'Oh, that figures.' Anita is Bob's super-efficient secretary. She has a dozen furry gonks on her desk and doesn't know the difference between 'practise' and 'practice', but is excellent at travel arrangements and making Bob's life run smoothly. I'm jealous. Not of Anita but of Bob. I want a secretary, I want someone to say, 'Leave it with me. I'll sort it.'

Kitty starts to cry.

'Is she hungry?' asks Bob.

'How should I know?' Recently, we have been trying to introduce Kitty to solid foods, but so far she has always spat them out contemptuously.

'Shall we try some baby rice?'

'If you like.' I undo my shirt and offer Kitty the only food she never refuses. At this rate, I can see myself breastfeeding until she leaves home to go to university. Kitty's sobs turn into contented little grunts and I lean back on the uncomfortable bench seat and look at Bob. He is standing there in his white T-shirt and khaki shorts but I can see that he is already mentally in his solicitor's suit, barking instructions at Anita and the rest of the team. He looks at me abstractedly, as if I am a particularly knotty clause in a contract. I stare back blankly. The doorbell makes us both jump.

I can hear Bob saying, 'Hello?' and then he presses the button to open the downstairs door. 'It's Luca.'

Luca comes in, bringing with him an almost tangible sense of the outside world, away from the claustrophobia of children and marriage. He is carrying a large carton of milk. 'I brought this,' he says, smiling at me. 'I thought you might need it, with the *bambina*.'

'She's OK,' says Bob ungraciously, 'but I could murder a cup of tea.'

'Ah, the English and their tea.'

'Would you like a cup?' I ask.

'Thank you. No milk.' He laughs shortly and sits next to me on the bench. Strangely, I don't feel embarrassed about my exposed breast, my dirty bare feet or tear-stained face.

Bob puts the kettle on the hob (the Italians have yet to discover the joys of the electric kettle) and sits down opposite us.

'So you are going home?' says Luca.

'Yes,' says Bob, rather defensively. 'It's my work.'

'You are a lawyer?'

'A solicitor. Yes.'

'I'm an accountant,' I say suddenly, putting Kitty over my shoulder and patting her back. 'I work in a corporate-finance department.' Kitty burps loudly.

Bob makes the tea and brings it to the table in mismatched rented-apartment mugs. Luca's has a picture of Snoopy, mine has one of those women with a disappearing bikini. Where on earth did Uncle Bruno find it?

Luca asks if he can hold Kitty, who is now asleep. I pass her to him and he takes her with almost nonchalant ease, propping her in the crook of his arm. Bob and I stare. This is so different from the behaviour of our childless male friends. Santa flatly refused to hold her until 'her head stops wobbling.'

'You're good with babies,' I say.

'I have lots of *nipoti* – how do you say? Nephews?'

'None of your own?' asks Bob – tactlessly, I feel.

Luca smiles the way he did when I asked if he was married. 'No. *Sfortunatamente.*'

There is a short silence. Then Luca says, 'So, I forgot. I came to tell you that I have tickets.'

'For the football?' I say.

'Yes, the derby.' He pronounces it to rhyme with 'Herbie'. 'Rome versus Lazio.'

'How many?'

'Four. The boys, Marco and Sergio, they want you to go with them.'

I am ridiculously touched. The boys know that I am the only woman in the family who likes football. Bob, who prefers rugby, always scoffs at me, saying that I'm a typical middle-class woman jumping on the Nick Hornby bandwagon, but it's not true. I've always liked football and I was the only member of the family to support Dad's team, Arsenal. When I was about ten, he began to take me to matches. They were magical times: cold winter afternoons, me in my Arsenal hat and scarf, Dad in his trademark trilby, always the same greasy spoon café for egg and chips, always the same stand (Dad putting his hands over my ears when the chanting became too ribald), trudging home in the dark with the other fans, the sense of shared euphoria or depression. More than that, they were times I shared alone with my dad, away from my sisters. On days when we couldn't go to the match, we would sit glued to the teleprinter on television. That soporific singsong: 'Brighton three: Portsmouth nil'. The heart-stopping moment when the Arsenal score came up. Dad's shout of: 'On the ball! Arsenal.' The pained indulgence of the other members of the family. Football was our thing and ours alone.

'They want me to come?'

'Yes, they say that you are the only true fan.'

I glance triumphantly at Bob. 'Yes, I am.'

Bob looks dubiously at Luca, who is still holding Kitty. She is lost in sleep: head back, mouth slightly open, lips shiny. Her arms are at her sides, her soft, red-gold hair is on end with static electricity. Luca bends his head and gently brushes her hair with his lips. I am shocked to feel a corresponding shiver run through me.

'Who gets the fourth ticket?' asks Bob.

'Why, me, of course,' smiles Luca.

CHAPTER TEN

Dad loved football. He supported Arsenal and his home team, Roma, and loved them almost equally. That had worried Marco and Sergio, who would ask him which team he would support if they ever had to play each other. Dad replied that he'd support whoever played best. Actually, that wasn't true: on the few occasions that Arsenal played Roma, Dad was one hundred per cent behind the latter. There are some things an Italian can never change.

Dad was a very Italian football supporter. It is not very common in England for a middle-aged university lecturer to be a passionate football fan, but in Italy it's the norm. You see them everywhere, sober-suited businessmen clutching briefcases and their bright pink copies of *La Gazzetta dello Sport*. One of my abiding memories of Dad will be of him at the kitchen table with a cup of espresso and his copy of *La Gazzetta* propped up against Keynes's *A Treatise on Money*, Volume 1.

The Stadio Olimpico is a million miles from Highbury. Unlike English stadia, which tend to squat unnoticed among housing estates, the Stadio Olimpico is visible for miles; situated on the banks of the Tiber, its modern white façade is flanked by two red marble buildings, which, Luca tells us, were built by Mussolini and known as the Foro dei Marmi, the Marble Forum. A huge crowd flows over the bridge and through the white gateway. Anything less like an English football crowd would be hard to imagine: lots of suede and leather (although it is still warm by English standards and the boys and I are in T-shirts), families pushing designer baby buggies, Gucci, Prada and pashminas. Absolutely no one has their face painted in team colours.

I become fascinated by the group next to us in the queue to go in, three boys and three girls. They must be Roma supporters because one of the boys is wearing a Totti T-shirt and one of the girls has a scarf in *giallo-rosso*, the team colours. But that is where the resemblance to an English football fan ends. All are talking quietly about basketball. One of the boys is on his mobile phone and I hear the tell-tale word 'Mamma'. As we wait, one of the girls gets a flask out of her (designer) tote bag and offers it round. I catch a delicious smell of coffee.

I want to turn round and say, 'Look, you've got it all *wrong*. In the first place, if you're going to a football match you don't bring your girlfriends. Second, well-cut jeans and chinos are not suitable football-fan clothing. Whatever happened to nylon tracksuits? Third, if you must use your phone, don't call your mother. Finally, if you're going to have a drink, *don't* make it coffee.' Instead, I smile weakly and the girl offers me some coffee.

When we pass through the turnstiles, Luca disappears and comes back with bottles of sparkling mineral water and delicious rolls with mozzarella and ham. I want to tell him that he's got it wrong too, that hamburgers and beer in plastic glasses are more suitable for a football match, but I say nothing: I'm too busy eating. For some reason – perhaps it's being in the open air, the sun warm on my face, the sky unfeasibly blue, perhaps it's being with the hundreds of people, none of whom are my sisters, or the fact that, for the first time in six months, I don't have a tiny creature pulling my hair, skin or breasts – I feel wonderfully free.

For Kitty, my body is her playground and part of me loves it: I trail my hair over her face, roll with her on the floor, tickle her, kiss her and nuzzle her. But it is also exhausting, dehumanising. I am Kitty's landscape, her mountains, her streams, her feather bed. It's exhausting, being a landscape.

Sometimes it's exhausting being married, and now I have a holiday from that too. Bob left this morning, kissing Kitty and me with the same slightly distracted affection. 'Is that it?' I asked.

'What do you mean, "Is that it"?' asked Bob.

'Nothing,' I said sulkily.

He came back to me and hugged me tightly. 'Oh, Gaby,' he said, rather despairingly, into my hair.

But that wasn't it. I wanted him to cling to me and say he couldn't bear to be parted from me. I wanted him to fling me on to the bed and make passionate love to me. But since Kitty was born, we've hardly made love at all, and when we do it's in silence at dead of night. So I smiled and waved cheerfully and said, 'Have a good flight and good luck with the deal,' and he smiled and said, 'Take care of yourself. Take care of our baby,' and then he was gone.

So now I sit back, take a swig of San Pellegrino and raise

my face to the sun. Next to me, Marco is looking at the programme, asking Luca for translations. Sergio plays a game on his mobile phone. In front of us, two elderly ladies are discussing holidays in Scotland. It seems they go there for the tartan and the shortbread.

Luca offers me his mobile – Italians seem more welded to their phones than any other nationality. Luca's is never out of his hand as he makes dinner reservations, does business deals and has muttered, intimate-sounding conversations, which, annoyingly, I can never quite follow. 'Do you want to ring your mother? See how the *bimba* is?'

I shake my head. It was hard leaving Kitty with my mother and sisters, even though they seized on her like three demented crones and swung her round in a manic whirlwind of nursery rhymes, songs and truly horrible snatches of 'Lord of the Dance'. I left two bottles of expressed milk and a list of instructions, all of which were ignored.

'If she cries, she might be too hot.'

'This is the way the gentlemen ride . . . hups a daisy . . .'

'She might want water instead of milk.'

' . . . and down we go. Who's Grandma's little angel, then? Who is?'

I gave up. Now I don't want to ring and hear that either she's having a wonderful time with the Three Degrees or that she's crying for her mummy and cannot be comforted. I just want to sit here in the sun, eating my roll, drinking my drink and thinking about nothing.

'Is good,' says Luca, pocketing his phone. 'They'll call if they need you.'

I look at him sideways, wondering how he always seems to understand even though, or perhaps because, he says so little. He is gazing intently at the empty pitch. With his broken nose and curly hair, he looks a little like Michelangelo's *David*. Remembering the statue's other attributes, I feel my cheeks redden. Luca's phone rings. Marco sits forward excitedly. The game is about to start.

I remember the one time Dad took me to an away match. It was in Manchester, an FA Cup game. Mum hadn't wanted me to go: Manchester was too far, the crowds were sure to be violent, etc., etc. But her unspoken reason, I think, was that I would have too much of Dad's attention. After all, she explained, with history-teacher logic, that weekend Anna had an orchestra practice and Maria had a swimming gala. Surely they were more important ('as important,' she corrected herself conscientiously) than a football match. 'It's not even the final,' she pointed out, reasonably. But Dad and I knew, as any football fan would, that when Arsenal and Man U met it was as good as a final. We had won these tickets in the club's lottery; we would probably never have a chance like that again. Dad listened to all Mum's objections and met them with his usual cool academic's reasoning. But I could see beyond the civilised lecturer to the crazed football fanatic. We were going to the match and no one on earth could stop us.

I don't know why he decided to drive to Manchester. Special trains had been laid on from London – perhaps he'd remembered the infamous Arsenal 'Inter-City Gang', and thought it wouldn't be safe. More likely he just wanted to drive. Dad loved cars and stubbornly refused to drive anything other than an Italian model. Now, Italian cars are wonderful – beautifully styled models of engineering, *brio* and class – but they are not best suited to damp seaside towns. Over the years we lost count of the Italian cars that rusted away outside the Lewes house where the salt wind drove in directly from the sea. Lancias, Alfas, Fiats, Dad tried them all. He had an unreliable mechanic friend called Lance who supplied them.

'Your Dealer,' Maria called him, with sinister capitals. Lance's cars never lasted long, and when the end came, he and Dad would open the rusty bonnet and gaze sadly at the pristine engine. 'Criminal, Enzo, that's what I call it,' Lance would say, sucking his teeth. 'That engine's as good as new.' Then he would tow away the car and bring back another shiny, unsuitable Italian car.

Anyway, on that trip Dad had a beautiful red Lancia Beta. 'She likes to go fast,' he said, as if the car were a temperamental but lovable racehorse. 'I can't stop her.' But neither could he start her. Morning after morning he cursed as the car hiccuped sadly in the road and Mum drove serenely past in her reliable, but *brio*-less, Japanese vehicle.

When Dad announced that we were going in the Lancia, I prepared myself for a morning of freezing in the car until Mum took us to the station, kindly refraining from commenting on the Lancia's shortcomings. But as we sat there in the dark at 5 a.m., wrapped in our Arsenal scarves, the car started easily and we drove off, hardly able to believe our luck.

'You see?' said Dad. 'She knows it's an important occasion.'

Our luck lasted as far as Three Bridges, an unlovely town

near Gatwick airport. Dad had just beaten three cars at the lights, 'including an Audi,' he told me proudly. We were heading on to the dual carriageway when the car faltered, coughed and died. Dad spun into the slip-road, breathing heavily.

'What's the matter, Daddy?'

'I don't know. Nothing much. I'll just have a look.'

When I think of that day, I remember sitting by the side of the road as all the boring Audis in the world drove past. Dad rang the AA and they towed us to a garage. The owner was kind and gave me a cuddly toy that was normally free only with ten gallons of petrol. He also let us listen to the match on his radio. Eventually, Dad and I took the train back to Brighton from Three Bridges. We played I-Spy and Twenty Questions. We bought plastic sandwiches from the buffet and drank tea in collapsing paper mugs. I was amazingly happy.

When we got back, Dad was just in time to see the end of Maria's swimming gala. He didn't see her win her race, but he pretended he had. I sat silently on the uncomfortable wooden bench by the pool, holding my cuddly toy from the garage. Then we all went home and had a celebration tea. Oh, and Arsenal lost, one–nil.

Here, the play is fast and furious. Mysteriously, the players seem both to move faster than English footballers and to have more time to kick the ball. At half-time the score is nil–nil but the crowd is happy, shouting jovial insults that I only half understand and singing lustily to the accompaniment of a drum, played by a huge man in a Roma T-shirt, sitting directly behind us. The beats are so loud that they take over your whole body. Doom doom. Doom doom.

It is a few seconds before I grasp that Marco is speaking to me. 'What?' I shout.

'Great game, isn't it?'

'Yes.'

'Better than Arsenal?' He looks at me sideways.

'Yes,' I admit. 'Better than Arsenal.'

'I don't think Nonno would have wanted to be scattered here,' he says. 'The football's too good.'

I know what he means. Arsenal are a world-class team – Man U fans would admit as much – but even with the best English football teams you know that the mediocre is not far away; a whiff of windy recreation grounds with anoraks for goalposts, fat men yelling on the touchline, mums with hot drinks in flasks. Even now, when Arsenal has hardly any British players, there is still that charming sense of the amateur. Perhaps they care too much. Roma are slick, assured and exciting . . . but when the players come out of the tunnel their faces have the bland expressions of professionals. In England, even a multi-millionaire goal-scorer can look like a little boy, wheeling around the ground with arms outstretched. Here they just raise their hands imperiously, as if calmly booking their places in the history books.

Marco is still staring at me, his head to one side. Suddenly he looks startlingly like Anna.

'No,' I say. 'I don't think he'd want to be scattered here.'

I had been so full of thoughts of Dad, football, Arsenal scarves, broken-down Lancias that it comes as a shock to realise, again, that he is dead. He isn't sitting beside me, marvelling at Totti's ball control and admiring Fabio Capello's trilby. I won't be able to go home and tell him all about it later. He is dead. He isn't here. He is dead.

The second half is as noisy and skilful as the first, but by the end my back is aching and my breasts feel as if they're about to burst. I can feel milk leaking on to my T-shirt and I pull on my jumper. Perhaps motherhood and football don't mix. 'Are you cold?' Luca asks.

'No,' I say. 'I'm OK.' I lean back and shut my eyes, thus missing the only goal of the match. Roma win one–nil.

Going back to Uncle Bruno's flat, in Luca's MPV, I let Marco and Sergio's post-match analysis wash over me. I can't wait to see Kitty, yet I wish that Luca would drive for ever. The solidly packed lanes of wildly hooting cars, the well-dressed crowds beginning their evening's *passeggiata*, the trams, the taxis, the Vespas, the Lycra-clad cyclists – it's all amazingly soothing. As if in Luca's car I'm safe from everything. Luca swerves to avoid a bus emblazoned, like all the buses in Rome, with the rather sinister Atak logo and I think of Dad and his desire to come back to Italy. Suddenly I wish I had his ashes with me so that I could throw them out of the window, over the cars, buses, Vespas, to be lost in Rome's rush-hour.

Back at Uncle Bruno's, real life returns with a vengeance. Kitty – angelic all day, according to my mother and sisters – bursts into tears at the sight of me. I rock her, sing to her, try to feed her: nothing works. 'Try a little sugared water,' suggests Auntie Carla, hovering at my elbow with a tray of food she has prepared for our return. ('Sandwiches!

They're not the same as a proper lunch.') I try to force down a mouthful of minestrone while Kitty wails in my ear, her face scarlet.

'She loved it when I sang to her,' says Anna. 'Give her to me.' She whisks Kitty away in a swirl of flowered skirts. I'm pleased to hear her howls redouble.

'She needs cranial massage,' says Maria, from beside the window, where she's painting her nails. 'To get her over the birth trauma.'

I mutter that if anyone needs help in getting over the birth trauma it's me. I take Kitty back and walk about with her over my shoulder. For a second she is silent so I stop in front of Auntie Carla's monstrous gilt mirror to look at her face. She is gathering her breath in preparation for another mighty roar. When it comes, the terrible scream makes Marco and Sergio leave the room, clutching their football programmes and slices of Auntie Carla's pizza.

'Darling,' says my mother faintly, 'I think you ought to stay here tonight. You can't cope with this all on your own.'

'Yes,' says Auntie Carla eagerly. 'Stay here. I'll make pasta with *piselli*. It was poor Enzo's favourite.'

'Stay,' says Anna. 'We can talk about tomorrow. I've asked Jonathan to come with us. He might be coming round later.'

'No,' I say. 'I want to go back to my apartment.'

Kitty falls asleep in the car, lulled, perhaps, by Luca's furious driving. He parks by the Trevi Fountain and we walk in silence through the crowds throwing in coins and taking photos to show the folks back home. The apartment is cool and quiet: even the noise of the tourists outside has faded to a faint hum. In the entrance hall, with its featureless white walls, Luca asks, 'Do you want me to come up?'

I haven't turned on the overhead light, so his face is in shadow. I stand on the first step of the staircase, with Kitty in my arms, and he smiles, his teeth gleaming white in the darkness.

'No,' I say, 'I'll be OK, thanks,' and I start to climb the stairs.

In the apartment I put Kitty into the cot lent by Auntie Carla, a beribboned relic of Franco's babyhood. I should take the opportunity to go to bed and get some sleep myself, but instead I have a shower, change into a clean T-shirt and knickers, pour myself a glass of wine – Uncle Bruno has put some in the fridge – and sit in the dark, staring out of the window. This is the first night that I have spent on my own with Kitty, and my whole body is tense and alert. I can feel my skin touching the T-shirt, and the air-conditioned breeze on my face is intense, intimate, as if someone were blowing at me. Outside, the crowds are leaving the fountain, wending their way to restaurants and hotels for supper. I love the idea that I'm sitting above them all, in this crumbling stucco building, part of the night, yet distant from it. The only light comes from the lit-up advertisements outside and the spotlit fountain. The brakelights of cars send darts of red around the room.

Kitty sleeps peacefully in her nest of frills and bows. Suddenly I feel all-powerful, the mother-figure, able to cope with anything. Rome is a masculine city: Romulus and Remus, countless emperors, gladiators and senators, Trajan and his mate St Peter, the Pope, all those young men on street corners staring at passing girls with dispassionate lechery. Over the last few days, the only women I have heard mentioned are the Vestal Virgins and, as Maria pointed out, even they didn't have too good a time of it. But for a moment I feel like the mother of all Rome, a fertility symbol older than the seven hills. It is a wonderful, yet frightening, sensation.

I look out into the night and feel a rush of almost sexual pleasure at being alone. Since Kitty was born I have been surrounded by people: midwives, health visitors, Bob, my mother, my sisters. All those words of advice, encouragement and (occasionally) censure: 'Don't let her sleep on her front. Don't give her formula milk. Let her cry. Don't let her cry. Give her solid food. Give her sugared water. Give her rusks to chew. She's teething. She's crying. She's hungry. She's too fat. She's too thin. She's got jaundice. She's got wind. She's just playing you up. You must show her who's boss. You. Are. Not. Doing. It. Right.'

Now, silence is wonderful.

When I get cold, I put on Bob's jumper and go back to sitting by the window. I don't switch on the lights. The jumper smells of Bob. I think of his red-blond hair (which Kitty has inherited), his smile, his hard, broad shoulders. Since Kitty was born we have made love fewer than ten times. Ten times in six months when we used to do it up to five times a night. Once, during a weekend in Venice, we stayed in bed for a whole day, making love over and over again as the gondoliers outside sang all the cheesy love songs in the world. It's not that I don't fancy Bob now, it's that I'm so bloody tired. All I can think of when I get to bed is sleep. Then Kitty's crying wakes me and I think, I wish I were dead and then, at least, I'd have some rest.

Maybe Bob is making love to someone else right now. The efficient Anita, one of the sharp-faced female lawyers on his team, his ex-girlfriend Tanya, who still send cards at Christmas addressed simply to 'Bobbie'. I don't believe he would do that to me. I know he loves me and I love him, but he seems so far away – not only when he is in a different country but when he is here in my bed. Kitty has drawn a veil between me and the rest of the world. I can still see people's shapes through the gauze, but it's always there and I can't push it aside.

Kitty stirs in her sleep and I cover her with a blanket. Before, I would have worried: Is she too hot? Too cold? Is the blanket too heavy? Not heavy enough? Now I just drop it casually over her sleeping form. Then I walk slowly to the kitchen and wash up my glass – I have drunk more than half of the bottle. I pour myself a glass of the chalky-tasting tap water, drink it all, pour myself some more, then go to the loo and brush my teeth. Then go into the bedroom, kiss Kitty's forehead and climb into bed. I know that neither of us will wake in the night.

CHAPTER ELEVEN

There seems to be a problem in translation between Luca and the aged nun in the dusty habit. Luca is at his most persuasive, head bent, hands cupped before him in a gesture of pleading, which is only half ironic. But the nun shakes her head and mumbles through toothless gums. The church is closed to visitors. We can't go in. End of story.

'What a waste of time this is,' grumbles Maria, sitting on a low stone wall outside the church. She takes off her straw hat and shakes out her hennaed hair in the sun. It is the afternoon of another glorious day.

We spent the morning at Campo de' Fiori, looking at the market stalls overflowing with wonderful fresh food from the country. I bought a new sunhat for Kitty, and Auntie

Carla, who was enjoying herself hugely, told me I paid three times too much. Marco and Sergio were fed up and sat sulkily on a wall surrounded by crates of wildly flapping ducks. Mosaic asked if she could have a duck as a pet and Marco had to be restrained from telling her of the birds' true destiny. An elderly man on a bicycle bought two and went off with them hanging from the handlebars in canvas bags.

Afterwards we walked past Via del Biscione, where Dad was born. It is a strange curved street, like the bow of a ship. Franco told us it was supposed to have been built over the ruins of an ancient Roman theatre by Pompey, Julius Caesar's enemy. Rome is a funny city. Sometimes the only clue to the past is in the shape of its walls and piazzas, like the Piazza Navona where you have to ignore the fountains, souvenir shops and men pretending to be statues, and look up until you can see the shape of the Roman stadium that used to be there.

As I gazed at the high walls of the Via del Biscione, I tried to imagine Dad living there as a child. The houses were austere and depressing, with peeling paint and crumbling stonework – but I knew, from experience, that inside they would be full of gleaming electrical gadgets and miles of marble floor – and I couldn't imagine Dad running down these dark streets with a hoop, or whatever they played with in those days, or up those cold stone stairs calling for his mother. I suppose that, although Dad's having been Italian was an important element of our family history, it's difficult for me to picture him as an Italian in Italy. To me he will always be the Italian in exile, complaining about the lack of fresh pasta in Lewes and sticking the prancing Ferrari horse to the back of his Fiat.

We walked to the end of the street and bought ice creams in a café. I gave Kitty some of mine and she smeared it into her hair and on to her new sunhat. Mosaic dropped hers and cried. Uncle Bruno, sunk in gloom at the sight of his childhood home, suggested we went home for lunch.

After a huge Auntie Carla meal I was sitting back in my chair, wondering whether I would ever move again, when the intercom buzzed. Auntie Carla gave a short cry of surprise and, for a moment, I thought, Could it possibly be Bob, back early from England? The door opened to reveal Jonathan's black-clad figure and I blinked stupidly as Auntie Carla bustled in, saying, 'Come in, Father. Have some lunch. There's plenty left.' *Father*. I still can't get used to Jonathan being called 'Father'. It's a name for white-haired old priests, for robed figures before distant altars. Jonathan is nobody's father.

'Hello, Gaby.' Jonathan sat down next to me. It was so disconcerting to have him there, amid the debris of a family meal, with Mosaic and Kyle playing table tennis on the balcony and Uncle Bruno asleep in his chair, that I hardly knew where to look. I took refuge in Kitty, who was asleep against my shoulder. I got up, saying I needed to put her into her cot. My voice sounded high-pitched and odd. Jonathan smiled but said nothing.

Anna strode over. 'Jonathan! How nice of you to come. I'm sure the nuns will take much more notice of us if you're there.' She simpered at him and tossed back her hair. I noticed that she didn't call him 'Father'.

'Where are we going?' asked Marco suspiciously.

'To the church of Maria Assumpta,' said Anna impressively, 'where Nonno was baptised.'

'Why?' asked Marco, even more suspiciously.

'Because we want to scatter Nonno's ashes there.'

'No, we don't,' said Maria, from the corner where she was sitting with Tara.

'Well, Trajan's Column was hardly suitable,' snapped Anna, with a placatory smile at Jonathan.

'Nor is some mouldy old church.'

'What do you think, Gaby?' asked Jonathan.

Everyone turned to look at me as I stood by the door with Kitty in my arms. I opened my mouth to speak, then shut it again. That question seemed to be the first real thing that Jonathan had said to me since we arrived. His expression was impossible to read. 'We should go to see the church,' I muttered.

Now, as we stand outside it, I wish I hadn't spoken. It is dark and forbidding, its heavy wooden doors barred with iron. The nun bars our way, too, a tiny but intimidating figure in dusty black. I push Kitty's buggy to and fro, scattering small stones. Maria and Mum sit together on the wall, each deep in their thoughts. Maria's sequined sandal draws slow circles in the gravel. Marco has escaped, pleading a headache. 'Too much sun this morning,' said Auntie Carla, eagerly. 'He'd better have a quiet afternoon in bed.' But we all knew that, as soon as we were safely out of the way, Marco would be back in GameBoy-land, blasting things. Ray, Tara, Bruno and Paola, Franco's wife, have also stayed at home. I wish I was at home, too – or, rather, back in the tiny apartment, just me and Kitty.

Luca makes another appealing gesture to the nun, and Maria snorts contemptuously. 'We might as well go home,' she says. 'That old crone's never going to play ball.'

Suddenly Anna sweeps forward, majestic in another of her Catholic-matron's dresses, dragging Jonathan behind her. I move aside to let them pass.

The nun recognises the unmistakable air of authority emanating from them and nods politely. Defeated, Luca steps back, grinning ruefully at us. Jonathan starts a conversation in his slightly too-perfect Italian. Anna stands beside him, nodding forcefully. Gradually the nun makes way, examines her rosary, smirks almost flirtatiously at Jonathan and beckons us into the church. Silently, we follow.

The church of Maria Assumpta is no longer a parish church, as it was when Dad was baptised there, all those years ago. Now, according to Jonathan, it's a convent, home to an enclosed order of nuns. Like the Vestal Virgins, the nuns are forbidden to leave their cloisters, except on special occasions, such as papal masses. The nun now showing us into the church is the only one allowed contact with the outside world and the sight of Luca with his mobile phone and winning smile must have been too much for her. She was soothed by the appearance of a genuine Catholic priest in the form of Jonathan. Now she bridles girlishly as Jonathan holds open one of the heavy wooden doors to allow her to precede him.

After the bright sunlight, the church is oppressively dark. Kitty whimpers and I tuck her blanket round her. Behind me, Sergio says, 'Bloody hell, it's a tomb!'

'Sssh, Sergio,' says Anna furiously.

But then, as our eyes grow accustomed to the dark, we catch sight of magnificent frescos stretching high above us, shimmering in the dust motes. I look down at my feet and see elaborate mosaics – fishes, crowns and serpents – disappearing into the darkness. The church is almost empty, apart from a few folding chairs by the altar, and the walk up the aisle is endless.

The altar is bare except for the tiny red light, which tells us that the Sacrament is still exposed there. In front of me, Jonathan genuflects. Despite myself, my knees quake but I hold on tightly to the buggy and stay upright. Next to me, my mother quivers but remains standing. David and Anna genuflect together, as if choreographed. At a glance from his mother, Sergio does the same. Maria ignores everyone and wanders off to look at the frescos.

Jonathan and Anna are gazing up at the fresco over the altar. I hear a soft voice in my ear. 'Is the coronation of the Virgin,' says Luca. 'She dies and goes straight up to heaven in her body. No one else does this.'

'The Assumption,' I say. 'A pretty bloody big assumption, if you ask me.' Luca looks at me quizzically. Suddenly I miss Bob. He would have got the joke. He would even have laughed. I look up at the fresco. In her lapis-blue robes, Mary rolls her eyes upwards in spiritual ecstasy. She looks as if she is on board a heavenly elevator. Two cherubim with a golden crown hover above her head.

'The crown of heaven,' says Luca. 'Mary is crowned Queen of heaven.'

I am transported to the May procession at school. May is supposed to be Mary's month, so Catholic schools mark the occasion by placing bunches of carnations in front of plaster statues of the Virgin. At my primary school, the girls in their first-communion year wore their long white dresses and one crowned the statue. Both Anna and Maria were chosen, but

I wasn't. In my year it was Siobhan O'Hara, whose dress had a real lace train and pearl beading. I remember blaming my dress – after all, it was third-hand by the time I got to wear it – but Maria said smugly, 'It's not the dress, it's who's wearing it. That's what counts.'

Anna is making her pitch to the nun. 'Our father . . .' she begins loudly, in schoolroom Italian. It sounds like the start of a prayer: 'Our Father, who art in heaven.' Well, he is, isn't he?

'Our father,' repeats Anna, then goes on, 'was baptised in *this very church*.' She pauses impressively and looks at the nun for approval. The nun, however, is staring at Jonathan. 'Now that our dear father has passed away,' Anna ploughs on, 'it was his dearest wish that his . . .' She is stuck for the word.

'*Ceneri*,' supplies Luca. Ashes.

' . . . ashes be scattered here. In this cloister.' She stops again, this time less confidently.

Maria comes forward from the shadows to hiss, 'It was *not* his dearest wish. It's yours.'

My mother is watching with apparent polite interest.

Jonathan's face is emotionless.

The nun's filmy, impassive gaze sweeps past them all

and, to my amazement, lands on me. She points a gnarled finger at Kitty's buggy. 'The *bambina*,' she says. 'You've had her baptised?'

At first, I am just surprised that she knows Kitty is a girl – unlike Italian girl babies, she is not swathed in frills and pink bows. Then, I can't believe what I heard. 'N-no,' I stammer.

The nun comes closer. She glares at me with the disregard of politeness common to the old or mad. Or the religious. 'You have her baptised,' she says, in broken English. 'You have her baptised or she no go to heaven. She stay in Limbo. For ever.'

Perhaps it is the shadows and the strangeness of the bare altar. Perhaps it is the nun, with her pointing finger and opaque stare. Perhaps it is Anna's nod of agreement. Perhaps it is because Bob isn't there. Perhaps it is because Jonathan is. All I know is that horror and revulsion rise up within me so violently that I feel I am about to be sick. The old nun is like the wicked fairy in *Sleeping Beauty*, appearing uninvited to curse the baby princess. I feel I must protect Kitty or die. I clap a hand to my mouth and push the buggy one-handed past the nun, Jonathan, my sisters, my mother, Luca. I am wild-eyed, desperate. I have to get away.

In the darkness beside the Lady altar, I find a door and push at it blindly. To my surprise, it opens. To my further surprise, it leads on to a cloister: symmetrical pillars and a square of grass as green and perfect as the church is dusty and neglected. It is like that bit in *Alice in Wonderland* where she sees the garden through the little door but can't get outside because she is too big. Somehow, I am in the magic garden. Breathless, I push the buggy right to the centre of the lawn and look back.

Slowly, the door opens again and Jonathan comes out. 'Gaby,' he says.

'Jonathan.'

For a moment, it seems that we are suspended in time and space, in the middle of this enchanted garden. I can hear birds singing but they are a long way off. Anna appears in the doorway, then goes away again. We are alone.

'I'm sorry about the Mother Superior,' he says. 'She shouldn't have said that to you.'

I am overcome with annoyance. The title 'Mother Superior' irritates me beyond measure. As does the fact that Jonathan doesn't actually say that the old witch was wrong.

'Mother Superior,' I repeat, with heavy sarcasm.

191

Jonathan flinches, as if I have struck him. 'She shouldn't have said that,' he repeats. 'The Church doesn't teach it now anyway. About Limbo and all that. As long as you have a baptism of desire . . .'

I raise my hand. I can't bear him to go on. All those stock Catholic phrases: the Church, Limbo, Baptism of Desire. It is just unspeakable to hear Jonathan, *my* Jonathan, talking in this manner. He sounds a hundred years old. I close my eyes and see if I can conjure up the old Jonathan with his wicked blue eyes and seducer's smile. I can't.

'Jonathan,' I say, 'forget it. It doesn't matter.'

'But it upset you,' says Jonathan softly.

'Why should you care?' I ask bleakly.

Jonathan takes a step forward and I take a step back, keeping the buggy between us. He stops and raises his hands in a curiously Italian gesture. 'I'm sorry,' he says.

Somehow this takes the wind out of my sails. I had expected him to come out with some guff about God's will and being part of a divine plan beyond our mortal understanding. He is watching me intently, frowning. I can see the little lines at the corners of his eyes. 'Jonathan,' I say abruptly, 'why did you come?'

He lets out a sigh, as if he was waiting for this. 'Anna asked me to.'

'I know, but why did you come to the airport?' I want to add, 'Why are you here, in the garden? Why are you hanging around my family? Why are you looking at me like that?'

'I suppose,' he says at last, 'I wanted to see you.'

He comes towards me again and somehow we find ourselves walking side by side round the cloistered walkway, as if we are on a stroll in the countryside. Briefly, my mother appears at the doorway into the church and vanishes again.

'I'm sorry about Enzo,' says Jonathan. 'I always liked him.'

'Thank you,' I say, not adding that this feeling was not reciprocated.

'I always liked your family. I loved visiting that house in Lewes. It was a real family home.'

I wonder if he knows he has said the word 'family' twice in one minute.

'Noisy, you mean?'

He grins. 'Yes. Noisy. Fun. People coming and going all the time. I liked that.'

'It drove me mad.'

'It was your family. That's why.'

We walk on, like some parody of a family ourselves, me pushing the buggy, Jonathan with his head down, hands in pockets.

'Are you happy?' Jonathan says at last.

It is growing dark and, in the shadows of the cloister, his face looks younger and softer, the clerical lines blurred.

'Of course, I'm happy,' I say too loudly.

'It's great to see you with your baby,' says Jonathan.

I look at him sharply. That sounded too much like something Anna would say: It's great to see you in your role, little woman at home with a baby, Martha not Mary. 'Yes,' I say spitefully. 'It's wonderful to have a child.' This, after all, is something he can never have.

'So you're happy?' he repeats, a shade wistfully.

'Yes,' I say again, and then, perhaps because at that moment he looks like the student Jonathan again, I say, 'Having a baby is lovely but it changes things.'

'Between you and your husband?'

'Bob. Yes.' Now that I have said his name, it seems that something is out in the open. I have stopped thrusting Bob between us, like the trophy husband, and admitted something that I have previously kept hidden, even from myself.

'He seems like a good bloke,' says Jonathan tentatively.

I laugh. 'Yes, he is. It's just . . . things change when you have a baby. It can't be the two of you. We were together for a long time before we had Kitty. It's hard to adjust.'

'But it must bring you closer,' persists Jonathan, 'having a child together.'

'Yes,' I say, 'it does, but it also drives you apart. It's hard to explain.' I think about Kitty having Bob's red hair and my smile. I think about the way that sometimes she looks like no one except herself. I think about how Bob has escaped back to our old life and that I can't follow him.

'Did you want that for us?' asks Jonathan suddenly. 'Marriage and babies?'

I stare at him. What can I say? That I wanted it more than anything else on earth but he left me for another man, albeit one with a good line in miracles? That I never wanted to marry him, that Bob is worth a million of him and, in Kitty, I have found my immortal soul at last? That twelve years ago he forfeited the right to ask that question?

'Yes,' I say at last. 'Yes. I did.'

We have stopped walking and are standing, facing each other. Then Jonathan grasps the buggy and starts to push it. It feels as if we have reached some sort of agreement. We walk on in silence for a few minutes, and then I say, 'What about you? Are you happy?'

'Yes,' says Jonathan, after a pause. 'I am happy. I'm glad I became a priest, but it's hard. If I had known how hard it would be, I wouldn't have started. You have to face yourself, your weaknesses. It's bloody difficult. You remember how I hate admitting that I've got any faults.'

'Me too,' I say. I can't believe he used the word 'bloody'.

He smiles. 'We're very similar, I think. That's why I don't think it would have worked out. You and me. Even without all this.'

'Do you miss it?' I ask. 'Having a relationship?' I want to say 'sexual relationship' but I don't have the nerve, standing in the cloisters, with the church bells ringing in the background. The shadows are lengthening. It must be nearly six o'clock.

For a moment, Jonathan says nothing. Then, when he looks up, his eyes are full of tears. 'Yes,' he says. 'I miss it desperately.'

Tears are rolling down my cheeks too. Jonathan puts out a hand and almost touches me, but doesn't quite. I back away. 'Goodbye, Jonathan,' I say. I pull the buggy away from him, walk briskly towards the door and stride through the church. Inside, my mother, Anna and Maria are sitting in the folding chairs, apparently in silence. As I march past them, they all get to their feet.

'Gaby!' calls Mum. I keep walking.

When I reach the main doors, I keep going, not knowing where to, just that I have to get away from my family, Jonathan, the church, everything.

As I bump the buggy down the shallow steps in front of the church, I hear another voice behind me. 'Gaby!' It is Luca.

I stop and turn. He has that half-ironic smile on his face. Once again, I have the impression that he understands everything.

'Gaby,' he says, 'let me take you away. We'll go out to dinner. Yes?'

'Yes,' I say.

CHAPTER TWELVE

Luca folds the buggy expertly and puts it into the boot of the MPV. I strap Kitty into her baby seat. In silence, Luca gets into the car and, crunching over the gravel, reverses out of the gates. I have no idea how the others will get home. I imagine them stranded in the empty church all night, with the eerie red light and the shadowy frescos, while the Mother Superior cackles outside. Perhaps when we are all gone she will transform into one of the stone gargoyles, faceless and crumbling, that guard the walls. Perhaps she never really existed; perhaps she was only a ghost of one of the former inhabitants. Shivering, I remember that when I came back into the church there was no sign of her. Had she ever been there at all?

I look at Luca's profile, comfortingly solid, as he steers the car through the early-evening traffic. 'Where are we going?' I ask.

'Trastevere,' says Luca. 'It's the best place to eat. But first we go to see the Tevere. It's where you want your father to rest, yes?'

It is a few minutes before I realise that 'Tevere' is Italian for 'Tiber', so beloved of Horatio and my dad. I wasn't aware that Luca knew about my plan for the ashes. I must have mentioned it at Uncle Bruno's or in the car but I hadn't realised Luca was listening. Sometimes, like the nun, it is hard to know if he is there or not.

Luca parks beside the river. 'Lungotevere', the road is called. Opposite I can see an impressive domed building. 'The synagogue,' says Luca. 'This is the Jewish quarter. It's very old. There used to be walls here. They were locked at dusk.'

'Why?'

'To keep the Jewish people in. Rich Roman ladies used to come in disguise to visit the Jewish fortune-tellers.'

I shiver. I don't like the sound of people being imprisoned behind ghetto walls. It reminds me of the Vestal Virgins and the locked doors of the convent.

When I lift Kitty out of the car, she is hot and cross. I put her into the buggy but she screams to be picked up. I carry her awkwardly in one arm and push the buggy with the other hand.

'Here. Let me.' I think that Luca is holding out his hand for the buggy but it is Kitty he wants. He puts her over his shoulder and perhaps it is the superior height or the strength of his arms but she falls asleep at once. Behind them, I can just see the tip of her hat nestled into Luca's neck.

We walk along the banks of the Tiber. Fast-flowing beige water swirls past us. In the middle of the river stands the remains of an ancient bridge, its arches reaching blindly into mid-air. The river must be very high because here and there I can see trees half submerged in the water. They give me a giddy, frightened feeling, as if the river is about to flood and drown us all. In fact, Luca tells me that these are artificial rapids, created for some environmental purpose that I don't understand. Instinctively, I move closer to him.

He points out a little boat-shaped island in the river. 'The Isola Tiberina.'

'What is that building on it?'

'A hospital. The Ospedale Fatebenefratelli.'

'Fatebenefratelli,' I repeat slowly. 'What does it mean?'

Luca pauses. '"Do well, brothers",' he says at last. 'The Hospital Do Well, Brothers.'

I like that. 'Do well, brothers.' It seems to cancel out the ill omen of the pale-eyed nun, the drowning trees and the bridge to nowhere.

We walk on. It is a beautiful evening, the shadows lengthening over the water, the buildings golden in the last of the light. The Romans are coming out to play: the streets are full of cars, the pavements awash with designer clothing. Five young men in an open-top Alfa swoop past us; one shouts to me.

'What did he say?' I ask Luca.

He grins. 'It was a compliment.'

We are crossing the Tiber now. I look at the abandoned bridge, sinister in the twilight, and read the words 'Pontifex Maximus' cut into the side.

'Pontifex Maximus,' I say. 'The Vestals' friend. What's he doing here?'

'Pontifex Maximus means "bridge-maker",' says Luca.

'I thought he was the high priest,' I say.

'Yes, but crossing water was important in Ancient Rome. People were thrown off bridges as a sacrifice to the river gods and the high priest was in charge of all bridges. It is a serious business, crossing a bridge in Rome.' We have now reached the end and he turns to smile at me. Does he hold my gaze just a fraction too long?

In typical Roman fashion, Luca marches me past any number of inviting restaurants, with tables set outside, fairy-lights in the trees and ambient music playing. He says these are only for tourists. Instead, he steers me into a dark little cavern, so unobtrusive that it doesn't even have a sign. Inside, the buggy bounces over the uneven floor and there are dark shelves full of dusty bottles, like a magician's store. Luca, Kitty still in his arms, begins an animated conversation with the owner, who has a sinister El Greco face, like a Mafia hitman.

Eventually Luca is satisfied ('*Va bene*') and, with a sardonic smile, the owner ushers us to a corner table. Luca puts Kitty back into her buggy. She doesn't wake.

The menu is handwritten on lined paper. I study it carefully, but when Luca orders, his choice mysteriously bears no relation to anything on it. He also orders a bottle of wine, which the waiter selects from a dusty rack above our heads and pours with a flourish. It tastes wonderful; I can almost feel it rushing straight to my head.

Luca tears at a piece of bread with those very white teeth. 'So,' he says, 'are you enjoying Roma?'

'Yes,' I say, taking another heady sip of wine. 'It's odd, though. It's almost like a holiday but it's not. I mean, here we are going round all these tourist attractions and all the time we're thinking about my dad. He's dead. That's why we're here.'

'You miss your father,' says Luca. He says it so gently that I feel tears coming to my eyes. Again.

'Yes,' I say. 'It's worse in Italy somehow. I keep seeing people who look like him – sitting outside cafés, taking dogs for walks, going to church, reading the paper on buses. Little old men with exactly the same sort of hat and coat that he always wore. A trilby and a sort of square overcoat. I suppose it's just a very Italian look.'

'When my father died,' says Luca, 'I kept thinking I saw him. Out of the corner of my eye and never his face, just a – how do you say it? – a glimpse ... grey hair, a scarf, a jacket like one of his. Then I thought, Maybe I am seeing him. Maybe he is still here after all.'

'How long ago did he die?'

'Two years. We didn't get on that well. He didn't want

me to leave the army. We kept arguing, the same old stuff, over and over. But now he is dead,' he laughs briefly, 'I keep having these conversations with him in my head and he always agrees with me. He tells me I did the right thing, that he is proud of me.'

'Maybe he's trying to tell you that you *did* do the right thing.'

'Maybe.' Luca smiles rather sadly. 'Maybe it is his ghost that keeps haunting me.'

'Do you believe in ghosts?'

'Not exactly. Shadows. Reflections. You say you see your father in the street. It is only like seeing him reflected in someone else. In your family, perhaps.'

Tradition has it that Anna looks like Dad, but I can't see it. He had thick hair, like hers, and the same blue eyes, but his usual expression was one of quizzical sweetness. Anna's is different. Then I think of Marco at the Stadio Olimpico, saying to me with a surprisingly gentle smile that the football was too good.

'Marco looks a bit like him,' I say. 'He's like him in character too. Laid back. Humorous.'

'What about Kitty?'

I think of Kitty's crumpled little face and spiky red hair. 'She doesn't look like anyone, really.'

'She is like your husband.'

'Yes,' I say. 'She is.'

The food arrives. My pasta, fettuccine with mushrooms and peas, is so good that a moan escapes me. For a few minutes we eat in silence. Then Luca says, 'What about the priest?'

'What priest?' I wipe my mouth. It's hard to eat fettuccine in an elegant way.

'The one who was there today. Jonathan.' He pronounces it with an exaggerated English accent. Jon-a-than.

'What about him?'

'What did he say to upset you?'

I shrug. 'It was nothing, really. We used to go out together. Ages ago.'

Luca looks at me enquiringly. 'Go out?'

'He was my boyfriend,' I say, and gulp some wine, then decide I may as well spell it out: 'My lover,' I add.

'*È vero*?' Luca is amazed – and perhaps amused too. 'But he is a priest!'

'Before he was a priest,' I say. 'When we were students.'

'So,' Luca leans back so that the waiter can take away his plate, 'is he still in love with you?'

He says it in such a matter-of-fact way that I forget to be embarrassed. I think of Jonathan in the cloisters of the church, his eyes filling with tears. I think of him at that party, years ago, asking me if I wanted to go for a walk. I think of standing in Bedford Square and hearing him say he was leaving me. I think of the wedding in Streatham and Jonathan at the altar, arms outstretched to heaven. 'No,' I say at last. 'I don't think he ever was, really.'

Over the next course, veal with tiny potatoes and green beans, Luca tells me about his girlfriend, Dagmar, who is German. 'She's always crying, asking me if I love her. It's terrible.'

'Do you love her?' I ask, emboldened by the wine.

He shrugs. 'What is love? It's just a word.'

I think of the hundreds of times I told Jonathan I loved him. All those words, that sea of sentiment, so easily washed away. 'You don't love her,' I say.

Luca laughs, not offended. 'Why does that matter? We have a good time together. Why does she want more? It's because she's German. They're a very emotional people.'

'In England,' I say, 'we think the Italians are emotional. Not the Germans.'

Luca shakes his head. 'The Italians are the coldest people in the world. When the Romans ruled the world, what did they do? Built straight roads and put in plumbing. Not very romantic.'

'Rome is romantic, though.'

'Rome,' says Luca, finishing his wine, 'is the most wonderful city on earth but the Romans are terrible people. Do you know what SPQR stands for?'

You see those initials everywhere, on man-hole covers, carved into fountains, on bus-stops and street signs. I dredge my mind for school history lessons. '*Senatus populus* . . .' I begin.

'No, no,' laughs Luca. 'It stands for: *Sono Porci Questi Romani*: These Romans are pigs.'

'But you're a Roman,' I say.

'Yes.' Luca sighs. 'But we're lovely too. It's just that we once ruled the world and we can never forget it.'

When we get up to leave, the restaurant is nearly empty and the sinister owner is sitting at one of the tables, watching football on a miniature TV and picking his teeth. Kitty is still sleeping, her cheeks flushed. I feel her forehead: it is hot and dry.

'Is she OK?' asks Luca, putting away his wallet. He has insisted on paying.

'I don't know. She feels a bit hot.'

He puts his large hand on her forehead. 'It's warm in here,' he says. 'Let's get her some fresh air.'

Outside it is a lovely mild night. The Romans swarm along the riverbanks, shouting and laughing. The Tiber flows smooth and dark below us. But all I can think of is Kitty. What if she is sick, here, in a strange city? Suddenly I feel that I would swap it all, the magical nighttime city, the floodlit fountains, the handsome stranger beside me, for one English chemist selling Calpol. The thought of the familiar bottle with its purple label makes me almost expire with homesickness. What wouldn't I give for a bottle of Calpol, Radio 4 – and Bob. I want Bob.

When we get to the car, I lift Kitty out of the buggy. She shivers, and the coldest shadow in all of parenthood sweeps over me. Meningitis. What are the signs? Temperature, stiff neck, fear of bright lights. I carry Kitty to a streetlight and she starts to cry angrily. I am shaking with fear.

'Gabriella?' says Luca. 'Let's get back to the apartment. I'll call Franco.'

Of course! Franco the doctor, the paediatrician. Thank God. I get into the car but I don't put Kitty into her car seat – I can't bear to let go of her. Luca steers one-handed through the teeming late-night traffic, his mobile pressed to his ear. He says something but I don't catch what it is.

'Have you spoken to him?' I ask.

'He's out. I leave a message.'

When we get to the apartment, the square is empty, the fountain limpid in the moonlight. I carry Kitty upstairs. Luca follows, punching numbers into his phone.

I put Kitty into her cot and she settles. I feel her forehead. Is she a bit cooler? Luca is standing by the door, blocking out the light. 'Luca,' I say, 'can you get me some paracetamol? For babies?'

'*Sì*,' he says at once. '*Paracetamolo*.'

'And, Luca . . .'

He turns.

'Please find Franco.'

'*Sì*,' he says again, and is gone.

I go back to Kitty. Her forehead is burning now. I go to

the bathroom and get a wet flannel. I don't wring it out enough and, when I put it on Kitty's forehead, it drips into her neck and makes her cry. Feverishly I pull off her clothes and examine her for the tell-tale meningitis rash. She is so tiny and vulnerable, lying naked in the preposterous frilly cot. She turns her head away from me. Oh, God, I think, fear of bright light.

I sponge her all over her body. She cries and arches away from me. Her hair is wet but her skin is still hot. Then she is shivering. I cover her with a blanket but she's so hot I take it off again and pick her up. 'Ssh Kitty,' I say. 'It's all right.' Why the hell should she believe me?

I walk about the apartment, following the same path that Bob and I took during our circular argument two days earlier. Jesus, only two days! Suddenly I'm filled with violent hatred for him. How dare he leave me here with a sick baby? How could he choose work above his family? It doesn't matter that Kitty was perfectly well when he left us, I feel as if he has abandoned us both to die. Tears run down my cheeks and fall on to Kitty's head. She sobs noiselessly. What am I going to do?

I put her down and sponge her again. I can hear the old

nun's voice: 'You have her baptised or she no go to heaven. She stay in Limbo. For ever.' Kitty is going to die and she won't go to heaven. That old witch has cursed her. Without knowing what I'm doing, I leave Kitty in her cot and go into the kitchen. On the wall a crude piece of ceramic depicts a bumpy-faced Virgin Mary. Below her there is a small container bearing the inscription: 'Holy water from Lourdes. Bless this house and all who live here.' I climb on to a chair and get down the plaque. In the bottom of the container there is about a centimetre of yellowish water. I hear Sister Immaculata's voice, as clear as a mission bell, in my head: 'In emergencies anyone can baptise a baby. It doesn't have to be a priest.'

I go back to Kitty. She is sleeping fitfully, murmuring. What is she thinking of? She has only been alive six months. Can she have dreams and memories? Does she even know how much I love her? Slowly I dip my finger into the holy water from Lourdes. Then, bending over Kitty, I make the sign of the cross on her forehead. 'Kitty, I baptise you in the name of the Father and of the Son and of the Holy Spirit. Amen.' Kitty sighs in her sleep. Outside, police sirens howl in the distance.

When Luca and Franco appear at the door, I am standing with Kitty in my arms. I don't need Luca's worried glance at Franco or Franco's quick professional nod to know that she needs to go to hospital.

CHAPTER THIRTEEN

Franco must have phoned ahead because the hospital parts before us like the Red Sea. We are ushered through the crowded emergency room and into another suite of rooms. A female doctor meets us at the door. She has short grey hair and a formidably unsympathetic manner. Franco greets her with exaggerated respect.

Kitty is put on to a bed while the grey-haired doctor shoots questions at me. I can't understand a word. The last few hours have made me forget.all the Italian I ever knew. I gaze at her blankly, feeling as if I am under water or behind glass, unable to make contact, able only to discern faint shapes, mouths opening and shutting, hands waving.

Luca comes to my rescue. He translates the doctor's questions, gripping my arms tightly, as if he is holding me together. How old is Kitty? Breastfed or bottle? Has she had all her inoculations? Has she got a rash? Can she recognise me? Is her crying different from normal? Has she had a fit? I try to answer as well as I can but it's so difficult. I just want to yell, 'Make her better!' I feel as if, for the first time, I can understand pictures of women at disaster scenes, howling and rending their garments. I want to howl and rend with all my might. Instead, I hold on to Luca and tell the doctor that she's five months old, she has had all her injections (nightmare surgery full of screaming toddlers wearing 'I was brave at the doctor's' badges), she's breastfed and usually sleeps well. No, I don't know what's wrong with her. My husband's not here and I just want to see her smile again. Please. I say it aloud, 'Please, please.'

Ignoring me, the doctor goes to Kitty and Franco comes to put his arm round me. 'They're giving her something for the temperature. They may need to put a drip in to get some liquids into her.'

'Is it meningitis?'

'They don't know. They're doing tests. Don't worry, you're in the right place. Dr Agostini,' he gestures at the grey-haired woman, now barking orders at a minion, 'is one of the best paediatricians in Europe. Kitty will be OK, I promise.'

'Bob,' I say. 'I want to ring Bob.'

Franco glances at Luca. 'I'll do it,' he says. 'Just give me the number and I'll go outside. I can't use the phone in here.' Poor Luca – no wonder he looks as if he has lost a limb.

I give him Bob's number, stumbling over the familiar digits. 'Just tell him to come,' I say.

'Yes,' says Luca, pushing his way through the swing doors. 'I will.'

'I want to see Kitty,' I say.

She looks tiny on the full-sized bed. She is wearing only a nappy and her skin is blotchy and dry. A doctor is fiddling with her arm, trying to fit a drip, but somehow she is still sleeping, brows knitted, breathing shallow. I stroke her hair. 'It's OK, Kitty Kat,' I say. 'You'll be OK.'

Franco stands behind me. 'That's right,' he says. 'Keep talking to her.'

I turn to him in panic. 'What shall I say?'

He smiles. 'It doesn't matter. It's the voice that counts. Your voice. The mother's voice.'

Then I hear something that, subconsciously, I must have

been listening for: *my* mother's voice. I had not asked Franco to bring her but she's here anyway. And not alone, judging by the chorus of authoritative female voices outside. There is a flurry in the corridor and my mother, Anna and Maria burst into the room, followed by Luca.

'I left a message,' Luca says to me. 'I'm sure he'll come soon.'

I think of Bob in a bar with his colleagues, Anita at his side, smiling discreetly at his jokes. Another wave of hatred sweeps over me. He should be here with me now. Tomorrow might be too late. If he's too late, I'll never forgive him. Meanwhile, Anna and Maria are haranguing the doctors. My mother comes over to me and looks down at Kitty. 'Poor little mite. Don't worry, darling, she'll be OK.'

'Do you think so?' I sniff.

'I'm sure. I remember having this with all three of you. Anna had measles so badly she was delirious for three days. Maria had a fit after her whooping-cough vaccination. You had a terrible reaction to honey. Went into shock. I had to call an ambulance.'

I stare at her, drinking it in. I can't believe that I was ever dismissive of these stories, that I ever hated the way that everything that happened to me had happened first to Anna and Maria. Now I'm so glad my mother had three children, that she has seen it all before. I want to hear it over and over again. 'But we were all right, weren't we?'

'Of course. By the time you got to hospital you were sitting up in bed asking for apple juice. And, funnily enough, you'd always hated apple juice. It was Maria who loved it. You and Anna preferred orange.'

The doctors around Kitty have gone into a huddle. I'm relieved that Franco is there, huddling with them. It seems amazing that Franco, with his toy cars and battleship obsession, should have become this person of quiet authority, at whose word nurses fetch and carry. If I close my eyes, he is the annoying nine-year-old Franco again; if I open them, he holds the secret of life and death. Perhaps sensing my thoughts, Franco gives me an encouraging smile. 'We've taken some bloods,' he says. 'They'll tell us what is the matter. Now we must try to get her temperature down.'

'Can I stay with her?'

'Of course. Keep talking to her. If she starts to shiver, hold her firmly and try to soothe her.'

'I'm staying too,' says my mother.

'Certainly,' says Franco appeasingly. He looks anxiously at Anna and Maria.

'We're staying,' says Anna. Franco turns back to his colleagues. He knows Anna too well to argue. 'All right,' he says. 'Just keep Gabriella calm. I'll see if I can hurry the results of the blood tests. Luca, why don't you try Bob again?'

Luca comes over to me. 'I'll get him. Don't worry. Is there anything you need from the apartment?'

I tell him what I want.

So we sit there, my mother, Anna, Maria and I. Kitty shivers in her sleep and I stroke her arms and tell her that everything's all right. My voice sounds strained and odd, nothing like a proper mother's voice. When I go to get a drink of water, Anna talks to Kitty but she doesn't like the change: she whimpers and arches her back.

'She wants her mum,' says Anna. 'It's not the same.' It feels like the nicest thing that Anna has ever said to me.

Soon it seems as if we have been in this room for ever: the white-faced clock on the wall, which tells me it's one o'clock, the poster showing the recovery position, the modern painting, so bland as to be almost invisible, the drooping pot-plant. I gaze at the plant and imagine myself going into the loo, filling a plastic cup with water and pouring it on to the parched soil. I imagine the soil drinking in the liquid, the brown-tipped leaves becoming strong and green. The fantasy is so strong that I can almost hear a faint gurgle. But I don't move from my chair.

'Take care of our baby,' was the last thing Bob said to me. 'Our baby'. It's funny, but he had never used those words before. When I was pregnant, I thought of whoever was inside me as belonging to both of us, but it was almost as if I had an extra responsibility because I was looking after something that was Bob's too. But since Kitty was born, I have started to think of her as belonging exclusively to me. I think it was the breastfeeding. Getting that right was some-thing Kitty and I achieved together, that sealed our bond. I can still see Bob standing in the vestry doorway at Dad's funeral. He was happy for us, but he was outside that intense experience. I think that was the moment that I started to move away from him.

It was Bob who wanted a baby. Even before we were mar-ried, he used to talk about, 'when we have children.' I liked it because it was so different from how Jonathan had been: he hadn't mentioned the future if he could avoid it. But

I suppose I never realised how important it was for him. Then, after we had been married a few years, Bob began to say things like 'We won't be able to have holidays like this when we have kids,' and 'We won't be able to lie in bed all morning when we have children.' He always spoke of them in relation to things we'd no longer be able to do. To me, parenthood sounded joyless and depressing. Not something to look forward to.

On my thirtieth birthday, he said, 'We need to talk.'

'Why?' I asked. We were getting ready to go out and I was putting on my make-up, which didn't go with the serious-ness of the discussion, me daubing on eyeliner and blowing lipstick kisses at myself.

'Now you're thirty . . .'

I could see Bob's face in the mirror. He was clearly nervous; it was such an unusual expression for him that it made his face look wrong.

'Yes?' I said, probably a trifle frostily. After all, I didn't want to be *continually* reminded that I was now thirty.

'Don't you think we should talk about having a baby?' Bob blurted out.

I swung round, lipstick in hand. He looked back at me,

not nervous now but very serious. I knew that this was it. I couldn't deflect this conversation with quips about nappies and morning sickness. I was going to have to face up to the question of whether or not I wanted a baby. I bleated the first thing that came into my head: 'I'm still too young.'

'You're thirty, for God's sake,' Bob snapped.

We never did go out to dinner that evening.

It sounded pathetic, but it was how I felt. Perhaps it was because I was the youngest in my family (Bob is in the middle: older sister, younger brother). Certainly my dad always treated me as if I were a lot younger than I was: calling me '*bambina*' until I was about twenty, refusing to believe that I was old enough to drive, bringing me chocolate when I was a thirty-five-year-old pregnant woman. At times, of course, this irritated the hell out of me. 'I'm not a baby!' I would shout at him. ('Oooh, you are,' Anna and Maria chorused. 'Little baby Gaby. Dear little Gaby baby.') But I suppose part of me must have believed it. Believed that, while Dad was alive, I could never grow up.

Bob and I had the same conversation many times during my early thirties. I kept saying that I did want children, just not yet – when I was more established at work, when we had more money, when I felt ready. But when I was thirty-four I got pregnant by accident. I was shocked. I had heard so many stories about women desperate for babies, about IVF and surrogacy, the agony of infertility, that I had almost forgotten it could happen like that. I felt a little tired, a little unwell, my breasts tingled. 'Do you think you might be pregnant?' asked Bob, ultra-casual, over breakfast one Saturday, watching me pour my coffee down the sink. And, of course, I was.

I was delighted. It was so wonderful to have the whole decision taken out of my hands. I was so happy. So proud of my body (it worked!), so proud of Bob and me as a team. I sailed through my pregnancy. After those first few weeks, I didn't feel ill. I had twice as much energy as usual, behaved so dynamically at work that my clients were terrified. Bob was in seventh heaven, treating me as if I were a piece of exceptionally delicate china. When I was five months pregnant, we went on holiday to St Lucia and I lay on the white sand feeling deliciously content. I had nothing to do but lie about in hammocks getting fatter and fatter. Being pregnant is the only time in your life that you can be busy doing absolutely nothing.

A nurse comes in, rubber soles pounding authoritatively.

She checks Kitty, looks at her chart, smiles encouragingly and goes out. Anna rushes after her. 'Well? Any change?' she barks in English.

The nurse smiles and says, 'Look after the *mamma*.'

The *mamma*. That's me. The entity that was so happy inside me for all those smug, contented months of pregnancy is now a separate person, in need of me. I kneel by the cot, stroking Kitty's hair and wishing, crazily, that I could take her back inside me and keep her safe.

About thirty minutes later, Luca appears. His hair is wet so it must be raining outside. He is carrying a jumper (I am freezing in the air-conditioned room) and a plain white plastic bag. 'Thank you,' I say. I put on the jumper and put the bag on my lap.

Maria looks over curiously. 'What on earth . . . ?'

A green plastic container and a rosary are inside the bag. Anna leans over to look. 'Is that . . . ?' Maria lets out a stifled gasp. Mum looks over quickly and then away again. Luca stands by the door, arms at his sides, ready for action. I ignore them all. I take out the container and say, in a demanding voice, a youngest daughter's voice, 'Daddy. Save my baby.'

*

It is three o'clock. Luca has taken my mother and sisters to find some coffee. The clock ticks loudly. The plant is still dying in the corner. Kitty mutters in her sleep, her eyes moving beneath their lids. I stroke her hair. I am alone, waiting, with Dad.

In my hand I am still holding the rosary, Nonna's rosary, given to me by Dad on my first-communion day. I don't know why I put it into the bag with his ashes, but it seemed wrong to have them there on their own in their green plastic holder, like something from a garden centre. I felt as if I should add something more solemn, something with history. So I thought of Nonna's rosary.

I have always loved the feel of it in my hand, the ivory beads and the gold cross clinking together, but I have never thought of it as anything more than a rather special piece of jewellery. I have never used it as old women use their rosaries at mass, passing the beads smoothly from one hand to the other, lips moving in prayer. I am not even sure what prayers you are meant to say. For the second time that night, I try to conjure Sister Immaculata's voice. Lourdes. The Virgin in the grotto. St Bernadette. The little consumptive girl and her vision. The nun dying in a haze of sanctity. 'Ten Hail Marys and one Our Father. A decade of the rosary.'

'Sister? Why only one Our Father? God's more important than Our Lady, isn't he?'

'Yes, but the best way to God is through His Blessed Mother. Haven't you ever asked your mother to change your father's mind about something?'

Not in our family. My dad was always the soft touch. Mum was cooler, more reserved, fair but unyielding. Dad was sometimes not very fair – 'No, you can't have your ears pierced. It doesn't matter what Maria does' – but he was always amenable to pleading, crying and emotional black-mail. 'That's my last word,' he would say, seconds before he came out with another few hundred. Then he would sigh, ruffle my hair and give in: 'All right. Don't cry. Just this once. Don't ask me again, OK?'

'No, Daddy, I won't. I promise.'

So many times. When I wanted to stay all night at a friend's house, when I wanted to wear ripped jeans to mass, when I wanted to go to a club in Brighton, the first time I wanted to go out with a boy. Dad always said no explosively: 'Out of the question. No! *Basta. Finito.*'

Mum would say, 'I don't think so, darling, it's really not appropriate.'

Then I would storm and cry and Dad would give in, sighing: 'Just this once.'

'Just this once, Daddy,' I whisper now.

One hand on Kitty's forehead, I hold the rosary in the other. I don't remember Nonna. She died when I was a baby. I remember Nonno, the doctor, who was always referred to as a saint. Nonna was not a saint. Even her name, Attilia, sounds aggressive and formidable. Dad said that Nonna got angry when Nonno treated his patients for nothing. 'They take advantage,' she said. 'They know you can't say no.' But apparently she was kind too – she took food and medicine to poor families in the neighbourhood, always dismissing her generosity with a matter-of-fact shrug: 'Someone's got to do it.' She had known sorrow too: she had lost a son. Anna told me that Nonna had a shrine in her bedroom with Uncle Armando's photograph surrounded by candles and flowers. In front of it she had a kneeler, the sort you have in church, and she prayed there every day. Come on, Attilia the Hun, help your great-granddaughter, the descendant of Genghis Khan.

'"Hail Mary,"' I begin, '"full of grace. The Lord is with thee."'

The words sound soothing, familiar – 'The blessed mutter

of the mass,' Robert Browning called it. '"Blessed art thou amongst women and blessed is the fruit of thy womb, Jesus."' I feel my head bowing at the name 'Jesus' in some curious remembered reflex, as if an unseen hand is pushing at the back of my neck.

Who am I praying to? I'm not sure. I think of that day, in the hospital, when Bob told me that Dad had died. I remember, when Bob had gone home, looking up at the ceiling of the ward, with its exposed pipes, peeling paint and single strand of tinsel left over from Christmas and speaking directly to God. 'You'd better bloody exist,' I told Him. The gurgling pipes and gently swaying tinsel made no reply. Do I believe that Dad is now in heaven, happy with the angels and saints, reunited with his parents and lost younger brother? I don't know. All I know is that Kitty is here now and I will do anything to save her. Anything. Even pray.

The door opens and somehow I know that Anna is behind me. Defiantly I keep my back turned. Prayer has always been her thing; she is the expert. She knows exactly how to bow her head with the right degree of humility. She is never embarrassed, even when praying in public, saying grace before meals or asking St Anthony to help her find something. I remember her telling me that at the funeral parlour she prayed beside Dad's body. At the time I thought, How *could* she? But now I understand: if you feel something enough, you don't care what anyone else thinks.

Anna comes to stand beside me. She puts her hand on Kitty's forehead. 'Gaby?' she says. I look up, expecting some saintly observation about the power of prayer or a demonstration of the right way to hold a rosary. Instead she says, 'Gaby, I think the fever's gone.'

A few minutes later, Franco comes in. He has the blood-test results. It isn't meningitis, just a viral infection. He takes Kitty's temperature. It is almost back to normal. My mother cries, burying her face in her hands. Luca crosses himself. Anna and Maria share a brief hug. I put the rosary back into my pocket. Then I go out to the loo, fill a cup with water, go back and water the plant.

Dawn is breaking when Luca drives me home. Kitty is out of danger but Franco says that she should stay in hospital for another day. 'It is more comfortable than the apartment and you can get some rest. Yes?' We drive past the hospital buildings in the aptly named Viale Policlinico, past vast ministries, shuttered and silent. As we reach the centre of Rome, the city is waking up. The flower-sellers are setting out their baskets in the market squares; the cobbles are still wet with the night's rain and a thousand puddles reflect the pale blue morning sky. As we pass the Piazza della Repubblica, church bells begin to ring.

I turn to Luca. 'Is it Sunday?'

'*Sì.*' He smiles at me, his yellow eyes kind. 'It is Sunday.'

And I understand something. I understand that we want happiness and wealth and love. We want work and sex and religion. We want our team to win at football and for our parents to love us. But, most of all, we want our children to live.

CHAPTER FOURTEEN

I am in a deep, deep sleep when the telephone wakes me. It is as if I am at the bottom of a dark well and have to clamber my way up to the surface. Unsteadily I cross the room and pick up the receiver.

'Gaby! It's Bob.'

'Bob,' I repeat sleepily.

'Gaby! What's all this about Kitty? What's happened to her? Is she OK?'

It takes a few seconds for everything to sink in, and when it does, it seems extraordinary that Bob doesn't know what has happened. That he wasn't in the hospital with the clock and the painting and the dying plant. That he didn't feel Kitty's burning forehead or see the fear in Franco's eyes and the urgency of the doctors. It is amazing that he doesn't know any of this. He is only in London but it feels as if he is a lifetime away.

'She'll be fine. She had a really high temperature and I thought it might be meningitis. She was all shivery and she was scared of the light, you know? Franco said take her to hospital. I've been there all night but they say she'll be fine. It's not meningitis. It's just a virus.'

'Gaby, my God.' There is an expensive international silence. Then Bob asks, in a sort of hushed, respectful voice, 'Is she still in hospital?'

'Yes, but it's just for a day, Franco says. To give her some rest. I can bring her home tomorrow.' Home. It sounds odd. But, in some ways, it seems that I have been in this tiny apartment, with the tritons blowing their horns outside, for ever.

'I'm coming back,' Bob says. 'I'll catch a plane today.'

'Where are you?'

'Home.' That word again: our flat with its wooden floors and framed posters. I can see Bob in the kitchen with the barstools and the postcards stuck on the fridge. We should move, I think, somewhere with a garden so Kitty can play.

'Gaby?' Bob is saying. 'Gaby? Are you all right?'

'I'm fine,' I say. 'Just tired.'

'I'm coming back,' Bob says again. 'Don't worry.'

'Where were you last night,' I ask, 'when Luca rang?'

'I was out . . .' There is a pause. 'We'd done the deal and . . . well, you know.'

Yes, I do. The adrenaline of the completed deal. The drinks in the pub, the drunken Indian meal, the taxi home. If you go home, that is.

'That's OK,' I say. 'I'll see you later.'

'Gaby?'

'Yes?'

'Give my love to Kitty.'

'Yes.'

Bob never says, 'I love you,' to me on the phone. I used to say it to him but now I don't. I feel too self-conscious somehow, even when I'm on my own.

'See you later,' I say again.

'Yes. Take care. I'll be with you soon.'

'Bye.'

'Bye.'

I put the phone down for a second, then ring the hospital. Franco has given me the number of the scary consultant. She comes on to the line, barking, *'Pronto!'* as if it's the name of a badly behaved dog. Somehow I find enough Italian to ask how Kitty is. She is fine, says the scary doctor, temperature down, drip out. She has had some water and a little food.

Blimey! I think. They've weaned her already. I feel a pang and my breasts twitch. 'Can I come to see her?'

'*Sì*. Come this afternoon.' And the receiver goes down. She is obviously too busy to say goodbye but I don't care: I worship her as if she is a goddess. The goddess of Rome. I look at my watch. It is only ten o'clock.

I go to the window. It is another beautiful day and the square is full of tourists throwing coins into the fountain. A group of Japanese girls are standing below me, having their photograph taken. When it is developed, it will show a pale-faced ghost in the top window, like a visitor from another world.

I am still wearing the clothes I had on last night – jeans, T-shirt and Bob's jumper. I feel wrinkled and dirty. I go into the luxurious bathroom (dark blue tiles and white marble, easily the nicest room in the apartment) and have a long, hot shower. I can almost feel the dirt streaming out of my hair. I stand there for a long time with my head back and the hot water pouring over me. Then I wrap myself in a large bath-towel and go into the kitchen to make myself a cup of coffee.

As I wait for the Dalek-shaped espresso machine to boil, I think about Bob in our little yellow kitchen. Is he perched at the uncomfortable breakfast bar, having tea and toast? He is a great tea drinker: he thinks coffee is the fuel of the devil. Is he frantically ringing the airlines or is he leafing through papers from work, sighing at the inconvenience of fatherhood? Is he on the phone to Anita or is she there, wearing one of Bob's shirts in that cute just-stayed-the-night way and using my toothbrush? Then I think, Christ, where did that thought come from?

The coffee is wonderful, shooting a caffeine kick behind my eyes. I blink and the room seems brighter than ever, full of light. I feel deeply disloyal, but, for a second, I savour the pleasure of being alone, a pleasure so intense it makes me shiver to the ends of my fingertips. How long is it since I've been alone, without even Kitty? Kitty! I haven't worried about her for ten minutes. I'm a monster mother. The caffeine high fades.

The doorbell rings, making me jump. I press the entry-phone and hear Anna's loud teacher's voice: 'Let us in, please,

Gaby.' Seconds later she bursts into the room, followed by Maria. Anna is holding a covered basket, like the wolf in *Little Red Riding Hood*. 'Food,' she says, 'from Auntie Carla. Aren't you dressed yet? I've already been to mass.'

'We thought we'd go out for lunch,' says Maria, flopping down on the sofa. 'Take your mind off things.'

Suddenly it seems so *strange* that they're here, without husbands or children, the three of us together in a strange apartment in a foreign city, that I want to laugh. They seem so bright and full of colour, Anna in a red shirt and white trousers, Maria in a long green sparkly dress, that I feel invisible by comparison. 'Come on,' Anna says, not unkindly. 'Hadn't you better be getting dressed?'

'We rang the hospital,' says Maria, opening a magazine. 'Kitty's fine.'

'I know,' I say, irritated. 'I rang too.'

'We can visit her in the afternoon,' says Anna.

'No, thanks,' I say. 'I want to go on my own.'

I get dressed quickly. Wanting to match their finery, I put on the only vaguely smart thing I brought with me: a sleeveless black dress. It's a bit tight in the bust so I drape a red scarf round my neck in an attempt to distract attention from the straining buttons. I haven't any smart shoes so I put on a pair of red flip-flops. My hair is curly from the shower so I brush it and hope for the best.

When I come back into the sitting room, Anna is washing my coffee cup and Maria is looking out of the window. 'Look at them all,' she says. 'Three coins in the fountain. Rossano Brazzi has a hell of a lot to answer for.'

Anna looks round. 'We'd better get going,' she says. 'Haven't you got any proper shoes?'

Perhaps in defiance of Franco and Luca, we choose the least secluded restaurant we can find, at the foot of the Spanish Steps, near the café where Anna and Maria once ate ice cream with the Golden Boys. Our restaurant is the full tourist Monty, with tables outside and a gypsy violinist. We drink cold white wine and watch the crowds flowing past us up the flower-strewn steps towards the Villa Medici Gardens.

'Imagine what it must have been like in August,' says Maria.

'Yes,' says Anna. 'It's so unfair that teachers have to go on holiday in the busiest months . . .'

Maria and I switch off. I take a chunk of bread and dip it in olive oil. I feel ravenously hungry. In one part of my mind,

I am thinking in *News of the World* speak: 'With her baby sick in hospital, heartless mum Gabriella de Angelis drinks in a four-star Italian restaurant . . .' In the other I want to enjoy it all. Kitty is safe. I am free to eat and drink in the sunshine. I shake out my hair and a handsome German at the next table smiles at me.

Maria notices. 'You haven't lost it, Gaby,' she says.

'Lost it?' I say. 'I never had it.'

'Rubbish,' says Maria. 'You always had loads of boyfriends.'

I gape at her. 'Me? You were the one with all the boy-friends. Don't you remember? Every boy in school was mad about you. And then you got Lee who was the best of the lot.'

'Yes,' says Maria sulkily. 'But then I was married in a grotty little flat while you were out on the town with a different boy each night. I was so envious. I used to cry myself to sleep every night.'

'*You* were envious of *me*?'

Anna cuts in, saying calmly, 'You both had loads of boy-friends. It was me who didn't. I was the good girl, going to mass, doing my homework, looking after my little sisters.'

We turn on her crossly. 'You *loved* all that.'

'Everyone thought you were wonderful.'

'"Sure and He broke the mould after He made Anna."'

'"Pity about the other two".'

'"Anna's the star, Anna will be prime minister one day."'

'Have you any idea how hard it was,' asks Anna, 'being the perfect one? Going to all those boring meetings, in charge of this, chair of that? Having Mum and Dad nagging me to go to Cambridge, get a brilliant degree, be prime minister?'

We stare at her dumbly. 'I thought you liked being perfect,' I say at last, rather lamely.

Anna breaks a breadstick neatly in two. 'Oh, I liked it,' she says, 'but sometimes I wanted to have fun too.'

'And then,' Maria says, with the air of having the final word, 'you got David.'

'And the boys,' I add.

'Oh, yes.' Anna shrugs, dismissing her soulmate and the fruits of their love with an airy wave of her hand. 'Oh, yes. I got married at twenty-two and was pregnant at twenty-five. What have I got to show for my life? I haven't got a career like you, Gaby. Or you . . .' she adds, as an afterthought, to Maria, who is aware that Anna has never considered her unique calling, which combines teaching Pilates with cleansing people's spiritual auras, as a proper job.

Our food has arrived. Maria spreads her napkin on her green-spangled lap and says, without rancour, 'Oh, I haven't got a career. Gaby's the one with a career.'

They stare at me – somewhat accusingly, I feel.

'You think my job's boring,' I say to Maria.

'Yes,' she says, sprinkling Parmesan. 'I do. I mean, accountancy – what could be more boring than that? But it's a proper career. You've got all the suits and everything.'

'And the company car,' chimes in Anna.

I'm shocked that *Anna* has noticed something so worldly – it's a silver-grey VW Golf, since you ask. 'You don't care about things like that,' I say feebly.

I'm talking to Anna but Maria answers: 'Oh, I don't care,' she says. 'Lots of negative vibes from all that money. People trapped on the hamster wheel. But you have to admit the clothes are nice.'

'Except that I can't get into them any more,' I say. A button has popped off my dress and my red scarf trails in my *spaghetti vongole*.

'No,' agrees Anna. 'Babies are great levellers.'

We are all silent, eating thoughtfully. The gypsy violinist comes over to our table but wanders away again as soon as he realises that we aren't lovers or a sight-seeing family, just a group of not-so-young women eating their lunch.

'Dad, though,' says Maria suddenly, as if we had been talking about him all along, 'he didn't make me feel a failure. He thought there was a lot of value in my rebirthing sessions.'

Anna sucks in her cheeks but doesn't speak. Her own, often-voiced, opinion of these sessions is that they are full of middle-class women who would be better off working in the local Oxfam shop rather than crawling out of imaginary vaginas on to Maria's distressed-oak floor.

'Dad liked Ray,' says Maria, 'but, then, he liked Lee too.'

'Dad liked David,' says Anna. 'He said he was one of the most intelligent people he knew. He liked to talk to him about philosophy and things.'

'He liked everyone,' I say.

'Except Margaret Thatcher,' says Maria.

'Oh, except her.'

'Dad didn't think my life was a failure either,' says Anna, after a pause. 'He said teaching was one of the most valuable careers you could have.'

'Well, he was a teacher,' says Maria.

'University – that's different. Mum used to say I should

have gone back to Cambridge and done a PhD but Dad never did. And he adored the boys.'

Suddenly a huge tear falls into my pasta. 'He never saw my baby.'

It's very embarrassing. Anna and Maria pass me napkins and pat my back as I cry and cry. The gypsy violinist comes over again and plays what he imagines is a cheering tune. Waiters offer glasses of water. I sob and gulp and hiccup. I haven't cried like this for years. When Dad died I cried a bit, now and then, but never with such a torrent, such an avalanche, of tears. It feels oddly cleansing, like one of Maria's aura laundry sessions, just sitting there with tears rolling down my face.

'It's your reaction,' says Anna briskly, 'to Kitty being ill.'

'It's a delayed reaction to Dad dying,' says Maria, passing over another napkin. 'Discharging, they call it.'

'It's just crying,' I say. 'I'm sorry.'

I cry all through pudding, but manage to eat it. I'm still sniffing when the tiny gold cups of espresso and tissue-twisted Amaretto biscuits arrive. The waiter comes over with three glasses of yellow liqueur. 'On the house,' he says, looking at me. 'For the *signora*.'

'Thank you,' I say. '*Grazie*.'

'Is good for the heart,' he says, gesturing.

'Thank you.'

'What is it?' whispers Anna.

'Limoncello,' says Maria, downing hers in one gulp. 'Disgusting.'

Maybe it's the Limoncello but I feel much better as I leave the restaurant. A little drunk, but pleasantly so, as if I'm floating a few feet above the ground. Anna holds my arm as if to pull me back to earth.

We wander aimlessly through the chattering, camera-clicking crowds. 'Where are we going?' asks Maria.

'I don't know,' says Anna. 'What's along here?'

'The river,' I say. 'The Tiber, Father Tiber.'

'You're drunk,' says Maria.

'A bit,' I admit. 'It's quite nice. I haven't drunk so much since Kitty was born.'

We wander along the banks of the river. In the distance is the Castel Sant' Angelo, the gold angel on its tower glinting in the sunshine. I think of the photo of Dad in front of the castle and of Mum telling us he wanted his ashes scattered in Rome.

Anna has been thinking of Dad too. 'You know,' she says suddenly, 'I always thought I was Dad's favourite.'

We stop and stare at her.

She goes on, rather defiantly, not looking at us but across at the castle, 'I was the eldest. I was the most like him. Academic and all that. He loved us all, I know, but I always thought I was his favourite.'

'I thought *I* was his favourite,' says Maria. 'I'm the most Italian – tempestuous, fiery. He used to say I was like Nonna.' She tosses her hair complacently.

The castle is reflected perfectly in the calm water: stone and water, life and death. I know I was his favourite. I was the youngest. I loved football. I was his baby, his companion, his mascot. But I say nothing.

Eventually, as we cross the river at Ponte Vittorio Emanuele, Anna says, 'I suppose it's quite good, really, that we both thought we were his favourite. Shows we both know he loved us.'

'Parents shouldn't have favourites anyway,' says Maria airily, clearly oblivious to her blatant bias towards Kyle. Anna and I exchange a look.

'Of course he loved us all,' I say loudly. 'He was a wonderful father.' Some passing English tourists laugh. Anna takes my arm again.

From *King Lear* to *Cinderella*, there is something special about three sisters. It is a magical combination, like seven sons. As a child, I used to identify with the youngest and most beautiful daughter, the one who always emerged triumphant in the end. It was not difficult to see myself as Cordelia, with Anna and Maria as Goneril and Regan. I was the one who really loved my dad: the other two just wanted to divide his kingdom between them and put his friends in the stocks. For all their external beauty, they were the Ugly Sisters and I was the heroine of the story. Now, in a rush of knowledge brought on by too much alcohol, I realise that they probably thought they were the heroines too. It is like that dizzying moment you have as a child when you discover that you are not the only person in the world. When you understand that all the people you see waiting drearily at bus stops, shopping or walking in the park, *all those people* have thoughts of their own and not one of them is thinking about you.

'I have three daughters,' Dad used to say, 'and I love each one better than the other.' I used to hope it was a cumulative thing: he loved Maria more than Anna and me more than both of them. Now I see that this might not have been what he meant, that it was something altogether more profound. That he loved Anna, Maria and me in a kind of circle: the more he loved one of us, the more he loved the other two. That his love was everlasting.

Outside the Vatican, I catch a taxi to the hospital. My last view of my sisters is of them standing in front of the Piazza San Pietro, red, white and green, like the Italian flag.

CHAPTER FIFTEEN

In the taxi, I lean back in a pleasant, mildly alcoholic haze, and think about my sisters. The conversation about Dad reminds me of something. Another time when Anna and Maria were in intense, yet unspoken competition. Another time when I was on the sidelines. Then the taxi stops at the lights and I see a poster on a bus stop, loopy writing against a garish picture of a big wheel: 'Luneur Park, Open All Year Round'. And then I remember. Luneur Park. The last time we saw the Golden Boys.

Luneur Park is a huge fairground at EUR, just outside Rome. EUR is the town built by Mussolini in imitation of Ancient Rome. It has a square, modern colosseum, vast, echoing squares and endless colonnades complete with mosaics of heroic-looking miners, soldiers and assembly-line workers.

Most important of all, it has Luneur Park, open twenty-four hours a day, blasting pop music over the sombre reminders of Fascism.

Dad took us to Luneur Park as a treat. He must have known that, Golden Boys apart, the holiday had not been much fun for us. He had been working, Mum had been hot and distracted, Auntie Carla had tried hard but she had been no compensation for the beaches and discos of Ostia. So Dad, although he hated loud music and fun-fairs, took us to Luneur Park on our last night in Rome.

It was wonderful. The steamy night was full of flashing lights, noise so loud it made your blood pump in time to its beat – and boys. Hundreds of boys: hot-eyed Roman youths who ogled Anna and Maria with open, if mocking, admiration, and begged them to come with them for a *giro*, a little ride round Rome – come on, get into the car, we'll have fun, yes? Dad took his elder daughters' arms and steered them past. Franco and I trailed along behind. Once, one of the boys shouted, to much laughter, 'I'll take the little one instead!' I turned and stuck out my tongue at him.

We saw them on the Big Wheel. We were queuing for our turn – Franco was scared so Anna and Maria had been forced to take me with them ('Do we *have* to, Dad?'). We were standing, looking up at the floodlit wheel, its lights strung out against the night sky, when we heard, 'Anna! Maria! Gabriella!' Giancarlo and Massimo were suspended high above us, making their car swing wildly as they waved at us. 'It's *them*,' hissed Anna unnecessarily. We hadn't seen the Golden Boys since that disastrous trip to the Forum. We had thought they'd disappeared to the seaside or the mountains, but there they were, large as life and several times as natural, calling to us from the heavens.

The boys descended and begged to be allowed to accompany us on our ride. Dad hesitated but he could hardly say no. It was me that was the problem. Giancarlo wanted to go with Anna and Massimo wanted to go with Maria, but nobody wanted to go with me. You couldn't have more than three in a car and both my sisters wanted desperately to avoid a threesome. I flushed hot with embarrassment as I waited in the queue, facing my sisters' disdain, my father's exasperated pity and Franco's half-comprehending amusement. But, still, some stubborn streak of cussedness stopped me giving up my ride. I wanted to go on the Big Wheel, so I would go. I didn't care if I did ruin my sisters' love-lives. Eventually Dad prevailed on Anna, as the eldest sister, to take me with her. She did, with bad grace, pulling me along behind her and ignoring me completely as the wheel began its creaking ascent.

The ride was terrifying. At the top, our car stopped, swinging precariously. Giancarlo stretched out his arm behind Anna and made the car rock even faster. I screamed and Anna pinched me. Maria and Massimo were just below us and Anna made me scream again by leaning over to see them. 'Shut *up*, Gaby,' she yelled, as the wheel began its heart-stopping, dizzying descent. Luneur Park, EUR, Rome: our very lives spun past us, faster and faster, as the hot night air shot into my open mouth and I shut my eyes so that all I could see was redness and all I could feel was the lurch as my stomach was left miles above us and all that remained was an empty space in my ribcage filled with screams and delicious fear.

Our car shuddered to a halt and Anna got out immediately, scorning the help of the Neanderthal man in overalls who stumbled over to undo our seatbelts.

'She screamed all the time,' she complained furiously to Dad. 'I'm never going on anything with her ever again.'

And she didn't. I went on the dodgems with Franco (embarrassingly slow) and with Dad (wonderfully fast). I had ice cream and Coke and a piece of pizza in a paper napkin. I went on the Waltzer and the American Twist and the deceptively stately-looking Sailboats. But I did not really see my sisters until the end of the evening. 'Stay in sight,' Dad told them, and they almost obeyed him. I kept seeing flashes of Anna's white T-shirt and Maria's pink shorts. I saw Massimo waving from the terrifying heights of the Cyclone, and once Giancarlo came close enough to drop into my hands a blue nylon rabbit he had won on the shooting range.

It was nearly eleven o'clock when Dad decided we should go home. Franco was yawning constantly and I had been sleepwalking for the past hour. We met Anna and Giancarlo at the pizza stall. Giancarlo was eating pizza with gusto and Anna was standing beside him looking tired and rather sulky. 'Where's your sister?' Dad demanded. Anna shrugged but Giancarlo volunteered, through his pizza, that he had seen Maria and Massimo on the Big Wheel. 'Go and get her, *cara*,' said Dad to Anna, and added, perhaps wanting to separate Anna and Giancarlo, 'Take Gaby with you.'

Not speaking, Anna and I made our way to the Big Wheel.

The fair was at its height and we had to push our way through the crowds, Anna dragging me behind her. When we got there we couldn't see them, but then Anna nudged me and pointed upwards. Maria and Massimo were at the highest point. We couldn't see their faces but they were locked in an embrace so fierce that even the wheel's death-defying descent could not break it. Their car stopped a few feet away from us, and I felt intensely proud of Maria. How could she, at only eleven, do such professional kissing? She and Massimo writhed and squirmed like two pop stars. Only the Neanderthal's tap on Massimo's shoulder broke them apart.

Maria opened her eyes. 'Oh, hi!' she said brightly. 'Is it time to go?'

Anna did not say a word on the journey home. In the neon light of the apartment lobby, she looked as if she had been crying but, if so, I thought it was odd that I hadn't heard her.

We never saw the Golden Boys again.

CHAPTER SIXTEEN

When I get to the hospital, Kitty is lying in her cot, gurgling at the ceiling. When she sees me, she lets out a great crow of delight. I pick her up and nuzzle her body. She is wearing a hospital nightgown and an unfamiliar nappy. She smells of milk and hospitals and, wonderfully, of herself. The nurse who was sitting beside her says, in English, 'She knows her mother.'

'Yes,' I answer smoothly in Italian. 'She knows me.'

Kitty pulls happily at my red scarf and another button falls off my dress.

The grey-haired consultant (doesn't she ever sleep?) emerges from a side room to tell me that Kitty is fully recovered. 'You can take her home now, if you like.'

'Now?'

'Yes, now. Have you got a car?'

'No.' I imagine taking Kitty back to Uncle Bruno's apartment and a heroine's welcome, tears of joy and prayers of thankfulness. Then I think of taking Kitty back to my empty apartment and sitting with her by the open window, listening to the tourists outside and doing nothing.

'No,' I say again, 'but I know someone who has.'

When he drove me home that Sunday morning, Luca handed me a piece of paper with his phone number again.

'Just in case,' he said, with his conspiratorial grin.

Luca takes a long time to answer the phone. I stand in the shiny reception area, holding Kitty tightly. She beams up at me and pulls my hair. In some miraculous way, she seems not only to have survived last night's ordeal but to have gained strength from it. Her red hair stands up in exuberant curls, like little bronze wires. I know my face must look a hundred times paler and more tired beside her rosy vitality.

'*Pronto.*' Luca's voice shocks me. I have almost forgotten why I am holding my phone.

'Luca. It's me, Gaby.' I lose my nerve and go back into English.

'Gaby! How is the *bambina*?'

'She's fine. They say she can go home and I was wondering . . . Can you give us a lift?'

'I'll be there in ten minutes,' says Luca.

I sit in the reception area with Kitty on my lap. She nuzzles at my chest and I lose a few more buttons as I feed her. The tinted windows give everything a green, underwater feeling. A kind receptionist swims over with a pile of bricks for Kitty, who laughs delightedly. I sit in a trance as she presses the little plastic shapes into my head, my cheeks, my neck. Every time they fall to the ground, she laughs again. I feel as if I have lost all power to move, even to pick up the bricks from the floor.

As I sit there, in that cool, tinted space, I think of my sisters wending their way home along the banks of the Tiber. Maria will want to stop for coffee but Anna will march her onwards, saying they can have a cup of tea at Uncle Bruno's apartment. Maria will grumble but she'll give in. I know this as certainly as if I were walking beside them, looking at the café awnings beckoning invitingly. Maria and I always give in to Anna; it hadn't occurred to me before that this, in its own way, is a burden. It hadn't occurred to me that the mantle of being the eldest, the cleverest and the best-behaved is difficult to bear. 'Sure and He broke the mould when He made Anna,' is what the nuns said, and now I thank God for it. Who wants to be made in someone else's pattern anyway? Maria and I were free to be ourselves and that, in a way, was thanks to Anna. There you are, Anna: sainthood at last.

And Maria. To me, she will always be the coolest girl in the school, hitching up her skirt to ride on Lee's motorbike or kissing Massimo so expertly amid the lights of Luneur Park. But now it seems Maria envies *me*, the accountant, the boring one who read maths at university, the one who was still a virgin at eighteen. I try to imagine myself as the sort of person whom Maria might envy, but I can't. I will always be in awe of her. She is still so beautiful in her gypsy skirts and floating scarves that I feel colourless beside her. I remember Lee sobbing on the garage roof in the rain and I still feel unequal to inspiring that sort of devotion. Maria might think I've got it sussed, with my good job and company car, but deep down I still want someone to stand on a garage roof for me.

Suddenly I see the receptionist look up and, instinctively, fluff out her hair. The automatic door slides open and Luca appears. He is wearing jeans, flip-flops and a white T-shirt. His curly hair is slightly wet, as if he has just had a shower.

'Gaby!' Suddenly I have the wild idea that he is going to kiss me, but instead he takes Kitty from me and lifts her into the air. She crows with delight and I start, slowly, to pick up the plastic bricks.

'Is different from yesterday,' says Luca.

'Yes,' I say, straightening. 'Very different.'

In the car, I put Kitty into her baby seat and sit in the back with her. As we drive, once more, through the teeming streets, I stare at the back of Luca's head with its damp curls and think of Dagmar, the emotional German girlfriend. Where is she on this lovely Roman evening? Has Luca just left her bed? Is that why he has showered? What must it feel like to be in love with Luca?

At the apartment Luca doesn't ask if he can come up, but when I reach my front door I know he's behind me. Inside, I put Kitty on the floor and give her my scarf to play with. Then I face Luca. He looks at my cleavage.

'My buttons came off,' I say.

He says nothing but then, slowly, does something that makes my heart skip a beat. He switches off his mobile.

'Coffee?' I say brightly.

Luca takes a step towards me. Kitty laughs in the background. I should go to her, pick her up, put her in front of me like a shield. I should scream, back away, call my mother. But I don't.

Luca is now so close that I can see the green lights in his extraordinary yellow eyes.

'We can't,' I say.

'No?' he asks, smiling. He bends his head towards me. As his lips touch mine I think, frantically, I should stop this, now. This is crazy. I can't do this. Instead, my arms snake round his neck and I am kissing him back.

And that is what Bob sees when he walks in through the open door.

CHAPTER SEVENTEEN

'For God's sake! Look out, Mum!'

Hands over my eyes, foot jammed on an imaginary brake, I sit beside my mother as we weave in and out of the Roman traffic. How long is it since I last drove with her? All of my memories are of driving with Dad. But I must have been in a car with my mother when I was a child. If so, it's a miracle I survived into adulthood.

'Watch out! The lights are red!'

'Oh, those silly little lights,' says my mother airily. 'They're too small to see.'

In the back, Kitty chortles in her baby seat. Has she come through all the traumas of the last two days only to die at my mother's hands in a multiple Fiat pile-up? 'Mum!' I say. 'Please go slower.'

She laughs. Her hair is tied up in a floaty blue scarf and she resembles a demented Isadora Duncan. When she asked me to go for this drive with her, I thought, Why not? It beats sitting alone in the apartment, wondering what Bob's doing. But now I'm not so sure. This morning I thought my marriage was over. Now I think it might be my life.

When Bob came in yesterday and saw Luca and me in that incriminating embrace, it felt like a dream. It had to be a nightmare. Surely a giant lobster would walk in from the bathroom any minute and Bob and Luca would waltz away in matching evening frocks. Instead Luca, seeing my face, drew gently away from me. He glanced at Bob, then at me, smiled apologetically and left the room without a word. Seconds later we heard the outside door slam. Neither of us had moved.

'It's not . . .' I began, and winced at the cliché.

Bob ignored me and went to pick up Kitty. 'How's my girl?' he said, his voice sounding loud and unnatural. 'How's my baby?'

I'm your girl, I wanted to say, I'm your baby. Instead, I said, 'Bob, I'm sorry.'

He turned to me. His face was ghastly, a greenish grey,

clashing horribly with his hair. He and Kitty stood facing me, two blue-eyed red-heads. I felt like an intruder.

'It's just . . .' Then the words came out too quickly: 'I've been so worried about Kitty and now she's all right and I was so relieved and I'd had lunch with Maria and Anna and I was a bit drunk and Luca drove us home and I was just so happy to have Kitty back and—'

'You got drunk with Maria and Anna, came home and snogged Luca,' said Bob, with his horrible lawyer's ability to separate the wheat from the chaff.

'No. No!' Suddenly I was really angry. 'No. You weren't here. I thought Kitty was going to die and you weren't here. Then she was better and I was so relieved. Wouldn't you have had a drink? After all, you were out all night drinking with your mates from work.'

'I wasn't "out all night",' said Bob, putting irritable quotation marks round the words. 'I just went out for a couple of drinks after work.'

'You weren't there,' I said, 'when Lu – when I tried to ring you.'

'That wasn't my fault,' said Bob. 'My mobile was low on power so I switched it off.'

'Very convenient.'

'Christ, Gaby!' His voice was so loud that Kitty, in his arms, jumped and started to cry. 'You were the one snogging the taxi driver.'

'He's not a taxi driver.'

'Whatever.' Bob turned away to soothe Kitty, 'It's all right, sweetie.'

I felt wrong-footed and resentful. It should be me holding the baby, facing Bob reproachfully, reminding him that he had abandoned me in my hour of need. Instead I was the scarlet woman, the wicked mother, caught with another man while my child played at my feet. I didn't like the role but how could I change it?

Now, signalling erratically, my mother zigzags her way through three lanes of traffic. 'Here we are,' she says calmly, pointing at a road sign high on an ancient stone wall. 'Lago di Vico. It's this way.'

I was surprised when Mum rang this morning and asked me to go for a drive with her. When had she last gone for an unspecified 'drive'? It is unlike her to embark on any journey without a clear destination, an AA map and a list of directions written in red ink. She hasn't even got a car in

Italy. But it turns out that she has arranged to borrow Paola's chic little Fiat and has a definite, but unspecified, agenda. 'Come on, Gaby,' she said. 'You need a break after the last few days.' You can say that again, I thought. And Bob had just told me he was going back to London so what did I have to lose?

On Sunday night, after arguing all evening, we went to bed. After all, what else could we do? For one thing we were both exhausted. I fed Kitty and put her down in the frilly cot. Then I went to the bathroom for my second shower of the day. When I got back, Bob was in bed with the sheets pulled up to his chin. Even though I must have undressed in front of him a hundred times, even though he watched as Kitty emerged, bloodily triumphant, from between my legs, I felt ridiculously self-conscious as I changed into my nightdress. When I got into bed beside him I saw that he was wearing a T-shirt and boxer shorts. He normally sleeps naked.

'Goodnight,' I said.

'Goodnight,' said Bob, and turned away from me.

And that was it. But as I lay there, listening to the traffic outside, I didn't feel too depressed. At least we were there, sleeping together with our baby beside us. Tomorrow was another day. Tomorrow Bob would understand that I had kissed Luca only because he was there, the age-old excuse of men caught in similar circumstances. He would understand that I loved only him and that the most important thing was that we were together and that our child was still alive.

But when I woke in the morning the bed was empty. Kitty's cot was empty too. In a panic I jumped up and went into the sitting room. Kitty was on the floor playing with a furry elephant given to her by Auntie Carla. Bob was sitting on the sofa, fully dressed, putting some papers into his overnight bag. 'I'm going back to London,' he said, without looking at me.

'No!' I said. I felt desperate. I had to do something, anything, to stop him leaving. If he goes out of the door, I thought wildly, that will be the end of everything.

'Why not?' Bob's voice was calm and cold, like a stone falling into a deep pool. 'You're both fine and there's a lot of paperwork to finish.'

'Someone else can do it,' I said, my voice rising. 'Please, Bob, I need you.'

'Do you?' Eyebrows raised. 'It doesn't seem like it.'

'Please, Bob!'

At my shout, Kitty started to cry. Bob picked her up and

placed her carefully in my arms. Then he kissed the top of her head. Unconsciously, I held up my face to be kissed, eyes shut, but when I heard Bob's voice again he was standing by the door, bag in hand.

'Goodbye, Gaby,' he said.

'*Goodbye, Gaby.*' I hear his voice again and again as Mum drives out through the depressing northern suburbs of Rome towards Tuscany. *Goodbye.* Could Bob really have left me for ever? Was this how marriages ended, without shouting and screaming, without *negotiation*? Could that one kiss really have been the end of everything? Anna is always going on and on about *Othello*, what a wonderful, moving tragedy it is, how Othello kills the one true thing in his life, the pearl worth all his tribe, or some such rubbish, but I have always thought it a silly story. All that tragedy arising from one little misunderstanding. All that anger and murder and suicide over a *handkerchief*. What rubbish! In real relationships people talk about things, they explain that they mislaid the precious handkerchief and, by the way, don't listen to Iago because he's a twat. But here was Bob, Clapham's ginger Othello, storming off home because his wife had been stupid and drunk and kissed a man she hardly knew. Just one kiss.

'Are you all right, Gaby?' says Mum. 'You're very quiet.'

'I'm fine,' I say, twisting round to give Kitty her elephant back. 'I've just got cramp from pressing a phantom brake.'

Mum laughs. 'I'm a good driver. Not like Daddy, bless him. He thought he was Michael Schumacher.'

'Tazio Nuvolari,' I say.

'Yes.' Mum laughs again. 'Thank God none of you was a boy. Dad would have wanted to call you Tazio.'

'It's quite a cool name,' I say.

We are now entering a densely wooded area. It's funny how Italy does this to you: one minute you're in the middle of a sprawling conurbation and at the next you're in the wilds, as if you had travelled in time as well as space. I think it's because Italy has so many mountains: it has a stubborn, untamed spine that stretches through all the elegant towns and quaint piazzas. In Italy there are still wolves and wild boar. There are still mountains that no one has climbed and forests that no one has penetrated. Once, a few years ago, on holiday in Tuscany with Bob, driving back to our rented villa near Siena, we saw a large cat-like animal cross the road in front of us, its eyes yellow in the headlights. 'Christ! What was that?' I said.

'God knows.' Bob was visibly shaken. There are still wild animals in Italy.

The road narrows dramatically and I pray that we don't meet any traffic coming the other way. The trees are dark at either side of us and there is nowhere to stop or turn round. I am just considering asking Mum where the hell we're going when she takes a sharp turn down an unmade road to our right. I close my eyes in sheer terror, and when I open them I feel, once again, that I must have strayed into a dream.

There is water all round us. Miles of clear blue water, still shrouded in the morning mist. Waves lap gently on a narrow beach of black, volcanic sand and, in the distance, the woods stretch, seemingly for ever.

'Lago di Vico,' says my mum, smugly. 'Lovely, isn't it?'

We park the car, take Kitty out and walk along the beach. It is a fresh morning, not cold but the faint breeze carries a warning that summer is nearly over. Despite this, a few Italian families are picnicking by the water's edge. In the shade of the trees, two elderly men have erected a card table and are playing *scopa*. Far out on the lake we can see pleasure boats with slides at one end, looming out of the mist like prehistoric monsters.

'It's extraordinary,' I say, 'that this is here. So near to Rome.'

'Yes,' says Mum. 'It's like a mirage, isn't it?'

After a while we sit down and Kitty plays happily with the coarse black sand. Mechanically, I stretch out a hand to stop her putting some into her mouth. The naturalness of the action pleases me. Perhaps I'm becoming a proper mother at last.

For a few minutes Mum is silent, looking out at the lake, inscrutable in her dark glasses. Then she says, 'I'll never forget the first time I came here. I was with your father. Actually, it was the first time I had been to Italy. We had just got engaged and Enzo took me to Rome to meet his family. I don't think I've ever been more terrified in my life. You won't be able to understand but, remember, I didn't have a big family. I was an only child and my parents were dead. There was just me and Aunt Ena. I'll never forget that at our wedding there was just Aunt Ena on my side of the church. There were lots more from Enzo's family, even though we got married in England. Anyway, the first time he took me to his parents' apartment, I was scared stiff. Literally stiff, like a doll. There was Attilia – Nonna.

Good grief, she was terrifying. Jet-black hair full of combs and pins. Masses of jewellery, made up to the nines, even though she was seventy if she was a day. Nonno was there, too, but he was sweet to me, kept telling Enzo how lucky he was to have found a 'real English rose,' as he put it. Bruno had just married Carla and they were frighteningly smart. Carla was wearing this amazing Dior dress, tight-fitting with a sort of bolero jacket. I was in my little English tweed skirt and twinset. I felt like an absolute mouse beside her. There were a couple of other aunts and uncles and this old doctor friend of Nonno's who was a bit doolally and kept asking who everyone was. It was like something out of *Alice in Wonderland*. The Mad Hatter's tea party, perhaps.'

'Didn't Dad look after you?' I ask, remembering the first time I met Bob's parents. His dad kept making bad puns ('You're from Sussex? Bright an' breezy, eh?') and his mum insisted on feeding me an apparently endless supply of scones. Only Bob made it bearable, swapping corny jokes with his dad and telling his mum I was full up, we'd already eaten, but it was all delicious, thanks very much.

Mum smiles. 'He tried. He told them I didn't speak Italian, that all girls dressed like that in England and that I wasn't used to big families. But they didn't take any notice. They all talked nineteen to the dozen. I found out later that Bruno and Carla spoke English but they didn't even try to speak it to me. Just kept talking in Italian louder and louder, smiling, gesturing, pointing. I sat there with this stupid smile glued on my face. I didn't understand a word. And the food! You think Auntie Carla cooks big meals, you should have seen Attilia's spreads. I had never seen so much food on one table in my life. I didn't eat much, in those days. I was a student and I didn't have any spare money. But when I did eat it was simple stuff – cheese on toast, baked beans, things like that. Attilia made stuffed mushrooms, ravioli, creamy sauces, beef rolled up with herbs inside. Oh, yes, it was delicious, but to me it was terrifying. I was so nervous that I couldn't eat anything so they kept trying to tempt me. '*Uno di questi*, Jane? *Uno di quelli*?' I thought I was going to be sick, right there in front of them all. Anyway, the meal seemed to go on all day. Four courses, a selection of cheeses – I'd never seen cheese like it, I'd only ever eaten Cheddar – coffee so strong it seemed almost solid, little sweets in shiny paper, Amaretto biscuits, red wine, white wine, grappa. When the meal was finally over, it was dark outside and Enzo said that he was going to take me for a drive.'

'And he brought you here?'

Mum is silent for a moment, with Kitty in her lap now, sifting black sand through her fingers. Then she says dreamily, 'We drove through the woods. It was so dark, so unfamiliar. I was quite scared. Then, suddenly, this lake was in front of us. The moon was shining on the water and it seemed magical. As if it had been created just for us.'

The sand falls through her fingers as if they were an hourglass. She holds up her face to the sun. 'We walked here on the sands,' she says. 'We were alone together at last.'

They made love, I think, by the lake in the moonlight. Traditionally, the thought of your parents having sex is supposed to make you feel ill, or at least embarrassed, but all I feel is happiness that my mum and dad had that time together. And sadness that Dad is dead and Mum has lost the person she loved most in the world. Because Mum loved Dad most – we always knew that. Some mothers love their children more than their husbands. Looking back, the only time when I have felt unfaithful to Bob was not when my lips touched Luca's for that infinitesimal second, but the first

273

time I looked from Kitty's face to Bob's: one so perfect, so vulnerable, the other so rough, so hairy, *so adult*. I felt that Kitty needed me more than Bob did, and because of that I loved her more. But I think that even as children we knew that, for Mum, Dad was the most important person in her life. Dad loved us all equally: that was his gift. Mum loves us, we know that, but she loved Dad more. And suddenly I feel something else – envy. Mum loved Dad and he knew it. I don't think Bob has any idea of how much I love him and maybe now I'll never have the chance to tell him.

'You want to scatter his ashes here, don't you?' I say to Mum.

She nods. The breeze lifts her hair and makes her look suddenly girlish. 'Yes,' she says. 'I think that is what he would have wanted.'

CHAPTER EIGHTEEN

The drive home through the rush-hour traffic is so terrifying that Kitty and I fall asleep in self-defence. When I wake we are in the underground car park at Uncle Bruno's apartment. The dark disorients me. 'Where are we?' I say stupidly. 'Where's Kitty? Where's Bob?'

'We're at Uncle Bruno's,' says Mum briskly. 'Kitty's in her car seat. I don't know where Bob is.'

'Nor do I,' I say sadly.

Mum looks at me oddly. 'What do you mean?'

'Nothing,' I say. 'Bob's had to go back to London on business. Didn't I tell you?'

'No, you didn't,' says Mum, still gazing intently at me. 'Are you OK?'

'Yes, of course.' I turn around to lift Kitty out.

The whole gang is at Uncle Bruno's: Bruno, Carla, Franco, Paola, Anna and Maria plus their husbands and families. Even Jonathan is lurking in the corner, discussing computer games with Sergio. No Luca, thank God. I think back to Mum's first visit to Rome and the room full of people, talking, laughing, gesticulating. Funny, I have never thought how it must have been for her, a little middle-class girl from the Midlands plunged into the chaos of an extended Italian family. And Bob, too. I've never wondered how difficult it must have been for him, the first time he met my family: Dad cracking jokes in Italian, my mother smiling distractedly, Anna talking about the Sacred Mysteries of the Rosary, Maria offering to read his aura. Not to mention two-year-old Sergio wanting to sit on his lap and eight-year-old Tara insisting on showing him all of her pony books. I didn't help him enough, I think. But then I remember Bob's face, relaxed and smiling, as he talked cars with Dad, pretended to be a dinosaur for Sergio and offered his star sign to Maria ('Virgo. A very bad match for Gaby'). Bob didn't need my help.

I watch Mum as she moves smoothly across the room, patting Auntie Carla's hand, dismissing Anna's strident concern, lifting Kyle on to her hip. She seems so much a part of the furniture that it is hard to imagine her as an outsider. Then she smiles at me and I know she's thinking the same thing. I smile back. We have never had a secret before.

Jonathan emerges from the gloom to sit beside me. Auntie Carla is starting to put another huge meal on the table. Paola and Anna are helping her but I'm safe because I'm holding Kitty. This is one of the best things about having a baby: it's a great excuse not to help around the house. Jonathan lifts a hand, presumably intending to pat Kitty's head in an avuncular fashion but loses his nerve and lets it fall back to the sofa.

'How's Kitty?' he asks.

'She's OK,' I say. 'It's amazing the way children recover. She's as good as new.' Once again, I find myself talking to Jonathan in a rather defensively hearty manner.

'I'm glad.' Then, lowering his voice, he says, 'I hope I didn't upset you the other day. At the church.'

It is a real wrench to bring my mind back to that day, before Kitty was ill, before I kissed Luca, before Bob left me. Oh, God, I hope Bob hasn't left me.

'I shouldn't have come,' says Jonathan. 'It was just . . . so nice to see you all again,' he ends lamely.

His face is in darkness but one of Auntie Carla's fringed, beaded lamps casts a circle of light over his hands: they are picking at the sofa cover, scraping away at the velvet. I don't think I have ever seen him nervous before. I feel dreadfully tired and it's an effort to speak. 'It's OK,' I say. 'It was nice to see you too. I think I was just over-emotional. It happens when you have a baby.'

'Oh, yes,' says Jonathan, eagerly seizing on the excuse, 'I'm sure it must be very . . . well, emotional, having a baby.'

'Yes,' I say, smiling slightly. 'It is.'

'And your husband,' says Jonathan, 'is he here?'

'No,' I say, and my next words seem actually to hurt my throat: 'He had to go back to England.'

Marco, who is at the other side of the room, sulkily putting mats on the table, hears this and comes over. 'What was that about Bob?' he asks.

'He's had to go back to London,' I say loudly, to the room in general.

Instant uproar. Why? How? What a shame when he'd only just got back. He works too hard. His firm must be full of bad karma (Maria), he must be so hungry (Carla), he must need a drink (Ray), he must be sad to be away from his wife and baby (Bruno), when is he coming back? (Marco), will he bring us a present, (Mosaic). I nod and smile and say I'm sure he'll be back soon and, if everyone will excuse me, I'm just about to call him on my mobile.

I smile apologetically at Jonathan, get up and go out on to the balcony. This is as big as another room, with lemon and olive trees in terracotta pots. I sit on a stone bench and dial Bob's number. A recorded female voice answers, with mechanical malice: 'The mobile phone you are calling has been switched off. Please leave a message after the tone.' I switch off my phone. What message could I possibly leave?

'Gaby!' calls Auntie Clara. 'Supper's ready.' I go inside and prepare myself for another marathon meal. I think of my mother facing that first trial by food at Nonna's house. Hard to think of Auntie Carla and Uncle Bruno as young urban sophisticates in designer clothes reducing my mother to awed silence. Uncle Bruno now looks older than Dad did: his hand shakes as he pours his wine and his heavy grey moustache gives his face a sardonic expression. He loved Dad, I know. Romulus and Remus, Dad said. How did it feel to be the only one left, to have lost both of his brothers? I glance involuntarily at Anna and Maria, talking respectively about RE teaching in schools and the importance, in your horoscope, of the position of the moon. The great thing about being the youngest is that you're protected from mortality.

Auntie Carla looks older too, but, like most Italian women, she is beautifully turned out. Discreetly tinted hair, subtle gold jewellery, a tasteful scarf round the neck to hide the tell-tale signs of ageing. Then she turns to me with such a sweet smile that I see her quite differently. I remember how kind she was, that summer with the Golden Boys. How she persuaded Dad to let Anna and Maria go out with them, how she took us to the Forum and was prepared to believe in Anna's ghosts. For the first time I wonder if she wanted a daughter.

After the plates have been cleared away and the adults are drinking coffee in tiny gold-rimmed cups, Mum tells everyone that she would like Dad's ashes to be scattered at Lago di Vico. There is a moment's silence. Then Maria says, rather aggressively, 'Why didn't you tell us this before?'

'Because none of you asked me,' says Mum, calmly reaching for the sugar. With a shock, I realise this is true.

'What about the religious element?' asks Anna crossly.

She turns to Jonathan. 'You can come with us, Jonathan, and say a few words.'

'You don't need a priest,' he says.

'What?' says Anna. This is directly opposed to her most deeply held view: that you always need a priest, if possible in full vestments and carrying a cross.

'You don't need a priest,' says Jonathan. 'You can make your own service. Say your own prayers. Just the family.'

I remember the dreadful moment when I took the holy water from Lourdes and baptised Kitty. 'I agree,' I say. 'We can say goodbye to Dad in our own way. We don't need a priest to say prayers. Surely we can say prayers ourselves?'

Unexpectedly Marco comes to my aid. 'Doesn't the Bible say something about "when two or three are gathered together"?'

'"For where two or three are gathered together in My name,"' supplies Jonathan, '"there I am in the midst of them."'

Anna is silent, torn, I am sure, between pride at her son coming up with an apt biblical quotation and irritation because the argument is slipping away from her.

'On the lake,' says Maria dreamily. 'I think that's rather beautiful. A bit like King Arthur.'

'Except Arthur didn't die,' Anna chimes in, unable to resist imparting information. 'In Malory's *Le Morte d'Arthur*—'

'Forget Malory for a moment, Anna,' says my mother briskly. 'This is what Enzo would have wanted. And it's what I want.'

We look instinctively at Uncle Bruno, as he was the most dubious of us about the whole undertaking. He looks at my mum, then raises his hands, palms upwards, in a particularly Italian gesture of acceptance and benediction.

'*Va bene*,' he says. 'We go to Lago di Vico.'

Later that evening Uncle Bruno drives Kitty and me back to our apartment. Tara and Marco come with us. Tara has arranged to meet some friends in a coffee bar and my guess is that Anna has put pressure on Tara to take Marco with her – she has probably noticed that Marco's a bit moody and bored. It can't be much fun for him, being with his family all the time. After all, he is sixteen.

Uncle Bruno drops me off at the apartment. The windows are dark and my heart sinks so rapidly that I think I'm about to be sick. It is only then that I realise how much I had hoped Bob would be there.

Kitty is asleep so I put her straight into her cot. Then I take out my mobile and call Bob again. No answer. My heart is beating so loudly that it seems to fill the tiny apartment like something from an Edgar Allen Poe story. Don't have a panic attack, I tell myself sternly. You have to look after Kitty. Breathe. I lace my hands across my chest and breathe in and out, watching my fingers come apart and back together. Breathe.

I call Bob again, then ring our flat in London. My voice on our answerphone gives me a terrible shock. Bob and I can't split up. We have a joint answerphone message, for God's sake. 'Neither Gaby nor Bob can talk to you at the moment . . .' When Kitty was born, Bob said we ought to change it to 'Gaby, Bob and Kitty . . .' but I thought that would be a bit naff, like having a 'Baby on Board' sticker in your car. Bob loved the 'Bimbo on board' stickers in Italy but, then, '*bimbo*' in Italian just means a baby boy.

Bob isn't at home. I have no idea where he is. That alone makes my heart beat too fast. Bob and I are married. Isn't part of being married knowing where your husband or wife is? 'Your better half,' that's what Bob's dad would say. 'Where's your better half today, Bob?' How can you lose half of yourself?

I search the apartment frantically in case Bob has left a note. I have hardly ever had a note from him. We've never been apart long enough to write to each other. Two weeks after we met in Crete, Bob and I moved in together. It wasn't planned. Mel and I were sharing a flat in Archway and one morning the ceiling fell in. The landlady was unreachable in India and we had nowhere to go. Mel went to stay with her boyfriend Peter, which led ultimately to them breaking up, and I went out to dinner with Bob. I told him about the ceiling, trying to make a funny story of it, and he said, 'Why don't you move in with me?' So I did. We went to collect my clothes and my special hypoallergenic duvet and I moved into his grotty flat in Elephant and Castle where the lift was always broken and the neighbours passed each other silver-foil packages on the stairs.

Jonathan and I used to write to each other. Long, impassioned letters during the university holidays. 'My darling Gaby, I love you more than words can say . . .' I used to look up quotes in Mum's *Dictionary of Quotations*: 'My bounty is as boundless as the sea, my love as deep.' All those words. Did they really just hide the fact that we had nothing to say to each other? That when one of us was going through something really life-changing, we had no words to describe it? How could Jonathan talk to God and not to me? How could I not know what he was going through?

From that first conversation on the beach, Bob and I have always talked in code with hidden allusions, half joking, half serious. Despite this, I feel I know him better than I ever knew Jonathan. I am sure Bob could never fall in love with God without my knowing it. Maybe that's why last night seemed such a betrayal. Bob would never have dreamed that I might kiss Luca. He had not noticed that I was falling . . . not in love, not even really in lust – but into *something* with Luca. I myself don't know what it was. Maybe it was just that Luca wasn't a member of my family. He was separate from the whole grim business of disposing of my dad's ashes. He was part of something else, part of Rome, part of being single, without children. *Sfortunatamente*.

Bob wouldn't have guessed that I would kiss Luca and I would never have guessed that he would go off like this. Bob is so reliable. That is part of what I love about him. Since Kitty was born, he has been at my side, ready to hold the baby, to fix the car seat, to warm a bottle, to tell me I'm doing it fine, that I'm a good mother. And now, over the worst two days of my life, he isn't here. OK, the first time it wasn't his fault, he had to work, but this *is* his fault. He should be here now.

I go to check on Kitty. She is sleeping peacefully. At least the last two days have taught me something. Now I know I'm a good mother without anyone having to reassure me. I knew Kitty was sick, so I took her to hospital and sat by her all night, stroking her brow and talking to her. Only my voice would do. Kitty and I came through it together and maybe I have grown up at last.

I have a shower and get ready for bed. I'm just getting a glass of water when I hear voices outside. The intercom buzzes and I hear a voice singing 'Smells Like Teen Spirit'. 'Marco,' I say, 'is that you?'

Tara's voice cuts in: 'For Christ's sake, Gaby, just let us in.'

In all big families, there are some pairings you just never see. In our family you would never, for example, see Anna and Ray together, or Maria and Sergio. Even though there are only three years between them, I have almost never seen Tara and Marco together. Although they are close in age, Tara and Marco belong to different worlds. Marco was born into the most secure Catholic family in the world; Tara was the child of two teenagers who split up almost before she came home from hospital. Marco spent his early years going to Montessori playgroups or mother-and-baby music sessions; Tara was shunted from her grandparents' house to her mother's student bed-sit to her new stepfather's home. Although Tara was not exactly deprived (my parents, at least, would have seen to that) she was always a little like a refugee. Marco had a covered sandpit from the Early Learning Centre in his garden; Tara's favourite toy was an old jewellery box of her mother's into which she would put shells and other less pleasing items found on Brighton beach. For years she carried it with her wherever she went. Now I wonder what's happened to it.

All through their childhoods, I never saw Marco and Tara together. Now, as Tara staggers into the room with Marco's arm round her neck, she looks as if she would have liked that to remain unchanged.

'What's going on?' I ask.

'He's drunk,' says Tara. 'It's so embarrassing. People just don't do this in Italy.'

Marco falls on to the sofa and grins up at us. His resemblance to Dad is marked.

'I had to bring him here,' says Tara defensively. 'I can't let Auntie Anna see him like this.'

'No,' I agree. Anna has never understood about drink. Even as a teenager she was unembarrassed about taking ginger ale to parties. I remember going to see her once in Cambridge and finding her and her friends drinking tea at six o'clock in the evening. *Tea.* It almost put me off going to university.

'I'll make some coffee,' I say. 'Would you like some coffee, Marco?'

'No,' says Marco. 'I'd like some more beer.'

'For God's sake!' Tara turns her back on him and follows me into the tiny kitchen. 'I'm sorry, Gaby,' she says. 'You were just going to bed.'

'It's OK,' I say. 'I could do with the company.'

Tara's smooth brown face crumples into a frown. 'Are you OK?' she asks. 'When's Bob coming back?'

'I don't know.' Suddenly I'm terrified that I'm going to cry. I turn to the Dalek coffee machine and talk into the steam. 'He's had to go back to London for work,' I say. 'I don't know when he'll be back.'

Tara says nothing. Another loud burst of singing comes from the sitting room. Kitty wakes up and yells.

'Oh, Christ,' says Tara. 'I'm sorry. You look after Kitty and I'll get the coffee.'

I fetch Kitty, who is scarlet-faced and furious. I carry her into the sitting room and dump her on Marco's lap. That'll put him off having children for a few years.

'Hello, baby,' says Marco amiably. Startled by this new, beery-smelling person, Kitty stops crying and stares dubiously into his face.

'Pretty baby,' says Marco. 'Pretty li'l baby.'

Tara comes in, carrying coffee and a packet of biscuits on a tray. I applaud her silently. Food is a good idea. 'For God's sake, Marco,' she says again, 'stop breathing beer fumes over that baby and have some coffee. We've got to sober you up.'

'Am sober,' says Marco. 'Sober as a lawyer.'

'As a judge,' snaps Tara, taking Kitty away from him. 'Sober as a judge.'

'Lawyer,' repeats Marco truculently. 'Lawyer. Like Bob. Where is Bob? I want to see Bob.'

'He's not here,' I say, wondering if these two have been sent by God to torment me. 'He's gone back to London.'

A lock of curly black hair has fallen into Marco's eyes. He is frowning in concentration. 'I like Bob,' he says. 'I don't like that Luca bloke. He's too bloody pleased with himself by half.'

I say nothing. Could he know? I ask myself. Could Marco, who spends half of his time with headphones on or staring at a computer screen, have noticed that I was attracted to Luca?

And if he noticed, who else did?

'I think Luca's gorgeous,' says Tara dreamily, jiggling Kitty on her lap. 'He's got the most amazing eyes.'

'Bob's got eyes too,' says Marco stubbornly.

This time I look at him sharply, trying to see if there's a double meaning behind his words, but Marco stares back innocently, his coffee dripping on to the floor.

I have always known that Marco and Sergio liked Bob. He has a younger brother so he knows how to talk their language: computer games, disaster movies, mutants, aliens, catchphrases from comedy shows. But it goes deeper than that. Bob has always spent time with them, helping Sergio to build a go-kart, taking Marco to a Grand Prix. While Ray has always been hearty and jokey with the boys, Bob has shown quietly that he likes their company. Now it seems as if Marco senses something is wrong. He doesn't know what but he knows it is to do with Bob. And he knows whose side he's on.

I take the coffee cup away from him. 'Shut up about Bob,' I say. 'I don't want to talk about it.' This comes out louder than I expect and there is a silence, broken only by Marco mechanically chomping biscuits.

'You should have seen Marco in the coffee bar,' says Tara at last. 'It was awful. My friend Jessica was there – Jessica Montanaro. And he kept telling her she was gorgeous and he wanted to go out with her. Then he started singing these dreadful songs and saying that Kurt Cobain was the first martyr of rock.'

'What's wrong with that?' asks Marco. 'He died for us!'

'I think you'll find that was Jesus,' says Tara smoothly.

I'm thinking of Dad. As a child, I always confused him with that other Father, the one with the thunderbolts and the long white dress. 'Our Father Who art in Lewes,' Maria used to say but, for me, it was more serious than that. Praying to God in church, 'Father, You are holy indeed and all creation rightly gives You praise,' I felt disloyal to my other father, the one with the rusty Italian car who thought that Liam Brady walked on water. Now a phrase from those churchgoing days comes back to me. 'He died that we might live.' Had my dad died for me? Had he died so that Kitty would live? Suddenly I feel dizzy, as if I have had a glimpse of something so big and terrifying that looking at it will make me lose my balance on the earth's surface.

'Gaby!' Tara's voice comes from a long way away. 'Are you OK?'

I blink hard and look at her. She is sitting by the window, Kitty asleep in her arms. The light falls on her golden hair and ripped jeans. She looks like a streetwise angel. 'Tara,' I say, 'what happened to that jewellery box?'

She stares at me for a second, then laughs. 'Oh, that,' she says. 'I've still got it. I keep my birth-control pills in it. Shall we make some more coffee? Sober Marco up some more?'

'I'm not drunk,' says Marco, with dignity. 'Jus' tired.' He falls sideways on to the sofa and goes instantly to sleep.

CHAPTER NINETEEN

It is a beautiful Rome evening when we go to Lago di Vico to scatter Dad's ashes. The woods are as dark as a fairy tale and the lake is wide and calm. As we drive along the gravel path, flocks of birds rise into the air, then disappear into the twilight. I walk along the black sand holding Kitty and thinking about Bob.

I haven't heard from him since that morning, two days ago, when he stood with his bag in his hand and told me he was going back to London. I have rung his mobile so often that the number is imprinted on the back of my eyelids when I fall asleep. I have let the phone ring and ring in our London flat as I imagine the rooms – our stereo, television, double bed, books, Kitty's cot – listening in stony silence. 'You can't ring here,' they say. 'This isn't your home any more.' I ring and ring, but I never leave a message. What is there to say?

How can I go home to the flat without Bob? Will he be there or will he have moved out? Am I now a single parent? An image comes back to me of Maria sitting in our parents' house, in her furry slippers, with baby Tara asleep at her feet. Maria was a single parent but that was her choice. She chose not to listen to Lee's voice at the window. I haven't chosen. I still want Bob. I want to open the door of our flat, with its yellow walls and studenty posters, and find him there, waiting for me.

I walk along, holding Kitty against my hip, feeling her weight pulling me to one side. That's it: I feel lopsided without Bob. That night, after my first trip to Lago di Vico, when we were all having supper, I was struck by how uneven the table was. Without Dad and Bob, there weren't enough men. Uncle Bruno is somehow too old and Marco and Sergio too young to count. Ray and David are men, I suppose, but they both seem neutered by association with my sisters. We needed Dad with his sudden laugh or Bob with his dry humour to dilute the atmosphere of babies and recipes and isn't-Sophia-Loren-marvellous-for-her-age? Together, my mother and sisters are too strong a feminine alliance; Dad and Bob are the only men I have ever seen resist their influence. Franco is still an outsider, as he was when he was a child. I remember him at Luneur Park, too scared to ride on the Big Wheel, too scared to join the heart-stopping process of falling in love. So much has changed, but still it is only as a doctor, in the hospital, that he really has any power. He alone was able to help Kitty, and I'll always be grateful to him for that.

And Jonathan. With a jolt, I remember that Jonathan was there that night. Perhaps he no longer seems like a man because he's a priest. I think of his dark face and strong hands, his blue eyes and reluctant smile. No, he's still a man. He must make the nuns' hearts flutter beneath their starched habits. But he no longer matters to me as a man. I realised that when I sat on the sofa beside him and thought of Bob.

Franco's car comes to a halt beside Uncle Bruno's, and Luca is in the passenger seat. It's the first time I've seen him since that kiss in the apartment. Now when I look at him it's like peering through the wrong end of a telescope. He seems immeasurably far away. How could I have thought him lion-like? He is just a man in a dark suit, aloof and formal, part of the scene and yet separate.

There was a heated discussion earlier in the day as to the appropriate dress code for the occasion.

'He wouldn't want us to wear black,' trilled Maria, wrapping rainbow-coloured chiffon round her neck.

'But we should show some respect,' countered Anna accusingly, with an eye on Mosaic's pink plastic sandals.

'I'm wearing my Arsenal shirt,' announced Sergio defiantly. 'Nonno loved Arsenal. He would have wanted me to wear it.' Marco, pale and unusually silent, said nothing. He was wearing a black T-shirt with Kurt Cobain's face on it, like the face of Jesus on the Turin Shroud.

'Girls, girls,' said Uncle Bruno placatingly. 'Let's all wear what we think best. Let's try to make it a happy occasion. A happy day for Enzo.' As he said this he looked sadder than any human being I've ever seen. Anna and Maria fell silent.

Now Luca crunches over the sand to collect the boat. He, of course, knew someone who could lend us one. The rest of the family wait by the shore, Ray skimming stones across the water, Mosaic and Kyle playing in the sand. Tara sits under a tree and stretches out her legs. I'm sure that Anna considers her skirt a good five inches too short. Instinctively, I look for Marco and Sergio but they are absent. My mother and I travelled with Uncle Bruno, Auntie Clara and Maria's family. Anna and David went with Franco. Where are the boys? Did the argument about Arsenal shirts intensify to the extent that they refused to come?

Suddenly I want to be away from the others, at least for a few moments, before Luca arrives with the boat and we are all together for the last time. The green plastic container has been replaced by a handsome plaster urn, which my mother is holding. Someone (Uncle Bruno? Marco?) has tied a red, white and green ribbon around the base. It flutters in the evening sunshine like a medieval banner.

I walk along the shore, Kitty on my shoulder. She is quiet, making little munching noises. Maybe she's hungry. Since her stay in hospital, she no longer rejects solid food. She has become addicted to baby rice and mashed banana. I take a rice cake from my handbag and give it to her to hold. How have I become this person who keeps rice cakes next to her lipstick?

Kitty gives a crow of pleasure. I look round expecting to see Uncle Bruno, for whom she has developed a passion. Instead I see three figures walking towards me across the volcanic sand. The two outside ones are wearing red shirts, like a uniform. The central figure is taller, with red hair lifting in the breeze.

'Bob!' My scream scatters the roosting birds and almost makes my mother drop the urn. Kitty bumps against my shoulder as I run crazily towards my husband.

Miraculously, like a scene from a movie, he runs towards me too. We stop, a few feet apart, and stare at each other.

'You came back,' I say stupidly.

'Of course,' says Bob. 'Did you think I wouldn't?'

'I don't know what I thought.' Tears start in my eyes. Bob puts his arms round me and I breathe in his wonderful comforting smell. He smells of home. 'How did you know where to come?' I ask, raising my head from his shirt.

'Marco told me.'

'*Marco*?'

'Yes, Marco. He got in touch with me.'

'But how?' I wail.

Marco and Sergio, the two figures in red Arsenal shirts, have now caught up with us.

'I sent him a text,' says Marco simply.

'A text?'

'Yes,' says Bob gravely.

'Cm bk Gby nds u.'

'Cm bk Gby nds u?'

'Says it all, doesn't it?' says Bob admiringly.

'I didn't know where he was, you see,' explains Marco patiently, 'so I thought I'd send him a text.'

'Where *were* you?' I ask petulantly, putting Kitty into Bob's arms. She laughs and spits rice cake into his neck.

'At a hotel by the airport. I didn't go home. I just . . . needed to think.'

'Me too,' I say.

'I love you,' says Bob.

'I love you too,' I say.

'So,' Marco continues, raising his voice, 'he texted me back and I said to meet me and Serg and we'd show him where to come. I knew he wouldn't want to miss scattering Nonno's ashes. After all, he's one of the family, isn't he?'

'Yes,' I say, and realise that this was what I thought when I saw the three figures walking along the lake shore. Bob is more than my husband: he is one of the family. He is my mother's son-in-law, Anna and Maria's brother-in-law, Marco and Sergio's uncle. He is bound to me now with so many ties that I couldn't sever them even if I wanted to. And I'm not the only person who loves him. Kitty loves him, my mother loves him, Marco loves him. And my dad loved him.

Luca guides the boat far out into the lake. In his dark suit he looks a little like Charon rowing across the River Styx. The water is still, silent, reflecting the blue twilight.

We reach the centre. The water is so clear that we can see the stony bed below, the fish gliding to and fro beneath us. The forest rises round us on all sides. Silently, my mother hands the urn to Uncle Bruno. He removes the lid, takes out a handful of ashes and bows his head. His lips move for a long time but when he speaks it is only to say a few words: '*Nelle tue mani, Signore.*' Into Your hands, Lord. Then he throws the ashes on to the lake.

Anna is next. She stands proudly in the prow of the boat, her black dress fluttering behind her. She says the Our Father, closes her eyes and throws ashes into the water.

Maria takes her place. Her rainbow scarf flaps defiantly in Anna's face. She holds her handful of ashes tightly. In the other hand, she holds a much-thumbed copy of *The Rubáiyát* of Omar Khayyám. I am slightly worried that we'll have to listen to reams of wisdom from this secular Bible, but Maria is mercifully brief. Unlike Anna, her voice is low, almost inaudible.

'Ah, make the most of what we yet may spend
Before we too into the Dust descend;
Dust unto Dust, and under Dust, to lie,
Sans Wine, sans Song, sans Singer, and – sans End.'

She holds out her hand over the water and lets the ashes sift gently between her fingers.

It is my turn. I was dreading putting my hand into the urn but the ashes feel dry and oddly comforting. I hold on to Bob tightly with the other. Although we are nowhere near the Tiber, I say Dad's favourite lines from his favourite poem:

'O Tiber! Father Tiber!
To whom the Romans pray,
A Roman's life, a Roman's arms,
Take thou in charge this day!'

Then something makes me draw my hand right back and take a mighty throw so that the ashes scatter like rain on the lake's surface.

My mother takes the urn. She stands quite still, holding it to her breast. For a moment, I think that she will refuse to let go but then she walks to the prow and tips the urn so that the rest of the ashes pour into the clear waters of the lake.

'Goodbye, my darling,' she says.

Luca turns the boat and we head back to the shore.

CHAPTER TWENTY

Two days later we gather for another ceremony. This time it is in a church, with a priest duly in attendance. And not just any priest: Jonathan is standing at the door to welcome us, smiling widely, robes brilliant in the sunshine.

I carry Kitty carefully, trying not to crush her beautiful white dress, a present from Auntie Carla. I, too, am wearing a new outfit, bought the day before: a long red skirt and a fitted black jacket. My hair has been cut and streaked. I feel five years younger and ten pounds lighter. I have even painted my nails the palest pearly pink. They peep at me from the open toes of my expensive new sandals. I can hardly walk but that isn't important somehow.

Tara came with me to advise on the haircutting and

clothes-buying. At the frightening salon, full of Roman women with long red nails and manes of expensively high-lighted hair, she sat beside me and I felt some comfort in the reflection of her youthful beauty. As I sat in front of the light-studded mirror, Tara said, 'Luca asked me out.'

'But he's got a girlfriend,' I said, before I realised that perhaps I shouldn't have known that.

Tara shrugged. 'I've got a boyfriend. It's only a date.'

'I didn't know you had a boyfriend.'

'Well, I didn't think it was fair to introduce him to all the family at once. Especially, you know, at a time like this.'

I grinned at her reflection. 'You were afraid.'

Tara smiled back, rather tensely. 'Well, my mum always flirts with my boyfriends. It's so embarrassing. And Auntie Anna will ask if he's a Catholic.'

'And is he?'

'Of course. He's Italian.'

The day before, I went with Anna to the Vatican City to see St Peter's Basilica. I hadn't wanted to go but Bob had gone with the boys to see a motor race and Mum said she would look after Kitty. Although I've been to Rome many times, I've always tried to avoid St Peter's. I've visited it, of course, and marvelled at the optical illusion of the columns in the piazza, which merge into one if you stand in the right place. I've climbed to the top of the dome and looked down on the roof-tops of Rome. I've worshipped at Michelangelo's *Pietà* and before the twisted Bernini columns of the high altar. But I've never really liked the place. It's too big, too full of tourists with whirring cameras. There's no sense that it's a church, much less the most important Catholic church in the world. 'Full in the panting heart of Rome, beneath St Peter's mighty dome . . .' went a hymn we sang half-heartedly at school, but I have never felt that St Peter's really is in the heart of Rome. I suppose that to me Rome is still a pagan city.

But Anna had got it into her head that she wanted to see St Peter's. More, she wanted to see the tombs underneath where the pagan and Christian dead lie side by side. Maria shuddered at the thought of so much bad karma in one place and even David thought he'd rather spend the morning dozing on Uncle Bruno's balcony, so I stepped up for the treat.

Anna swept past the columns, fountains and obelisk, intent on reaching the basilica. I trailed behind her, getting in the way of a thousand photographs, avoiding street salesmen trying to sell me T-shirts with those touching fingers from the Sistine Chapel on the front. Anna was waiting impatiently by the bronze doors. 'Hurry up, Gaby – we haven't much time!'

'We have all the time in the world,' I said mutinously. 'It's the eternal city, after all.' Anna ignored me.

At the altar, lit by a million flickering candles, Anna genuflected. I sat behind her, wondering who puts out the candles at night. Perhaps I should light one for Dad. That's what you're supposed to do, after all. But he was at peace, on Lago di Vico, not there, in that gloomy, magnificent building. He wasn't really a man for church. It's outside a church that I will remember him, hovering in the porch, smiling enigmatically, ready to ask the priest tricky questions about original sin.

Because Dad died suddenly, he didn't receive the last rites. At the time, this worried Anna dreadfully. 'Well, Anna,' my mother would say patiently, 'we could hardly have ordered it on the off-chance. He wasn't expecting to die. He was just going out to pick some roses.' It was only weeks afterwards that I realised the roses would have been for me. Dad was anticipating celebrating the birth of my baby. He was planning to give me flowers.

My guidebook tells me that Vatican means 'prophecy'. It

is built on the eighth hill of Rome, where the ancient kings used to consult the sibyls. Here Caligula built a circus, added to by Nero. Christianity is only a recent addition, a crisp white icing on an old, rich cake.

'Come on, Gaby.' Anna was hurrying me again. 'Let's get to the necropolis.' Great, I thought. I can't wait.

It was cold among the tombs. Apparently the pagan graves overlooked the circus, so the dead could enjoy the games. I can't believe how bright the tombs are, red, gold and blue, 'little sitting rooms for the soul', as someone described them. Anna paused before one and pointed out Christ depicted as the sun god Helios. Pagan and Christian fused together.

As we walked through the street of graves, I asked her, 'How can you be so sure that there is life after death?'

Anna's face was shadowy in the darkness. 'Who says I'm sure?'

I gaped at her. I wanted to say, 'But, if you're not sure, who is?' In our family, Anna *is* Catholicism. We moan about her and respect her as if she is the Mother Church herself. Her word is law on all matters religious. She is surely magnificently free of doubt. 'Aren't you sure?' I whispered at last.

'Oh, I have doubts,' she said rather proudly. 'I have lots

of doubts. Once, when I was at school, I thought I believed in God but not in the Catholic Church. Now I think I might believe in the Catholic Church but not in God. Do you know what I mean?'

'Sort of,' I said. The Church, in all its cake-baking, flower-arranging reality, does not loom as large in my life as it does in Anna's.

'I envy you,' said Anna. 'You really believe, don't you?'

'Me?' I said, amazed.

'Yes. When I came into that hospital room and saw you with your rosary, praying, I thought how lucky you were to believe so completely.'

Praying? Was that really what I was doing? I thought back to that terrible charged night and saw myself standing at Kitty's bedside, holding a rosary, looking for all the world like those headscarved women you see at the back of Catholic churches anywhere in the world. Women with faded prayer-books, the pages blistered from overuse, women who still cover their heads at mass, even though this hasn't been the rule for over thirty years. I knew I didn't belong to that mumbling, bead-clicking regiment, but I no longer belonged in the clean light of scepticism either.

We were near the place where St Peter is meant to be buried. Jammed around him were the tombs of people anxious to be near the greatest Apostle. Inside the Vatican itself, there is a statue of St Peter in black marble. The foot has been worn smooth by the kisses of millions of pilgrims over the years. Distorted with love. St Peter, pray for us. Vicar of Christ, pray for us. How stupid, you think, how ignorant, how superstitious. And then, a little voice inside you says . . . and yet, and yet . . .

'I don't know what I believe,' I said.

This church could not be more different from the morbid splendour of St Peter's or the sepulchral beauty of the convent of Maria Assumpta. It is a modern, rather ugly building round the corner from Uncle Bruno's apartment. White-painted walls display modern Stations of the Cross in chrome and glass. 'Blimey,' says Bob, peering at one. 'No wonder he was cross.'

My mother, Uncle Bruno and Auntie Carla are inside the church. This is Auntie Carla's territory and she is everywhere: kissing a passing nun, lighting candles at a side altar and soothing the elderly parish priest, who is plainly rather disgruntled at having Jonathan usurp his role. 'He is an old family friend,' I hear Auntie Carla hiss. But he isn't. Not really.

Maria and Ray arrive with Tara, stunning in a white trouser suit. Mosaic and Kyle are playing with toy cars given to them by Uncle Bruno. Kyle sings, 'The wheels on the bus go round and round,' and I am reminded of Dad's funeral. I remember one of his university colleagues, a woman called Marisa, singing, 'Va, pensiero' from Verdi's *Nabucco*, the song of the Hebrew slaves longing for their homeland and the unofficial Italian anthem. At the time I wondered why my mother had chosen it but now I understand. Dad wanted to come home. I might not have been able to imagine him living in Italy but this was where he felt he belonged. Like Horatius on the bridge he was a Roman first and last. 'Never forget,' he said to me that night on the Spanish Steps, 'this is my city.'

Now Franco and Paola are here with Anna and David on their heels. Next come Marco and Sergio, Marco wearing a Ferrari T-shirt. Jonathan greets Anna with a kiss on the cheek. When he approaches me, I hold out my hand and he clasps it with priestly warmth. Bob shakes his hand too, his face bland. Kitty starts to cry.

Bob and I, jiggling our child, move into the front pew. I

remember our wedding day, me laughing with Dad as we walked up the aisle. Funny how you walk up the aisle a daughter and walk back a wife. But, then, the whole service is designed to exclude the woman herself as much as possible. You are given away by one man to another, all dolled up in sacrificial white. 'Having given Anna away,' said my dad, 'I've decided to raffle the next two.'

Jonathan gazes down at us with the perfect face, solemn yet serene. I wonder if he practises it in front of a mirror. 'What name have you given to this child?' he asks.

'Kitty,' say Bob and I. Then we look at each other. 'Kitty Anna-Maria,' I say. I can't resist a glance at my sisters. Anna is staring straight ahead but Maria's face breaks into a wide grin so that she looks exactly like the teenage Maria, the one who used to ride pillion on Lee's motorbike.

As I hear the name out loud for the first time, it occurs to me that not only have we given Kitty my sisters' names, we have also given her an Italian identity. As Kitty Duncan she was a normal British baby, not too posh or too common, not too outlandish or too ordinary. She was your perfect middle-class baby, standard issue at playgroups around the country. But now she is Kitty Anna-Maria, a child with Italian heritage. And just as Mrs Duncan was not me, plain Kitty Duncan is no longer my baby. Now she is Kitty Anna-Maria. She belongs to England and to Italy. Just like me.

Jonathan asks the parents and godparents to gather round the font. We have asked Franco and Tara to be Kitty's godparents. I had thought of asking Anna and Maria to be joint godmothers but they are her aunts. She will have them all her life, just as I will. So I asked Franco, who will always be associated in my mind with saving Kitty's life and Tara whom I love like a . . . not like a daughter, not like a sister, but a sort of combination of the two. Like a niece, I suppose.

Jonathan blesses the water, then asks us to make the baptismal promises on Kitty's behalf. Our voices sound strong in the half-empty church.

'Do you reject Satan?'

'I do.'

'And all his works?'

'I do.'

'And all his empty promises?'

'I do.'

As Bob said earlier, 'Tricky one.'

'Do you believe in the Holy Spirit, the holy Catholic

Church, the communion of saints, the forgiveness of sins, the resurrection of the body and life everlasting?'

'I do,' we say. After all, what harm can it do?

Kitty cries lustily as Jonathan splashes the holy water on her head. 'Kitty Anna-Maria, I baptise you in the name of the Father, the Son and the Holy Spirit.' Dad always said it was a good sign if a baby cries at its baptism as it's getting rid of the devil. Kitty is certainly banishing her devil to the far corners of the earth. Jonathan is pale and flustered. As I said, babies really aren't his thing.

Raising his voice over Kitty's wails, Jonathan directs Bob to light a candle from the fat Easter candle on the altar. He holds it carefully as we go back to our seats. 'Receive the Light of Christ,' says Jonathan, solemnly, evidently relieved that he is no longer holding Kitty.

He is now on the home stretch and gabbles the last words of the service, something about a new birth by water and the forgiveness of sins. Kitty's sobs are decreasing in volume, like the Big Wheel starting its descent. I find myself breathing in rhythm with her, willing her to be quiet. Then I hear Anna behind me saying, 'Amen,' loudly and it is over. Jonathan smiles at us from the altar but doesn't come closer. Auntie

Carla is sobbing happily. Kitty gets hold of my newly smart hair and pulls hard. I yelp and everyone laughs. Bob takes Kitty and holds her up so she can see everyone. He looks like a victorious football manager holding aloft the FA Cup. Marco and Sergio must think so, too, because they start to hum the theme from *Match of the Day*.

As we leave the church, I find myself walking beside Maria. She is wearing a cream linen dress and something – maybe the lack of sequins, beads and necklaces – makes her look younger than usual and rather vulnerable. Then I realise that the cream dress reminds me of our joint first-communion dress. Today, with her hennaed hair tied back in a scarf, she could be the Maria who posed in our garden with her prayer book and rosary beside Dad's beloved roses.

'That was nice,' she says abruptly, 'giving Kitty our names.'

'That's OK,' I say, embarrassed. 'They're nice names.'

'Should have been me first, though,' she says, more in her usual manner. 'Maria-Anna. That sounds better.'

'Maria,' I say suddenly, 'do you remember the Golden Boys?'

'Who?'

'The boys in the apartment below us. That summer in Rome. Giancarlo and Massimo.'

Maria's face eases into a slow smile. 'Giancarlo and Massimo. The ones who took us to the Spanish Steps. The ones we met at Luneur Park.'

'You snogged Massimo. Don't you remember?'

Kyle runs up to us and leaps on to Maria's back, almost overbalancing her. When she straightens, she says vaguely, 'No . . . I don't think so. I think I liked the other one anyway.'

'Do you remember when Anna saw that ghost? At the Forum?'

'Yes,' says Maria. 'That I do remember. I saw it too.'

She says it so matter-of-factly, standing by the church steps in the bright September sunshine, that even knowing Maria's capacity to believe in the supernatural, I stare dumbly at her. 'You saw it?'

'Yes. A sort of misty figure in white robes gliding down the steps.'

'The steps that weren't there?'

'Yes,' she says briskly, dispatching Kyle to play with Mosaic. 'Why? Didn't you believe us?'

'No,' I say lamely. 'I thought you were making it up.'

'Well, we weren't.'

For a moment, I feel slightly put out. Excluded again, outside the action. Gaby and the girls. But then I feel rather cheered. If the ghost exists, then who is to say what else does? God? Eternal life? Auntie Carla's pigeon spirit?

Maria is looking at me curiously. 'Have you asked Anna about the ghost?' she asks.

'No.'

'Oh, well,' says Maria, unconcerned. 'She doesn't believe in anything now. Only God.'

It's on the tip of my tongue to say that I'm not so sure now what Anna believes, but I don't. Instead I say, 'What about you? What do you believe in?'

Maria grins, her old, irresistible grin. 'Me? I believe in everything. Just to be on the safe side.'

Back at Uncle Bruno's apartment we have yet another huge meal. Kitty Anna-Maria so enjoys being the centre of attention in her frilly white dress that I wonder how she'll cope when we get home and all she has to entertain her are me, the *Teletubbies* and a weekly mother-and-baby group at the

Methodist church hall. And what about when I go back to work? What then?

It is very hot in the crowded apartment and, after tiramisu, ice cream and a truly sumptuous christening cake, I go out on to the balcony for some fresh air and to surreptitiously loosen my new skirt. Kitty has fallen asleep on the sofa and Bob is playing cards with Marco, Sergio and Auntie Carla. This is a brave move as Auntie Carla is an absolute whizz at cards, a cold-eyed Vegas gambler hidden within the body of a sweet elderly lady.

I am standing there among the lemon trees, watching night fall on Rome when I hear a step behind me. It's Jonathan.

'Beautiful evening,' he says.

'Yes.'

'Are you going back tomorrow?'

'Bob and I have decided to stay on for a few days.'

We are silent. I'm thinking how odd it still sounds to say 'Bob and I' in that married-couple way. Will I ever get used to saying 'We think' and 'We've decided' or will I always feel like a fraud?

'I'm glad it went so well,' says Jonathan, at last.

'The christening?'

'No. I meant finding a resting place for your father.'

'Lago di Vico is beautiful.'

'It is,' says Jonathan, turning to look at me for what feels like the first time since that party in Paddington so many years ago. 'But your father isn't there. He's in you. Never forget that. He's in you, in Kitty, in all your family.'

I study him for a minute. 'Jonathan,' I say, 'you made a terrible boyfriend but you're a pretty good priest.' Then I kiss his cheek quickly and go in to join my family.

CHAPTER TWENTY-ONE

Fiumicino airport. Once again, Bob and I are standing at a check-in desk, surrounded by our luggage. This time it includes several carrier bags of new clothes for Kitty and me, plus a bag from the Ferrari souvenir shop for Bob. It doesn't include the green plastic container, whose contents we have left behind. '*Arrivederci, Roma*', the song goes. Goodbye to Rome. Only I don't feel as if we're saying goodbye.

Yesterday Bob and I took Kitty to Lago di Vico for a picnic. I was worried that this might seem a morbid choice for a day out, but in the event it was lovely. The weather had suddenly become hot again and Kitty sat naked in the clear waters of the lake. Bob and I lounged on the beach, basking in the last sun of the year. As I sifted the black sand between my fingers, I felt as if I were lying on a sea of mortality. All the rocks that, over millions of years, had become worn into sand. All the volcanic ash from the long-extinct volcano, whose crater now formed the lake in front of us. All the people, from Ancient Romans to Victorian travellers via Romantic poets like Keats, who had come to Rome to die; all the millions of people who have visited Rome over the years. Even in ancient times the city had a population of a million. All those people. Now dust and ashes. Somehow, lying there under the hot Italian sun, it was a strangely comforting thought.

Afterwards, we drove round the lake in our little hired Fiat and found a children's playground, run down, full of rusting slides shaped like dinosaurs and sea creatures. Next to it a café was attached to a huge open-air stage where, peeling posters informed us, Zippo's circus was soon to appear. The place had an abandoned feel, like a modern-day Pompeii. I got into conversation with a couple at the next table who told me that Lago di Vico used to be popular with rich young people, the *rampanti*, as they are called in Italy, but now it is no longer the place to be and the cafés, restaurants and children's play areas are falling into disrepair.

'Would you like to buy a holiday house here?' asked Bob. Like many couples, one of our favourite conversations is about where we would have our holiday home, if we decided to buy one. So far the locations have ranged from Tuscany and the Dordogne to Bulgaria and the Scottish Highlands.

'What – you mean now it's no longer fashionable?'

'Well, property might be cheaper.'

'I don't know,' I said, looking out over the lake, which today was full of little boats. 'It's a lovely place but maybe we'd get bored after a while.'

Then Kitty signalled that she was bored by starting to cry and we got up and took her to the swings.

When we had got back from scattering Dad's ashes on the lake, Bob and I talked all night.

'I didn't really fancy Luca,' I said. 'He was just . . . there. Like the Colosseum.'

'He fancied you,' said Bob. 'His eyes were on you all the time. All that "Would you like a baby seat?", "Let me help with the *bambina*," "I've brought you some milk." He never stopped watching you.'

I remember Luca's strange yellow eyes. I had thought he was a lion but now I reckon he's more like a wolf. It's a suitably Roman comparison.

'Anyway,' Bob said later, 'I wasn't that worried about Luca.

I mean, I was angry and everything, but I knew it wasn't anything serious. I was more worried about the other one.'

'Which other one?'

'The priest. St Francis of Assisi. You know.'

It's funny, but I'd never thought Bob might be jealous of Jonathan. He always dismissed him with a joke: 'a bloke in a skirt,' 'Father Brown,' 'Holy Joe.' When I first told Bob, all those years ago, on the beach in Crete, that my last boyfriend had left me to become a priest, he said, 'Blimey. Is that what happens to all your exes?' At the time I had been a bit hurt by the way he dismissed my great tragedy, but I also felt intense relief. Bob thought it was funny. Maybe it wasn't the huge, all-consuming grief I had imagined. Maybe Jonathan's choice wasn't the stuff of grand opera but of comedy.

Now it turns out that Bob had taken him seriously, after all.

'When anyone mentioned him, you went all silent and twitchy. I thought you were still in love with him.'

'Of course I wasn't!' I snapped, too quickly.

'He was so bloody romantic. Swooping around like a sodding great crow. Looking all tortured and heroic.'

I laughed. 'I suppose I did think he was romantic once but then, talking to him, he seemed a bit sad. It's a lonely life, being a priest.'

Bob shrugged. 'I don't see that. All those nuns fluttering around you. All those women like your sister.'

'No children,' I said.

We were lying on the bed by Kitty's cot and, by mutual unspoken agreement, we got up to look at her. She was sleeping deeply, cheeks flushed, arms flung over her head.

'No,' Bob agreed. 'No children.'

Today it is Bob, our child and me. Just the three of us. As soon as Kitty was born I worried that Bob and I weren't spending enough time together as a couple. All the magazines had warned me about this. Bob would start seeing me as a mother rather than as a wife, our sex life would lose its sparkle, we would become one of those couples with nothing to say to each other in restaurants. In the first months, I made a big effort to get babysitters so that Bob and I could go out together in the evenings. Invariably it was a disaster. I would feel anxious at being away from Kitty, my breasts would ache and leak, I would become tearful and want to come home. Our lovely intimate conversations would descend into bickering about who was the tiredest: Bob, after a ten-hour day at the office, or me, having looked after Kitty all day. The only time we would grow animated was in discussing Kitty: how she was prettier than any other baby at the mother-and-baby group, how she had sat up weeks before the books said she should, how she understood every word we said.

Now, pushing her on a baby swing, it seemed that we were, at last, together again. We were a family, a threesome. There was no point in trying to pretend that Kitty didn't exist. Bob and I had to accept that we were going to be boring about babies for a while, that neither of us would get enough sleep, that we would lose some of our (childless) friends, that we might have to move to a house with a garden, that we might not be able to go skiing every year. Perhaps we were sinking into dull domesticity but, then, it felt as right as our feet sinking into the warm sand as we walked along the shore.

On the drive back to the hotel, I told Bob I wanted to return to work part-time. I missed the office, I wanted to wear my suits again and sit behind my own desk (after I'd forcibly ejected Toby). But it was no good my pretending that everything would be the same. I didn't want to work until nine every night and only see Kitty when she was asleep. I didn't want to be in New York or Frankfurt when she took her first steps or said her first words. I wanted her and I wanted my work. It was the first time in my life that I had ever wanted two opposite things simultaneously.

'Why don't I give up work and look after her?' asked Bob, only half joking.

'You earn more money,' I said. This is a sore point between us. 'And, besides, I suppose I don't want you to.'

I have learned a lot of things during the last few days in Italy. I have learned that I would rather be married to Bob than to Jonathan. I have learned that my nieces and nephews are no longer children, and that even Anna has doubts. I have learned that I would support Arsenal over Roma and that I do believe in God. But the most important thing I have learned is that I am the centre of Kitty's world. At first I resented this. I felt I had no life of my own – everything was Kitty's: my body, my time, my sleep. But now I feel a sort of pride in my absorption in her. I have looked after her on my own; I have sat by her bed and willed her back into life, when only my touch and voice would do. Of course, I know that that wasn't because I am special: it was because I was there.

If Bob looked after Kitty all the time, he would be the one. Later on, he would be the one she called in the night, the one whose kiss could cure her scraped knees and the only one who could do Pooh Bear's voice in exactly the right way. And although Kitty's need for me at times feels too intense and claustrophobic, I can't give it up.

'Did you really want a third child?' I asked my mother, at some time during that endless night at the hospital.

'Of course!' she said, shocked. 'We both loved babies.'

'But you'd just got your life together. You'd gone back to work.'

Mum laughed. 'You can have a life and be a mother, you know.'

'Did you resent us holding you back in your career?' I asked.

'No,' said my mother, 'but I wanted both. I wanted you and a career. Is that so bad?'

I had had a working mother and I'd survived. Kitty will survive too. I know I'm really thinking of myself. I don't want to give her up, let someone else become the centre of her world. But, equally, I don't want to give up work and being someone else outside the home, being Gabriella de Angelis again. So

I'm going to try to do both things and risk doing them badly. Perhaps that's what is meant by the phrase 'having it all'.

Bob and I check in our luggage and the escalator carries us smoothly up towards the departure lounge. We are rising above everything: above Rome, Italy, my family, work, all the everyday worries of the world. We are leaving everything behind – everything except Kitty, who is strapped smugly to Bob's chest. Wherever we go now, she goes with us, in spirit if not in flesh. When I'm away from her, I can feel the physical imprint of her body, the smoothness of her cheek against mine, the smell of her hair, the scratch of her fingernails. My body feels used in a way it never has before, my hair is pulled and my back aches, yet I also feel alive in a way I never have before. When we got back from Lago di Vico that last time and had put Kitty to bed, Bob and I made love on the sitting-room floor while outside the tourists shouted, laughed and threw coins into the fountain. And our love-making was more intense, more exciting, more *alive* than it had ever been. It was as if we had been on separate journeys, full of danger and temptation, and reached our destination changed but closer than ever, more aware of our need for each other.

Our flight is called and we gather our things together,

self-conscious at being given priority in boarding the plane. 'Families with children first.' We feel the hatred of other passengers boring into our backs and exchange guilty smiles with the other parents, those struggling with hot, angry children and an array of frightening plastic toys. We have all this to look forward to. At the moment, Kitty is fast asleep and our parenthood seems a serene and manageable thing. I'm sure this will change when the flight is in progress and Kitty screams because her ears hurt. I can already feel the sympathetic glances of the other parents as I give in and press the scarlet little face to my breast. At present, though, I feel pleasantly free as I carry the nappy-bag and let Bob hold our sleeping baby. The evening air is warm as we walk towards the plane, its red, white and green livery reminding me of the ribbon fluttering on the urn as we scattered Dad's ashes. We climb the steps on to the plane and I forget to look back and say goodbye to Italy.

As the plane climbs into the clouds, I think that at last I know who I am. I am Italian and English. I am an Arsenal supporter and a Catholic. I am an accountant and a mother. I am a daughter, a sister and an aunt. I am a wife. I am myself. I am Gabriella de Angelis.

My father is dead but I am still alive.

ACKNOWLEDGEMENTS

With thanks to Mary-Anne Harrington for her sensitive and inspiring editing and to all at Review for their hard work on my behalf. Thanks also to my wonderful agent, Tif Loenhis. Special thanks to Mandy Merron for telling me about accountancy and for being living proof that accountants aren't boring. Thanks also to Heather Williams because it wouldn't be the same without her.

Love and thanks always to my children, Alexander and Juliet, and my husband, Andrew, to whom this book is dedicated.

Thanks to Anna Furlan Robinson for correcting my Italian, and to my sister Giulia for being the perfect companion in Rome.

Read on for the first chapters of

The Secret of Villa Serena

CHAPTER 1

Thoughts from Tuscany
By Emily Robertson

Today, I have been thinking about the rush hour. About my journey to work in London: the brisk walk through petrol fumes and flapping bin bags, the brief but violent struggle to board the tube, the journey spent snugly wedged under somebody's armpit, apologising whenever people tread on me, the surge up the escalator, and finally the arrival, exhausted, at my desk.

My journey to work now is as follows: awake to the operatic sound of my neighbours' new cockerel, throw open the heavy wooden shutters and allow the morning sun to infiltrate every wood-beamed, stone-floored inch of the bedroom, go downstairs to a cup of espresso, a slice of ripe *melone* and a handful of figs, shower in the bathroom *which looks out onto four uninterrupted acres of breathtaking Tuscan hillside, dress in a thin cotton skirt and T-shirt, then walk slowly to my table on the terrazzo under the olive trees. Sit. Think. Breathe.*

On days like this I don't worry about Spouse's latest idea to buy a pig and set up as a truffle hunter. I don't worry about Eldest Daughter's predilection for sitting in the piazza eyeing up passing Italian youths, or Younger Daughter's refusal to eat anything other than peeled grapes and Mars bars. I don't worry that dear old Romano has told us that we must start the olive oil harvest when the moon is in Taurus. Or that the acqua minerale *which flows, amazingly, from our very own well has slowed to a sulky trickle. No, I don't worry about anything. I sit and I think.*

And, when I think of the rush hour, I smile.

'Mum. The water's gone off again.'

Emily Robertson looks at her elder daughter who is standing in a patch of golden sunlight. Behind her the silvery olive grove merges with the pale-yellow hills, deepening to ochre where they meet the sky, the pine trees are almost mesmerisingly dark and the house itself, terracotta in the evening light, is now bleached to the palest pink. It is all relentlessly beautiful and it gives Emily no pleasure at all.

'Oh dear,' she says weakly. On the table in front of her the laptop glints and she presses 'send'. Another 'Thoughts from Tuscany' is dispatched.

'Oh dear? Is that it? Oh dear? Is that all you can say?' Siena's righteous fury threatens to catapult her into the air, like a modern-day Assumption of the Virgin. 'I've got to meet Giancarlo in an hour and I can't finish washing my hair. There's no water anywhere in this stupid house. Christ! No wonder Dad doesn't spend any time here.'

'He's coming home tomorrow,' says Emily, assailed by a tiny, a very tiny, twinge of fear.

Siena ignores this. 'What about my hair?'

'There's some water in the kettle,' says Emily. 'I'll get that.'

Emily rises from the table and winces as she steps out from the shade of the terrace. It is nearly midday and the sun is at its hottest. Emily feels it pounding on her head as she crosses the parched grass and climbs the shallow stone steps to the kitchen door. Siena follows her, silent and watchful, refusing to be placated.

The kitchen is dark and cool. Emily's bare feet shrink with delight as they touch the cold stone floor. The remains of breakfast, cornflakes, Marmite, Coco Pops, all brought from

England, are still on the table. The kettle on the gas hob (impossible to find electric kettles in Italy) is still half full of water. Emily offers this humbly to Siena.

Siena mutters grudging thanks and makes her way out of the kitchen towards the narrow staircase that leads to the bedrooms. In the doorway she stops. Parting shots are her speciality.

'By the way, Mum,' she says. 'Your skirt's ripped at the back. Did you notice?'

Emily's younger daughter, Paris, writes in her diary. *O dark, dark, dark, amid the blaze of noon.* She pauses for a moment to look at the words, satisfyingly black against the empty page, and to think that there is probably not a thirteen-year-old in the world who could quote *Samson Agonistes* in such an offhand yet utterly relevant way. After all, here she is, with the horrible, white-hot Italian sun blazing in through her window (not quite noon, true, but all great writers take liberties with the facts) and she is, quite simply, in *black despair.*

Slightly comforted at the thought of the blackness of her despair, Paris rolls over onto her back and stares at the ceiling. She is wearing just a white vest and football shorts but she is boiling; limp and exhausted from the heat. Her mother has given her a fan for her bedroom but all it seems to do is move the hot air to different places. The ceilings of the house are Emily's pride and joy, dark beams arching across authentic brickwork, like a cathedral, Emily says. But, to Paris, looking up, it feels more like being inside the rib-cage of some prehistoric monster. Unspoilt, Mum says, like going back in time. That's just it: going back and back until, in the end, you are just nothingness, just floating in some awful dark matter. The sun shines and the crickets sing and nothing ever happens, except that she, Paris, gets more and more unhappy and nobody ever notices.

I hate this house, she writes for what feels like the fifty millionth time. *I hate Tuscany and I hate Italy and I hate having no friends and nothing to do and just lying on my bed waiting for it to get cooler so that I might, perhaps, go out for a walk.* She pauses, thinking how much she hates the phrase 'go out for a walk'. Her mum used to use it when they still lived in London: Sunday afternoons, too much lunch, football on the telly, 'Let's go out for a walk.' Dad was always too tired after a week at work, Charlie was too little and it was no good even asking Siena to do anything that sounded like exercise so it was always just her and Mum. The long, tedious slog past the shuttered shops, up to the common where families tried to fly kites in the windless air and small, shaven-headed boys played football with what looked like random violence. If they had had a dog, it might have been different, a dog would give purpose to a walk but Charlie (of course!) had asthma. 'Another reason to move to a warmer climate,' Mum had trilled. Another reason to hate Charlie.

A walk, she writes. *You can't even walk in these stupid hills because they're full of horrible loose stones and bits of tree roots and, just as soon as you get to the bottom of one hill, there's another one right there in front of you. There's not one flat bit of land in the whole of Tuscany and, if there was, the boys at school would build a football pitch on it because football is literally* all *they ever think about.*

She lies back, exhausted with hatred, and the door opens (no knock, of course) and Siena drifts in, wet hair plastered against her shoulders.

'Paris, can I borrow your red scrunchy?'

'No,' answers Paris, eyes closed.

'Oh, for God's sake!' Siena is furious though not, deep down, actually surprised. 'What do you need it for anyway? You can't use it now that your hair's so short.'

'I'm keeping it as an ornament,' says Paris, eyes still closed.

'Christ, you're pathetic,' Siena retreats to the door where she tries one last, desperate parting short. 'I'll tell Mum.'

Paris lets out a snort of contemptuous laughter. It is meant to silence Siena once and for all – and it does.

Olimpia, Emily's cleaner and part-time childminder, parks her wheezing, three-wheeled van outside the open door of the kitchen. Then she tenderly lifts down three-year-old Charlie who fell asleep on the drive home from his nursery school, where he goes three mornings a week to sing Italian songs and create pictures out of dried pasta and glittery glue.

'*Caríssimo*,' Olimpia drops a kiss on his tousled, blond head. Charlie wakes up and pulls away irritably. Sometimes, when he is in a good mood or wants to annoy his mother, he will sit on Olimpia's lap and let her sing to him about a cricket and a grasshopper who are getting married. At other times he is cold and distant to his mother and to Olimpia, who both continue to adore him unreservedly. 'It's not even as if he's especially interesting,' wail Siena and Paris, united on this subject as on no other.

'He's nothing special,' Paris points out. 'He's just small. Midgets are small.'

'He's a boy,' replies Siena darkly.

In the kitchen, Emily is dispiritedly repairing her dress. She can't be bothered to take it off so she has twisted it round and is sewing up the spilt with large, untidy stitches. Olimpia, Charlie in her arms, watches critically.

'*Uno strappo*,' explains Emily apologetically. She feels that Italian women would never tear their clothes and, if they did, they would have little women (probably Albanians) to mend them. Anyway, no Italian woman would be seen dead in ankle-length floral cotton.

'*Carlito é stanco*,' counters Olimpia. Sometimes, she will only speak to Emily in Italian, at other times she demonstrates considerable, though colloquial, fluency in English.

'Charlie! Baby!' Emily's face changes completely. Paris, watching from the doorway, thinks that her mother's face goes slack and pouchy whenever she looks at her youngest child. She prefers Emily's face tight and animated, every emotion signalled in advance, as it had been in the golden days before Charlie's birth. When they had lived in London.

'Want chocolate,' demands Charlie, in the whine he has developed since discovering that it works in two languages.

'Baby,' says Emily, 'we agreed. Only a tiny piece after your lunch. Now what have we got for lunch? Pasta? Eggy?'

It is no good. Charlie's mouth goes square and he howls to the newly restored ceiling that he wants chocolate and he wants it now, he does, he does, he does. Neither he nor Olimpia think it worth mentioning that he had two fingers of a Kit-Kat in the car.

Paris glides from the room like a ghost. When she was a child they had only had chocolate for a treat, at birthdays or at Christmas. She still remembers the taste of the chocolate money that they had in their stockings at Christmas, milky and foreign, not like proper chocolate at all. Come to think of it, not unlike Italian chocolate. Mum says that Italian chocolate is better than English because it contains fewer additives. It has become obvious to Paris that it is the additives that make it nice. She thinks of Italian chocolate, ponced up in blue and silver bags and tied with bows, and she thinks of Mars bars, as solid and vivid in their black and red livery as the God of War himself. Her mouth waters. It seems a long time since breakfast (three perfectly peeled grapes and a breadstick) but she has promised herself not to eat anything else. More than that, it's a kind of deal. If she doesn't eat, things will get better: Mum will stop mooning over Charlie and ignoring everyone else, Dad will come home more, and Siena will just simply go away. It's all linked, in some complicated way that she doesn't quite understand, to the gnawing feeling in her stomach. A feeling which, uncomfortable though it might be, has become almost company, almost a friend.

As Paris reaches the kitchen door, the mosquito whine of a Vespa announces the arrival of Giancarlo. Thin and almost frighteningly dark, he grins at Paris before calling loudly for Siena. Don't come running, Paris silently urges her sister, make him get off his bloody bike at least. But an ecstatic cry of, '*Pronta*' floats down through the house and, in a cloud of Mum's best perfume, Siena appears. As the Vespa squeals its way back down the drive, Paris gets a glimpse of the stolen scrunchy.

In the kitchen, Charlie sits happily at the table eating a bar of chocolate. Emily is sitting opposite, chopping tomatoes. Olimpia is noisily sweeping the hall.

'What shall we have for lunch, Paris? What about a lovely salad?'

'I loathe salad.'

'Oh darling.' That face again. 'You used to love it so. Remember when you went to Rebecca's for tea and asked for salad? I was so proud of you.'

'Mum, I was five.'

'That's what made it so unusual,' says Emily earnestly. 'When you think what most five-year-olds eat.'

'I'm trying not to,' says Paris, staring pointedly at Charlie's chocolate-smeared face.

'What about a pizza then?' persists her mother, not getting it at all.

'Mum, I'm just not hungry. It's too hot to eat.'

'At least have a cold drink.'

To shut her up, Paris goes to the tap over the authentic farmhouse sink (designed in Milan and ordered on the internet). A sad trickle of brown water splutters out.

'Mum! The water's gone off again.'

Far away, though not perhaps quite as far away as it feels, Petra McAllister sits in the basement kitchen of her Brighton home and reads the paper. Outside, horizontal grey rain lashes the deserted seafront. The few holidaymakers who have braved the pier huddle under its curly Victorian awnings, the lights from the rides barely visible in the fog, and the all-pervading music from the pier's very own DJ giving the whole scene a strange, surreal feel. The loudspeakers blare a jolly, summer song about fun and laughter and free drinks. Meanwhile the rain falls relentlessly from the lowering skies.

Petra hardly notices the rain, or the pier or the sodden tourists. She is used to Brighton in the summer. Besides, from her subterranean window, all she can see are feet hurrying past. Wet, cold feet in unsuitable sandals, smug feet in wellingtons and, occasionally, the bare feet of the army of homeless people who sleep in the nearby square.

Petra pours herself another cup of coffee and spreads the paper out on the table. She can hear the boys in the playroom upstairs and although there are raised voices, she judges these to be assumed for the purposes of play. 'How dare you break my track,' Jake is yelling, but Harry's nasal rendition of the Thomas the Tank Engine theme tune does not falter. That's all right then.

344

From habit, she flicks straight to the 'Thoughts from Tuscany' column. Next to it is a tasteful pencil drawing of a Tuscan villa, stark against the hillside, with one perfect olive tree growing beside it. Petra puts her coffee mug on top of the Tuscan house, noticing with satisfaction that some liquid has spilled over onto its picturesquely sloping gables.

'*Summer in the Villa Serena has a rhythm of its own*', she reads. '*I wake at six in the shimmering beauty of the dawn, eat a slice of cool watermelon, do as many chores as I feel like and, by midday, I am ready for a siesta. I am convinced that I sleep better in those few hours than I ever did in London. Heavy, scented sleep, lulled by the crickets outside and the tinny whirr of my bedroom fan. I wake in the long afternoon and, finally, as night falls, we eat our first meal of the day, sitting out on the terrazzo as the stars come out.*'

Petra sighs and puts down her coffee cup. She can't remember when she last had a good night's sleep, scented or not. She thinks of Emily Robertson, who has been her friend since university. On the one hand, she is happy that Emily is having such a wonderful time in Italy, on the other she wants to slap her sun-kissed face very hard indeed. She also misses her very much.

Idly, Petra turns the pages. It is the Sunday paper (though

today is Tuesday) and the pages are huge and unwieldy. Her cat, named Thomas by Harry but called the Fat Controller by the rest of the family, jumps heavily on the paper. Petra pushes him out of the way and begins to read an article about the dangers of drinking too much coffee. Then she stops. She pushes Thomas's fluffy bulk further and sees, under his left paw, a picture of a man, in his forties, good-looking, half-smiling. '*Dr Michael Bartnicki*', she reads, '*consultant in neurology at King's College, London . . .*' Then she reads it again.

'Michael,' she says aloud. 'So that's where you got to.'

In Tuscany, Emily is having a frustrating few hours trying to sort out the water situation. First she rings the Idraulica, the water company, situated in futuristic splendour a mere few hills away. However, though she has carefully composed a few Italian phrases in her head ('*non abbiamo acqua*'), the woman at the other end of the phone seems to have no idea what she is saying and preserves an incredulous electronic silence. Eventually, Emily scoops Charlie up (Olimpia has gone home) and trudges out to her tiny Fiat. 'Paris!' she calls. 'Do you want to come for a drive?' Another incredulous silence followed by a snort, which Emily takes (rightly) for an answer in the negative.

The car is boiling. Charlie shrieks when his bare legs make contact with the seat. Frantically, Emily winds down the windows. 'It'll be better when we get going,' she promises. Charlie looks at her sulkily beneath lowered eyelashes. Paul's car has air conditioning but it is at Pisa airport, awaiting its master's return. 'Be sensible, darling,' Paul said.' You can't expect me to meet clients in a Fiat Panda.' Emily gave in immediately. He had invoked the C word; clients are sacred in their family.

Now, as they wind their way down the drive, hot air blows in through the windows as if a giant hairdryer were pointing at them. At least Charlie cheers up, especially when Emily puts on his favourite tape, nursery rhymes sung by a relentlessly cheery trio with comforting northern accents. At home, Charlie had condemned this tape as hopelessly babyish but here he clings to it like the aural equivalent of a security blanket. Perhaps it is the voices, so cheerfully English with their flat vowel sounds and breathless intonation. Emily doesn't like to admit that she, too, finds the voices obscurely comforting.

The Idraulica is only a few miles away, but because it, like the Villa Serena, is built on top of a hill, this means going down one hill and up at least three others. The Mountains of the Moon, this area is called, the Alpe delia Luna. It's a place of densely wooded hills, with an occasional gleam of white stone, startlingly flat plains and scattered hilltop towns, walled like fortresses. The nearest town to the Villa Serena is Monte Albano, a medieval citadel built around a square tower and a picturesque, cobbled piazza. Emily laboriously negotiates its narrow streets, entering through a low, stone archway and scattering tourists as she bumps the wrong way down several streets marked *senso unico* (she has been in Italy long enough to know that this is allowable, if not essential). Out the other side through another archway, down the hill through a succession of dusty hairpin bends, each one offering a brief, terrifying view of spectacular beauty. On the tape, jolly voices sing about double-decker buses. It all seems a million miles away.

Hands sweating on the wheel, she drives on through several equally beautiful hill towns, each with its biblical backdrop of cypresses and mountains, past countless churches and wayside grottos (grotti?), on and on past perfect view after perfect view. When they had first arrived in Tuscany, Emily used to exclaim at each crumbling archway or lapis-blue Madonna, until Siena and Paris began to mimic her savagely, 'Oh look! A dustbin. How charming! Oh look, a typical Italian drug addict. *Che carina!*' Paul had laughed and Emily lapsed into hurt silence. She still does think it all beautiful, really, but she has to admit that you can get used to beauty so that it becomes just another daily duty: make beds, cook lunch, sweep floors, admire view.

Like a modern castle, the Idraulica is visible for miles around, its new white walls shining painfully in the sun. 'Azienda Idraulica Comunale' reads the sign in small, unfriendly letters. Emily drives past rows of tankers and parks her car in front of the grandiose marble entrance. As she lifts Charlie out, he looks up in awe. 'Is this a palace?' he asks.

After the heat of the afternoon, the Idraulica's reception area is freezing. Weird, thinks Emily, shivering, how in a second your body can forget that it was ever hot. They cross what feels like acres of orange marble and stop in front of a desk grotesquely decorated with bronze snakes. The ornate furnishings and the icy cold are beginning to make Emily feel as if she is inside a tomb. A glamorous receptionist, barricaded behind the snakes, eyes them without interest.

Emily begins hesitantly, '*Scusi. Abito a Villa Serena. Non abbiamo acqua.*'

'Have you paid the bill?' asks the receptionist in perfect English, drumming her elegant nails.

'Yes,' says Emily lapsing meekly into English, 'we pay by direct . . .'

The receptionist taps her details into the computer. 'Last month's payment is overdue,' she says, unsmiling.

'Is it? But the bank . . .'

'Better you pay me now,' says the receptionist flatly, 'and take it up with the bank.'

Emily empties her battered handbag (she can feel the receptionist looking at it with horror, she probably favours a minimalist Gucci number made from an endangered species) and finally unearths her chequebook. She writes a cheque for a dizzying amount of money and hands it over. Throughout all this, Charlie looks on, open-mouthed.

The receptionist prints out a receipt. '*Carino,*' she says, pointing to Charlie, and then turns back to her computer. There seems nothing more to say.

Back at the Villa Serena, the water gushes triumphantly from the taps. In delight, Emily has a shower and bathes Charlie. Afterwards she sits outside on the terrace and watches Charlie play in the dusty earth under the olive trees. The faintest shiver of a breeze lifts her wet hair. She closes her eyes and feels that perhaps, somehow, maybe this is paradise after all. It is a few seconds before she realises that Paris is speaking to her.

'Mum? Your mobile was bleeping. You've got a message.'

Emily reaches out a hand for her phone. It must be Paul, she thinks, he is addicted to text messages and, indeed, to all forms of electronic communication. She hopes he isn't bringing clients home with him tomorrow. She doesn't think she can face hours of making crostini and *saltimbocca* while German businessmen drink Montepulciano and talk about motorways. I must be a better wife, she tells herself. I must welcome people into my gracious home, warm with home cooking and family life. Nobody minds a bit of untidiness. I must not be neurotic.

She clicks on the message icon. The text is brief: *sorry darling, not coming home, am leaving you. p.*

CHAPTER 2

Thoughts from Tuscany
By Emily Robertson

Friday night is pasta e fagioli *night. In Italy, the custom of no meat on Fridays is still strong. The local* pescivendolo *does a roaring trade in* gamberetti, *scallops and little grey fish like sardines. Even some restaurants refuse to serve meat, which, admittedly, is no sacrifice in a country so rich in other culinary delights. Italy really is paradise for the vegetarian. Even Daughter Number 2 who, in England, dined sullenly on congealed baked beans and beige toast, is suddenly devouring pizza napolitana and* spaghetti con aglio.

Pasta e fagioli is a traditional Tuscan dish (the Tuscans are known in Italy as 'the bean-eaters') which comes to us courtesy of Olimpia, our Treasure. Olimpia is an angel in a headscarf and pinny who came on our first day to 'help us out' and has become a member of the family. She cooks for us, cleans for us and scolds us constantly but we couldn't live without her. She has enriched our lives in so many ways but in no way more than in bequeathing us the recipe for pasta e fagioli, *a heady fusion of borlotti beans, tomatoes, garlic and herbs. The recipe is actually meant to include bacon, which Olimpia devoutly omits on a Friday, but sometimes I surreptitiously add a dash of pancetta fat and don't tell Number 2.*

So, on Friday night, the pasta e fagioli *is simmering on the stove. An earthenware pitcher of the local Chianti stands on the scrubbed wooden table. Crusty ciabatte (the Italian word, incidentally, for slippers), fresh out of the oven, sit steaming in their plaited basket. Spouse, who has been away for a week on business, stands in the doorway and sniffs appreciatively. 'Now I know I'm home,' he says.*

To: Petra McAllister
From: Emily Robertson
Subject: None
Paul has left me. Bugger.

To: Petra McAllister
From: Emily Robertson
Subject: Thank you

Thank you so much for ringing last night. It meant so much just to hear another human voice. I mean, I know the kids are human, but I can't really talk about it to them. I've just told them that Dad has been delayed at work and, God knows, they're used to that. I think Siena knows that something's up. She keeps asking questions, which is really unlike her. Usually she's totally absorbed in her own life: Giancarlo, school, clothes, etc. But now she keeps asking when Dad will be back, why hasn't he rung, what's this important meeting he had to go to. On and on. It's driving me mad. Paris says nothing but then she never does.

You asked if this was a surprise and I said, yes, of course it was. I was even quite cross with you for asking. But actually I don't think it was really. I mean, I didn't think Paul would leave me like that, without any warning, but I've known for ages that something was up. Last night, I couldn't sleep so I just sat outside on the terrace all night thinking and thinking. Once I heard this howl quite near me (do you know they still have wolves in Italy?) and I thought, serve Paul right if I get eaten by a wolf and it's all his fault. But actually it wouldn't serve him right at all, only make it easier for him to start a new life with whoever she is. And yes, I am sure there is a whoever she is. I just know him so well. He might be fed up with me but he'd never go to all the trouble of leaving me if there wasn't something better on offer. I remember, when we first met, he always had something lined up for Saturday night. If something better came along, he'd cancel the first date but he'd never do that unless he had a better offer. So I'm sure he wouldn't walk out on one woman unless he had a better one lined up.

Oh God, Pete, what a long, depressing email. I'd press delete if I were you. Wish I could press delete on the whole of yesterday, on the whole of the last five years if that wouldn't mean losing my darling Charlie. Life's a bitch, as they say. Remember; Michael used to say, 'Life's a beach and then you fry'? Sometimes nostalgia hurts more than anything.

Take care

Em

xxxx

On Monday morning, Emily sits on her terrace trying to ignore Olimpia who is inside muttering about the dirty habits of the English ('What is a bidet?' she mimics in a vicious falsetto). Emily is staring at her laptop. The file at the top of the screen reads 'ThoughtsfromTuscany50'. Her fiftieth column about the delights of Tuscan life. Dispiritedly she types in a title, 'Summer nights at the Villa Serena', then clicks on the icon to underline it. She sighs. She can't think of a single thing to say about summer nights at the Villa Serena. Olimpia's Hoover whines from inside the house. The Microsoft flag waves at her jauntily from the bottom of the screen.

Siena and Paris have gone to the local swimming pool (Paris making up a threesome with Giancarlo under protest). Charlie is having his siesta. Emily's copy is due tomorrow yet her mind seems vast and empty, filled just with one tiny scrabbling gerbil of a thought: *Paul has left me, Paul has left me*. Because she is so used to being without Paul, his absence doesn't impinge on her everyday routine; it is not as if she misses his shoes under the bed, his body in the shower, his whisper in the night. It is as if she needs this ridiculous gerbil thought, just to remind her of how serious things are. *Paul has left me, he has left me*.

In desperation, Emily types a string of key words about Tuscany: light, heat, olive oil, sun-dried, wine, terracotta, hills, vines, piazza, antipasti, rustic, unspoilt, cappuccino. Then she tries to form these into elegant, elegiac sentences: 'We ate antipasti under the vines in the rustic piazza', 'Sun-dried tomatoes, sprinkled with a little virgin oil, make the perfect antipasti', 'Cappuccino drunk in the heat of the morning in the beautiful local piazza'. She groans and presses delete, delete, delete. Then she types another list of words: shit, fuck, bugger, bastard, wanker.

The sun is hot on the back of her neck so she shifts round until she is in the shade of the beautiful, rustic, etc., etc., vine. Bunches of grapes dangle in front of her like some illustration of plenty (though she knows that, in fact, they are not yet good to eat, being sour and hard). Two hunting dogs with bells round their necks crash through the undergrowth and disappear around the side of the house, intent on business of their own. A lizard suns itself on the baking stones, shutting its eyes with prehistoric calm. Emily, too, shuts her eyes and thinks about her husband. *He's left me, he's left me.*

'I'm not leaving the kids,' Paul explained kindly when

she finally reached him on the phone late on Friday night. 'I'm leaving you.'

'But why?' Emily asked for the hundredth time.

'Our marriage is over,' pronounced Paul as if this were an indisputable fact, one which Emily had been wilfully denying for some time.

'How can you say that? We've never even talked.'

'Emily,' said Paul, with awful heaviness, 'I don't want to discuss this any more.'

'Don't you? Well I do! After all, you've just told me that our seventeen-year marriage is over. Don't you think I deserve an explanation?'

'Don't get hysterical, Emily.'

'I'm not hysterical,' said Emily. 'I'm fucking furious.'

Then she had slammed down the phone and spent the next two hours trying to ring him back. His phone was switched off. Panicking, she phoned his parents in Portsmouth, 'Neither Derek nor Anthea is able to take your call right now,' then his brother in Gravesend.

'But it's the middle of the night, Emily,' Anthony kept saying.

'I know. Your brother's just left me. I need to talk to him. Do you know where he is?'

'But it's the middle of the—'

She had hung up on him and sat in the dark sitting room of the Villa Serena (all exposed beams and giant fireplace), trying to breathe calmly. Then she texted Paul (*bstrd!*) and wrote him an email. Then she deleted the email and sent one to Petra instead. She went into the kitchen and poured herself a large glass of wine. Drinking was difficult because her throat seemed to have closed up but she persevered, sip by sip. Why had Paul left her? They had been happy, hadn't they? Of course it had been a strain coming to live in a new country but, she told herself, that was only to be expected. OK, Italy was her idea but Paul owed her that much surely, after the Affair? And Paul had seemed happy enough; it had fitted in with his idea, of his own lifestyle (villa in Tuscany, skiing in Klosters, Christmas shopping in New York). He had even set up his own company, selling Italian property to starry-eyed English families. And she had got a job writing about how wonderful it all was. Paul was lucky to have her. She had looked after the children, made the house look lovely; she was the one stuck here all the bloody time. Self-pity was dangerous. She took another deep breath. What was going to happen to her now?

The phone had rung and she raced across the hallway to answer it. In those few seconds she lived through the entire reconciliation: Paul's tearful apologies, her own gracious understanding, their ecstatic reunion. A second (or third) honeymoon, somewhere exotic (not Italy), away from the children. A new start. Perhaps even a fourth baby.

But it wasn't Paul, it was Petra.

Now she sits frozen in the sun and thinks, I might never see Paul again.

She will, of course. Paul finally rang back on Saturday night and proposed flying to Italy the next weekend so they could 'discuss things more sensibly.'

'Discuss what?'

'Well, access, solicitors, that sort of thing.'

Emily had been dumbstruck. 'Access' had such a worn, legalistic ring. How could Paul, who had once, in a Siena hotel room, compared her to Botticelli's Venus, be talking to her about *access*?

'Emily? Are you there?'

'Yes. Don't you think you're moving rather fast? Yesterday I had no idea that anything was wrong and now you're talking to me about access and solicitors.'

'Emily.' Deep sigh. 'You must have known for years that something was wrong.'

'Well, I didn't.'

Emily traces her name in the dust on the terrace wall and thinks: did she really know all along? All right, they had had what they always referred to as their 'rough patch'. Siena had been twelve and Paris ten and Emily was just resigning herself to the fact that she wouldn't have any more children. Paul was working all hours starting a new company and Emily felt lonely and neglected. Siena was at secondary school, Paris would follow next year. She remembers how much she dreaded losing the comforting routine of the school gates. But then it turned out that Paul would miss it even more as he was having an affair with one of the teachers, a woman he had actually met during a parent–teacher consultation. Emily had left him, gone to Brighton, asked for a divorce. But then they had got back together. It had been Paul who wanted the reconciliation, she thinks sourly; he had come racing after her, begged her to go back to him. She remembers, at the time, feeling quite strong and determined about the whole thing. She was going to divorce Paul and start a new life with the girls.

But Paul had arrived, begging her for a second chance, and she had relented. This time it must work, she had told herself. And, for a while, it had. Paul had been lovely to her, wooing her all over again, and eventually she had begun to love him again. She suddenly became consumed with desire for a third child and Paul had agreed, with hardly any persuasion. They had had darling Charlie and they were both besotted with him. Then Emily had her big idea. They should go to Italy, start a new life, just the five of them. A perfect new life in the sun. She remembers how the vision of this perfect new life, the children playing under the olive trees, tranquil evenings in the cool of the terrace, the view of the hills at sunrise, had sustained her for months, had carried her through all the actual horrors of moving, the children's hysterics, Paul's boredom, her own, suppressed feelings of panic and inadequacy. It is only now that she wonders if this vision was ever really shared by her husband.

He had loved the house, though. They had fallen in love with it together, during that magical holiday in Siena. Leaving the children with Emily's parents, they had embarked on a second honeymoon: visiting crumbling properties by day, eating in the famous piazza in the evening, making love all night to the sounds of Tuscany (church bells, scooters whizzing past, the cries of Italian youth at play). One evening they had seen the Villa Serena, dusky pink in the evening sun, and they knew they had come home. But then they actually moved to Tuscany and their idyllic tourist days were over. Emily had thrown herself into the renovations but she knew that Paul was bored and irritated by the mess and chaos involved making the Villa Serena a Tuscan paradise. He spent more and more time away, returning only to complain about the workmen and, increasingly, about Tuscany itself. Too late Emily realised that Paul, the urban wheeler-dealer, was never at his best in the country.

Yes, of course she knew.

Emily sighs again and turns her laptop away from the sun. She opens 'ThoughtsfromTuscany50' once more and types: '*Summer evenings in Tuscany, drinking cold white wine and watching the stars appear over the distant hills . . .*'

Paris sits by the side of the swimming pool, in the only available shade (half an umbrella). She adjusts her peaked cap and pulls her T-shirt down over her knees. She is not going to get skin cancer, thank you very much, not like that idiot

Siena, sitting on the baked concrete in the full glare of the sun, pulling her bikini straps down over her shoulders. Just asking for melanomas, thinks Paris sourly; she is sure that mole wasn't there last week. A beauty spot, Siena calls it. The Lake District is a beauty spot, mocks the running commentary in Paris's head, *that* is the grim reaper, my sweet. The Lake District sounds so wonderfully cold and English that she has to close her eyes for a moment to stop herself feeling dizzy with homesickness.

Siena saunters over, her blue bikini now just clinging to the bottom half of her breasts. Paris had never realised before just how *fat* Siena was getting. Her boobs are huge, all sweaty and glistening with suntan oil, and there is a definite roll above her bikini bottoms. Not a roll, almost a *tyre*. Paris shuts her eyes.

'Paris! Do you want an ice cream?'

'No thanks,' says Paris, eyes shut.

'A drink then. You ought to, it's so hot.'

'No thanks.'

'You ought to,' Siena persists.

'OK,' says Paris, to get rid of her. 'Water.'

'*Con gas?*' asks Siena with an affected Italian accent.

'Still,' says Paris, through gritted teeth.

Siena wanders over to the café where she is joined by Giancarlo and his friends. Then they start that whole loud, horseplay thing that Italians seem to do at the drop of a hat: throaty cries ('*Aiee! Hai!*'), extravagant hand gestures, lots of pushing and shoving and laughter. What in God's name, thinks Paris, have they got to laugh at? Giancarlo, the pastry chef's son, doomed to a lifetime of cooking biscotti in ninety-degree heat. Massimo, the farmer's son, whose parents have never travelled outside Tuscany. Pretty Francesca, already engaged to sullen Mauro, the mechanic. Clever Andrea, who will probably never get to Pisa University to study medicine. Why the hell do they look so pleased with themselves, wrestling with each other at the pool's edge, drops of water like jewels shining on their brown legs and arms? OK, they're good-looking, if you like that smug, well-fed look, which Paris doesn't. But is that everything? Is that *enough*?

If they were English, she would think they were drunk, the way Dad and his friends sometimes got on a Sunday afternoon after watching the rugby. But Italians didn't seem to drink, alcohol that is. She'd heard Mum saying that it was impossible for a woman to get a second glass of wine in Italy.

Well, that was OK. She hated Mum to drink wine. It made her face softer and vaguer than ever. When Mum and Dad both drank wine it was unbearable. They'd either argue or get all kissy and stupid. But Giancarlo and his friends were all kissy and stupid on two cans of lemon soda and an *acqua minerale*. Weird.

Siena hands her a bottle of mineral water, still sweating from the freezer. Paris opens it and takes a tiny sip. She is experimenting with taking smaller and smaller amounts of food and liquid. She can almost feel the water trickling slowly past her larynx and sliding gently down her throat, drop by drop.

'Hey, Parigi!' This is Giancarlo, using a version of her name that she hates. She ignores him.

'You want to swim?'

He stands in front of her, all skinny brown body, baggy swimming trunks and beaded necklace. How *can* Siena find him attractive?

'No thanks,' she says.

Giancarlo lifts both hands in an operatic gesture of acceptance. He turns back to Siena and Paris hears him say, 'Your sister. She hates me.'

She cannot hear Siena's reply but there is a lot of giggling and head-tossing. Paris lies down in the shade of the umbrella and closes her eyes.

At the Villa Serena, Emily makes scrambled eggs and attempts to arrange her thoughts. Paul has left me, she begins briskly. Things to do:

Sell house

Move back to England

Get a proper job

Organise childcare

Get a divorce.

She stops because she is crying. Charlie, sitting stolidly at the table waiting for his eggs, says, 'Mummy's face is wet.'

'It's the cooking,' says Emily. Charlie stares at her as if this answer is beneath his contempt. Emily stirs the eggs with a wooden spoon and adds salt and pepper.

'No black bits,' says Charlie sharply.

Emily starts to pick out the pieces of pepper. Paul has left me, she begins again. I have three children without a father. No great change there, she thinks. Paul was away most weeks, travelling to London or Frankfurt on business.

She is used to living without him, she tells herself, she'll hardly miss him at all.

But then she stops herself, staring at the congealing egg, pale yellow against the heavy iron frying pan. There is a big difference between your husband being away on business and your husband leaving you. A vast, yawning gulf of a difference. Paul may not have been with her physically during those long, hot afternoons when the washing machine broke down and Paris broke her arm jumping from the terrace, but he had been there somewhere, in the background, a phone call away. Someone to moan to about the kids, safe because he was the only other person in the world who loved them as much as she did.

Dispiritedly, Emily spoons the scrambled egg onto a Postman Pat plate. It looks disgusting, she thinks, but Charlie, watching her through narrowed eyes, consents to eat a spoonful. She does not feel like eating. In fact, she feels as if she will never eat again. At least then she will lose some weight. She just *knows*, somewhere deep in her heart, that Paul has left her for someone slimmer.

She is sure that he has another woman, just as she is sure, even deeper in her heart, that the Affair with the teacher was not the only one. Paul is attractive to women, with his mesmeric blue eyes and his habit of sitting just a little bit too close. She has seen it so often, with strangers, colleagues, even with friends, women who criticised Paul behind his back ('He doesn't *deserve* you, Emily') but became curiously skittish and playful in his presence.

Slowly, deliberately, Charlie tips his drink over. Bending down to clear it up, Emily says brightly, 'What shall we do this afternoon, Charlie Bear? Shall we play with your train track?'

'No train track.'

'What about a lovely walk? We could go and look at Anna-Luisa's hens.'

'No walk. Horrible hens.'

Afternoons in Italy, with no parks, no soft play areas and no children's television have begun to assume monstrous proportions in Emily's mind. Hour after hour of hot walks to see the hens or endless games running wooden cars along stone floors. All the thousands of times she has looked at her watch to find that only ten minutes has passed. All the tears, tantrums and capitulations. Emily sighs.

'What about a video?'

Ten minutes later they are sitting in the cool, high-ceilinged sitting room watching *The Jungle Book*. Charlie looks up from the screen as Mowgli is adopted by the wolf family. The Father Wolf is standing on a rock laying down the law about something, the Mother Wolf is looking at him apprehensively.

'When's Daddy coming home?' asks Charlie.